Madeline's Secret

Enjoy

June 2018

Kevin Weisbeck

Kevin Weisbeck

Madeline's Secret

An Owlstone Book

All Rights Reserved

Published as a Print-on-Demand book through CreateSpace, an Amazon Company, for the author Kevin Weisbeck.

Cover design by Dan Huckle, Okotoks, AB Canada
Danhuckle.com

Final Editing by Marius Oelschig

Copyright © 2018 Kevin Weisbeck
ISBN 978-0-9917566-2-9
First printing, May 2018

Kevin Weisbeck

Dedication

I need to start by thanking all my Beta readers: My Father, Aunt Diane, Jessika, Jamie, Colleen, Kim, Janet, Barb, Janice and Katie Moon. You not only read it, but your critiques made it better.

A special thanks to all the members of the *Write Away* writer's group. Your endless hours of listening helped me to believe.

I'd like to thank everyone in the *Writer/Author in Residence* programs. It's a great program for all writers.

Thank you, Dan Huckle for this amazing cover.

And I couldn't have published this novel without Marius Oelschig. Thank you. Your help was bigger than you know.

And finally, I have to thank Sherry. We had too many conversations like these ones:

"Do you want to go for a walk?"
"Not right now, Dear. Just need to finish this chapter."

"Kevin, supper's ready."
"Be right down. Just need to edit five more paragraphs."

"I think I just cut my leg off with your chainsaw."
"That's nice. Do you spell apocalypse with one 'p' or two?"

Kevin Weisbeck

Chapter One

Snowflakes, as light as goose down, settled on the streets of Paris. Pretty as they were, the darn things were cold, icy, and made driving treacherous. Twice the Mercedes had wiggled, and twice I'd managed to straighten it. Only four kilometres to go.

I loosened my grip on the wheel, allowing the colour to return to my knuckles before turning down one of the side streets. The cobblestone lanes were lost in a blanket of white.

Father had always called snow 'God's dandruff.' I imagined the words being whispered in my ear and allowed a smile to find my face, albeit half hidden. For me, snow had always brought an odd beauty. I used to watch it fall from the window of our farmhouse back in Chilliwack, British Columbia. The flakes would spiral and flutter in a dance with gravity and where my father saw dandruff, I saw each one as a lost little child enjoying the freedom to frolic and seek out their destiny. If only I could have told them that gravity was an inescapable force. Their fate couldn't escape the inevitable.

My sister sat in the passenger seat with little Nicolas. She was oblivious to everything except for the fact that Nicolas had just been sick.

He'd lost his lunch back at the children's clothing store and instead of heading home, my sister had talked me into taking him to our parent's house. I balked at the idea, but she insisted our mother would know what to do. I figured we could handle it. Bottom line, she wanted to go, and I didn't have the energy to fight her. Getting her way was as expected as the rains in April.

But this April the crocuses were getting a solid dusting of snow. For me this was proof that there was always an exception to the rule. And with that exception, maybe my good fortune could break out and find centre stage.

I had picked up an adorable black dress and modelled it for her. Her baby blue eyes darkened the moment she saw it. Ouch. Was that envy? I surely hoped so. This was a rare and rewarding moment for me, the girl who had always lived life in her shadows.

"Dad is going to freak when he finds out how much you paid," she said.

Of course she'd want to ruin this for me. "That's why we're not going to tell him," I replied.

"What? You mean I can't say anything?"

"Damn it, Sis." I took a hand off the wheel and gave her leg a playful swat. "Quit stirring things up for me. I've finally found a taste of your world and I'd like to hang on to it for a while, at least until I get around to screwing things up myself."

She thought about that for a second. "And what if you don't?"

"Then I guess I'll live happily ever after, just like you. Can't we both be Cinderella for a change?"

"But, that would mean sharing our parents."

"It does."

"But…"

"Oh, ye of little faith." I looked over and rolled my eyes. "Look, Sis. I'm twenty-four going on twelve, remember? It won't take me long to screw things up. You know I always do. This will all be over before Christmas. I promise."

Her nose scrunched left, then right. "You know, I can see that."

Hoping she wasn't serious, but knowing better, I had to laugh. "Hey, be nice."

"I won't have to wait an entire year, will I?"

"Probably not, and we're already four months into it." I quickly added, "you're getting a bargain."

"That's fair."

She gave me a rare smile, the one I hadn't seen in months. It didn't put a crack in her face, like she had feared. I knew it wouldn't.

"I miss this," she added. "This reminds me of our days back home, when we were kids."

The comment almost brought a tear to my eye. I knew what she meant. Since the birth of Nicolas, we were on different pages in our lives, living in different worlds. I never would have guessed there'd be such a distance between us, physically or mentally, but life never stayed still.

I grabbed her hand and gave it a squeeze. "Things change. We need to make sure we don't."

The Mercedes continued to slip and slide its way toward our parent's house. As it did, little Nicolas started to cry. The poor boy had an empty stomach. We should have gone back to the house and fed him. Instead, as the early evening skies darkened, I continued to drive us further away. Two kilometres to go.

Too bad she wasn't the one driving. Then I could have held him. He never cries when I hold him. But, as I'd mentioned, what my sister wants is all that matters. There wasn't a lot of compromise. Life for her had become effortless. For some strange reason we'd all just bent to suit her. I'd spent a lifetime wondering what that felt like, to have all that attention and acceptance. In a way, she had earned it. She'd spent a lifetime doing everything right, unlike me, who'd done an excellent job of testing everyone's patience by doing everything wrong. I was an 'A' student, but it was at the school of hard knocks.

"Hey, you missed the turn off." She chuffed.

"What?" I plucked myself from the bewildering pool of my sister's life and looked back at the lane we'd just passed. "Was that the one?"

"It sure was. Are you okay?"

"I'm good." Which was a lie. She didn't buy it, so I sheepishly added, "Maybe?" This was also a lie but bent in a more believable direction.

My sister stared at me with one eyebrow cocked.

"Okay, let's go with no." This was when we all should have jumped up and yelled out 'bingo.'

You see, my life had been a mess since birth. In truth, I didn't know anymore now than I did when I had no idea, if that makes any sense. Unlike my sister's well-executed life, mine had meandered off the path at an early age, leaving me behind. I had tried to follow the path that she had chosen. I sucked up to teachers, listened to my parents, and I even studied for tests. None of that worked for me, so I stopped doing it. I've been trying to find my own life-trail ever since. And recently, hiding in a park filled with ducks, my life simply jumped out of the weeds and reacquainted itself with me. I had to admit it wasn't what I expected, but I had welcomed it, begrudgingly of course.

"What's bugging you?" she asked.

"My head's in a weird place." I took a right on the next lane. "That's all."

"I thought Dr. Schewe was supposed to be helping you with that."

"That guy knows shit," I snapped. Oops, there's that anger again—must remember my homework assignments. "The man thinks I have self-confidence issues."

"Self-confidence?" She laughed. "He obviously doesn't know you."

"I know, right?"

"You wanna know what I think?"

I took a deep breath, rolled my eyes, and waited.

"It's your hormones. They're acting up."

"It's not hormones."

"Think about it. You've had a lot happen. It's okay if life has you a touch scattered."

A touch scattered? She spoke the words as if this was a fad and that I'd grow out of . I looked over at little Nicolas. I hoped she was wrong. I'd spent a lifetime trying to find my way and even though I found it overwhelming, it was a beautiful find. My life, once black and white with emotions, had come to me in the form of a rainbow. For years I had kept my head down and trudged along, never expecting to find love again. Nobody told me that hiding from it didn't work. When it's time, it finds you.

"I'm good," I said. "Not as good as you, but good."

My sister had created her rainbow and meticulously sculpted it. It was a future she truly loved, truly deserved. She had chipped and chiselled until she had the world right where she wanted it. I was proud of her, and often a little jealous.

This time it was her hand lovingly patting my leg. "I know you're good."

I looked over to see her smile as it spread from ear to ear. It was a sisterly moment like the ones we used to share so many times as kids, before we'd moved to Paris all those years ago. As our lives pulled us in different directions, these moments had become rare, but essentially she was my rock, and I was hers.

"Shit!" Her eyes widened as she threw her hands up in front of her face.

"What—"

My head slammed against the driver's door. The window shattered in an explosion of fictitious diamonds. My hands, now stripped from the steering wheel, flayed wildly for control. The seat belt tightened against my chest.

Through a tangle of hair, I could see the sidewalk coming up fast. A throbbing from my left temple had my mind grappled for answers. "What just hap…?"

The car's tires met the sidewalk with a jarring thud, sending waves of shock up my spine. Momentum tossed the car up on its side, pressing me into the seat. We'd be late now. I could see our mother waiting at the window, arms crossed, and I'd be the one blamed. I always am. Why does she hate me?

The continuous rumble of twisting metal howled through my head. It reminded me of the thunder that used to blast through the Fraser Valley. The accompanying lightning from those storms could be the searing pain shooting down my side.

A kaleidoscope of colours danced before me. The flashes of light slapped me around as the car crumpled around us. Half strangled by the strap as it rode up my neck, my body tried its darndest to break free. My legs slammed against the dashboard's underside and then swung outward. The door opened briefly before slamming shut again. Both knees hammered hard against the steering column. Plastic shrouds snapped free, sailing upward past my face.

Slow motion, clusters of irrelevant thoughts, everything fragmented. My eyes burned, my nose found the sugar-sweet steam that filled the air. It was cold air, snow slapping me in the face cold. When the back window popped it sounded like a champagne cork. Was that a metal chair sailing across the hood?

A dull crack pierced my sanity as the car's momentum spun me around. The doorpost had found my left temple and that knock echoed through my body several times before drowning in the chaos. Abstracted thoughts, flickering as if charged by a frayed wire, sparked a couple times, and then vanished.

Tethered behind the wheel, I had wanted the madness to stop. It didn't. I was a passenger from that first impact as the flood of horror threatened an eternity. A terminal jarring impact finally granted my wish.

Twisted in my seat, I faced the driver's side window. I strained to focus. A white delivery truck sat in the middle of a blurred intersection. The grill was crumpled like a discarded love letter.

The car had landed back on its wheels. We had rolled once, maybe twice. I couldn't say with any certainty. Regardless, we had ended up against the front of a building. Chairs and tables, that I prayed were empty, had been tossed about, bent, and crushed.

But now, everything was calm. The once whirlwind of glistening diamonds and menacing noises had found their way to some far away ether. A cold and a distant chiming of church bells was all that remained.

I strained to look over my right shoulder. There was a woman sitting there. Her blonde hair was matted with blood. Maybe in her twenties, she was beautiful, but she wasn't moving. I tried to will my seatbelt off. I couldn't. Determined, I fumbled at the latch and freed myself. I gave her a shake. "Are you okay?"

Blankly staring out the badly splintered windshield, she didn't respond.

My arms were clumsy, as if waking from a deep sleep. One flopped awkwardly around her and I tried to draw her close. Her head teetered and fell against mine. That was when a scented breeze drifted past my nose. It carried a mix of blood and a familiar perfume. Who was this woman?

I felt the warmth of my tears as they found their way down my face. I wasn't crying. They thickened a fog that had blanketed any hope of understanding what had happened. I wanted to stop them, wipe them away, but I couldn't. They weren't tears.

My snarled hair was pasted against my face. The tangles allowed the ruby red tears to follow the path from my forehead to my cheek, and ultimately down my neck. An elegant black dress, embroidered with a sea of sequins, absorbed the coagulating blood like the cherry filling from some demonic Black Forest cake. Mesmerised by the sight, it forced me to wonder why I was wearing it. Had I planned on wearing this dress to some fancy dinner party? Too bad. It looked like shit now. Where was I going?

Distant crying, like that of a child unable to find its suckie, eased its way through the confusion. It side-stepped the ringing in my ears and drew my eyes downward to the blanket strewn on the seat between the woman and myself. The arm of a child was protruding from it. Tiny fingers opened and closed, searching, frightened. Lost in the knitted folds of crimson and periwinkle, this child had survived. I let the small hand grip my bloodied finger. There was strength and that was good.

I looked up to find an answer amongst the broken glass and bent steel. It wasn't there. Instead I saw the last orange and red rays of sun as it cut through the backlit bodies that were flocking to get a better view.

They gathered in an indifferent silence, frozen at our peril, unwilling to help. Cigarettes hung from their mouths, hung from their fingers. The bluish-grey death drifted inside the car, finding me through the chilled air. The smoky aroma comforted me. Suddenly I wanted one.

I turned to the rear-view mirror and found a girl in her mid twenties staring at me. She was badly bloodied and looked much like the woman beside me. There was life in her blue eyes. It was lost, but it was there.

Out of nowhere, the siren's wailing started, drew closer, and stopped. Several arms reached for the quiet body that had once rested against mine. I struggled to hold onto this conscious world as the woman was taken from me. It was a fight I wasn't meant to win.

"*Ma'am, pouvez-vous me dire où ça fait mal?*"

The fog was rolling in thicker now. It folded its arms around me, telling me it was time to concede, time to sleep. I was tired now and I was ready for that sleep.

"Ma'am, do you speak English? You must try and stay with us. What is your name?"

Long ago I had heard a child crying. I'd felt its grip on my finger, hadn't I? I was almost sure of it. It was gone now, along with the ringing of the church bells. Had the arms taken it? I looked to find comfort in the faces, but their eyes had melted into the shadows. Only the cloying smell of the cigarettes brought calm.

"Ma'am, what is your name?"

My consciousness continued to drip from my scalp, down my cheek, and into my once beautiful dress. And as the last rays of the sun dissolved into darkness, so did I, shedding my one final thought—what was my name?

Chapter Two

It was the smell of freshly starched linen that welcomed me from a slumber that had hung around like an unwelcome houseguest. And while my body felt rested, my brain felt like it needed to tap the snooze button a few more times. I swear the mush in my head was no smarter than thick lumpy gravy, my skull acting the part of the gravy boat. My name, where I was, or what day it might have been, were all things lost in the gooey brown abyss.

I looked around slowly and let my eyes adjust to the light pouring in from a lone, but large window that had been stained with the grime of age. Green treetops rose up as if growing from the windowsills.

I'm not sure how I knew this, but I've always loved trees. They're so strong and revered as they reach to the heavens. At night they stand like sentries, warding off any dangers that might be hiding in the dark. Like a forest of big brothers, if I have any, I'd expect them to stand tall and protect me now.

Being able to see the treetops meant that this wasn't the ground floor. That was a clue. The creamy walls came into focus next. As dismal as they were, they held no answers. My eyes went on a mad scramble for anything that might be helpful. What was this place?

Fluorescent lights bathed the room and cast shadows of simplicity and drear. That wasn't something I'd ever be a part of, was it? The bed was hard, which was also not by my choice. Then there was the string with a worn mustard-coloured tassel on the end of it. It might have been a bright gold many years ago. Someone had left it resting on my shoulder. I pulled it and a light came on behind me. Room service? This was definitely not my bedroom.

Fate had abandoned me in this place and it had made sure it took a part of my mind with it when it left. I tried to lift myself out of bed, hoping to find a calendar or my wallet. An intense pain, starting in my shoulder and shooting down my side, dropped me back to the bed. Slowly a handful of fragments from the accident started to surface.

It had been snowing. There was a large truck with the front grill damaged. The blood of this beast's cooling system formed a steaming green pool in the snow beneath it. I remembered that. I also remembered that the driver, barely shook-up, was on the radio and looking across at me as if I was an inconvenience.

Flakes of snow had been swirling through the car, landing on my dress. They turned pink before they melted. It was a beautiful dress.

There had also been a small hand emerging from a blue blanket. It had held my finger. My mind quickly flashed to the other woman. Suddenly there was doubt. Was I holding him, or was she? How do I know this child is a boy? He was though, and he had been watching the large snowflakes as they drifted from the sky.

Suddenly a store was twisting its way into my thoughts. We were standing by the front window. It was a clothing store and I was holding him in my arms. I was showing him my wedding rings. They dazzled us as I held my hand up to the light.

I pulled my left hand out from the underneath the covers and found the same rings. "So, I'm married."

I vaguely recalled someone, perhaps my husband? Glimpses of his presence had floated around in the gravy. It was a handsome glimpse, but God, his image was so far away right now. This boy must belong to us. His large blue eyes had been staring at the snow with such amazement, such innocence. He never cries when I hold him. I know that because he's my son. Then there was the woman beside us in the car. Where were they?

"Doctor! The woman is awake!" She hurried to my side and grabbed my wrist for a pulse. The twisting hurt, making me wince.

The doctor materialised as if he'd been summoned from a nearby broom closet. I half expected him to appear in tights and a cape. With a slight accent he asked, "So Madeline, how are we feeling today?"

I wasn't quite sure how *he* was feeling, but I was happy to get a name. I quickly added another question to the growing list—who was this Madeline person? It was a nice enough name and maybe I'd keep it. Do I have any say in that? My mouth opened, and nothing came out. Even though I knew I was capable, I didn't know what to ask or where to start. Both the doctor's and nurse's English were laden with heavy French accents. Was this France? Outside the sun was shining, but I distinctly remembered snow.

"Don't get up on my account." The doctor's order came with a light-hearted laugh.

Was this man for real? I wanted to give a head nod for his effort, but my neck hurt. Hell, my brain hurt.

"I'll start by telling you that you're going to be fine. I just need to check you over. You took quite a knock to the head. Do you remember the accident?"

"No, maybe a little. Was there a…" The words drifted from my mouth as if tired, as if they also found it hard to wake up. I wanted to ask if there was a baby. Instead I shook the thought and let him continue.

"It doesn't surprise me that you're having difficulty remembering. The paramedics said you couldn't recall your name. This is characteristic of amnesia. The next four weeks should allow for most, if not all of it, to return. I mean that's not a certainty, but it is a common occurrence. We need to remain hopeful."

He gently squeezed my shoulder and it hurt a little. He squeezed a little harder and that had me pull away from him. "Sorry. You had a partial dislocation. I was just checking for swelling. It's healing nicely. You've also cracked a few ribs and have a hairline fracture of the right leg. It wasn't bad enough to cast. Other than that, it's all bruises and lacerations. You were lucky."

All bruises and lacerations—just another day at the office, except I'd lost absolutely everything to do with my life. It's funny how that works, my heart beats, but this Madeline person is gone. Her life has become a scramble of bewildered thoughts and questions. I guess I own that life now. Doc says that over the next few weeks she may return to me. So, what do I do if she doesn't? A cold breeze swept across my face, clearing my thoughts.

The nurse turned to me from the window she'd just opened. "Doctor, should we tell her about—"

He stopped her. "No. We'll leave that to her parents. See if they're here yet. And go get Nicolas. He should be able to help."

"Nicolas?" Was he another doctor, perhaps a specialist?

"If this guy doesn't jog a few memories then nothing will."

Nicolas was brought in and he was adorable. I did have a son, the baby in the blue blanket. It was hard to believe that this little bundle of cute was all mine. He had just finished a nap and was in a playful mood. True to my memories he didn't cry when I held him.

A handful of little fingers gripped my thumb and they held on with all their strength. Nicolas, what a treasure, all a woman could ever want. His eyes, full of life and unconditional love, melted the guilt from not remembering his birth. I'm sure I'll remember all of that in time. A mother needs those things. His presence was strong. It allowed me to believe that things would be okay.

"Is he hungry?" I used a finger to brush one of his golden locks behind his ear. "Should I try feeding him?"

"That's quite okay. You've been unconscious for a couple weeks and need your strength. Besides he's on soft foods. As you can see, he's not lacking."

My little boy was doing well. Still he looked so young. "Thank you. Maybe this is a stupid question, but how old is he?"

"He's a year and a half." The doctor hooked my chart back onto the bed and turned to leave.

I noticed two strangers, frozen in the doorway. The nurse introduced them as the doctor slipped out of the room. "This is George and Elizabeth Harrows."

I simply stared. "Okay."

"They're your parents, Madeline."

"My what?"

"Look, Honey. It's true. Madeline's awake." The man raced to my side. "How are you feeling, Dear?" His big hand wrapped itself around mine. It was warm and welcoming. I liked him instantly.

"Considering everything, I'm feeling quite well, groggy, but well."

He was a robust man, six-foot-and-a-bit tall. His full head of hair, grey and a little long for his age, seemed familiar, but I couldn't say I knew him. The plump woman, Elizabeth, had cropped hair, curled, and dyed a standard chestnut brown and she didn't look quite as familiar, or as welcoming. She was a woman on her guard. Both of them had eyes weary from the tears they'd shed. Were they worried I wasn't going to make it?

I could build on these emotions. These two were as eager to fit me into their lives as I was to find one. "So, you know me? I have this adorable boy. I'm guessing you know him?"

I watched as they drew on each other for strength. The man continued to do the talking. "Well Dear, your name is Madeline, Madeline Trembley. You gave birth to Nicolas almost two years ago."

My mother kept her distance as my father went on to tell me about the slightly premature birth and my stay in the other hospital. It mustered no memories. Then he started to tell me about the freak snowstorm. A truck had slammed into the car causing it to clip the curb and roll into a building.

"We? So, Nicolas was with me? I had thought he was. And there was a girl, wasn't there? She was my age."

Now the man had my hand firmly in both of his. He held it nervously and that was when I noticed he was crying.

"It's okay, Sir. I'm fine. I'm right here." Then a flash of the other woman came to me. There was so much blood. She never made it.

He took a minute to explain how the accident had taken the life of Rebecca, my sister. She was the other girl in the car that day. She also looked like the girl in the rear-view mirror. They had attended her funeral and said their good-byes only a week ago. It had been forced on them like a child's dose of cod liver oil. In doing so, it had opened a void that could never be filled. I imagined them putting on brave faces for family and friends while a part of them got buried in the Earth.

"Was my sister younger or older?"

"You were forty-five seconds older." My mother answered.

Hearing that I had a twin and that she'd died sent a wave of horror coursing through my body. I remembered the image of her, bloodied and lifeless, but I didn't feel what a sister should. There was guilt from the accident, but I didn't miss her. I didn't know her.

"I'm so sorry for your loss." The words sounded wrong the second they came out. How inappropriate, she was family, my family. We were probably close. I just didn't feel it. She might as well have belonged to the family in the next room. I looked up at him as my form of an apology. His eyes were sympathetic and held me close. My mothers remained on the sidelines, watching, studying.

I tried hard not to sound disconnected when I talked, but I needed answers. Was that selfish? "Am I...like, where am...?"

My father answered. His French was terrible. "You're at La Hospital Lariboisiere."

He made it sound like La Brassiere. I wanted to laugh, but his cheeks were still damp, and there was a headache starting at the base of my skull. "So, I'm in France." Oddly that didn't surprise me. My mind felt comfortable with that.

"Paris, Madeline." A faint-hearted fear began to settle in his eyes. He was suddenly lost in the realisation that I honestly didn't know them. He was losing his other daughter as we spoke. "You live here in Paris. Try and remember. Please, try hard."

The trying was the easy part, but nothing fit. The idea of France was fine, but I didn't feel French. He didn't look French. Still, it wasn't that foreign to me. "*Puis-je parler Français?*"

"No, Madeline," the woman quickly corrected as she stared off at the sky. "We speak English."

Initially this woman had studied me. Her eyes had pressed mine for the truth. The sudden apprehension had me wondering if we ever got along. Her curt glances reminded me of an early memory when I was being scolded for tracking dirt into the house. It wasn't France, and I wasn't more than five years old at the time. But in this vision, it was her eyes. Like it or not, this woman was indeed my mother.

The hours passed as the three of us continued to talk. Nicolas gave an occasional coo and slowly they became Mom and Dad, albeit a fostered version. As the morning shifted into late afternoon my life was gently unveiled. The doctor encouraged the bombardment of my past. He said it was the best therapy even though nothing they said belonged.

My mother filled me in on Lawrence, a husband that had to take a quick overnight business trip to London. He hadn't expected me to awaken. While she spoke highly of him, Dad did not. There was something about hearing his name that gave me goose bumps. They weren't the fun kind. For the life of me I didn't know why. They saw my squirming on the topic of him and kept the conversation at a safe distance.

"I need you to do me a favour?"

My father answered. "Sure, what do you need?"

"None of this has been easy, for you or for me. It sounds like I have a lot to learn about my life, maybe too much for right now. This Lawrence guy, can you keep him away from me for a day or two? I'm not ready to deal with a husband just yet. Instead, I'd prefer a few pictures. I think I need to know who I am before my husband and I get plunged into each other's lives."

Mom was reluctant but wouldn't say why. Eventually they agreed and decided to go home. They'd grab a bite of supper and bring the pictures with them when they came back. After they left, the nurse came in and took my son. His eyes were heavy, and he needed a nap.

Left alone, I let my eyes close. As I drifted in and out of sleep the snowflakes began falling again. I slept as their image rolled through my mind like albino frogs in a Hitchcock movie. They splattered against the windshield and covered the road with a layer of frozen milky goo swirled with enough blood to wrench my stomach.

Were they the murderous little bastards that had killed my sister and taken my life? When my eyes reopened, Dad was at my bedside with my photos.

My mother had taken her place in the shadows by the window.

Chapter Three

E ven when my mother wasn't looking my way, the uneasiness in her eyes lingered. It thickened the mood in my stomach as if I'd swallowed a hand full of tadpoles. Every time our eyes met she politely smiled as if she'd been caught sneaking one too many cookies at the church bazaar. Then she'd look away.

Dad was comfortable on the bed beside me and immediately took my hand in his. "How are you feeling, Madeline? Any memories surfacing?"

"No." I wanted to tell them there weren't that many to begin with, but I knew they were trying. I appreciated that. There had been a couple of small glimpses of my husband, the accident, and my son watching the snow. These were only glimpses and nothing more. "You have the pictures?"

He handed me an envelope. "Your mother pulled a few out of our photo album. These ones came from your wedding."

"Thank you." I gave her an awkward smile and set them on the bed beside me. "And Lawrence?"

My father gave me an apathetic shrug. "We couldn't get a hold of him, but we'll keep trying."

I found it odd, and I was sure I was missing something, but shouldn't a husband be with his wife after such a bad accident? Again, hearing his name sent a shiver up my spine. Strangely, the flashes I'd been getting of him had been good ones. They calmed me. Maybe I should see him. The man was my husband, the man I loved. It was just that name, 'Lawrence', that unsettled me. Perhaps if I called him Larry. That name didn't bother me as much.

"Look, your mother and I only stopped by to drop off the pictures. We think you need a little space, you know, to sort everything out. I can't imagine how you're coping. Just know we're here for you and we'll pop in for another visit tomorrow." He gave me a playful pat on the leg as he got up. "You won't be able to get rid of us."

"I'm glad to hear that, Dad." Calling him that made us both smile. I could see it becoming as natural as sitting on a dock with him fishing, or sharing a bag of popcorn over a movie. Had we ever done that? I looked over to my mother. I doubt I would have done anything like that with her.

As they left, they both gave me a reassuring hug. It was comforting to know I wasn't alone in this world. Mother turned back to me at the doorway. Her eyes met mine and for the first time I saw the emotions of a parent. They were full of compassion and what seemed like regret. I swear they were apologising, but for what?

Whatever she was hiding behind those eyes would have to be put on the pile with the rest of the mysteries, like where my husband might be, or who my sister was. If there were clues in these pictures, I'd find them.

The first photo was of a bride. She looked beautiful in her gown. She had long loosely curled blonde hair, a slimming lace dress and the face of an angel. And then there were the flowers, red and pink roses with baby white carnations. I've always loved carnations. This woman was a princess in every way, except she looked like she'd been crying. And was that a bruise hiding behind the layers of make-up or just a camera's shadow? Why would I be crying on my wedding day?

In the second photo I saw my family. They looked out of place. It was like they'd taken a wrong turn on a vacation and were now staying at the only place that had a vacancy. Horror movies often started out in places like that. My sister, Rebecca, looked lovely as her smile lit her face. She also looked a little on edge. I guess weddings do that to the best of us.

In a third photo, my husband and I were cutting the cake. I held the knife while his hands enveloped mine. I couldn't see his face, but I could mine. In it I saw uncertainty. At first glance I didn't notice it, masked by the obedience of a good wife. Looking closer it was hard to miss. Could it have been the expenses from the wedding? Was it the expectations of the honeymoon?

I was about to look at the fourth picture when my mother interrupted me. "Hi, Madeline. Dad's downstairs, I only have a second."

"I thought you left."

"I told your father that I forgot my scarf." She pulled it from her purse and wrapped it around her neck. "There's little time."

"Time?"

"You need a head's up. Lawrence is down in the lobby. I was hoping to keep him from you until you were feeling better."

Suddenly my chest felt like it was full of cement. "He's here?"

"Listen to me. Lawrence isn't the easiest man to…" she struggled for a nice enough word, "to handle. He's strong-minded and expects things to go his way. You seem a little lost but trust me when I say it's in your best interest to follow along."

"Why, is he dangerous?"

"No, but he is Nicolas's father. And he's your husband. I know you haven't come to terms with that yet. You will. I just don't want you to do or say anything hasty. You may not see it in him at first, but he's a good father and a good husband."

"What should I expect?"

"He loves you, it's just not always evident."

"Not to worry. I'll be nice." My mother was an obvious victim of old school ways and by the sounds of it, so was my husband. I was expected to be a good housewife and mother, nothing more. This sounded like the requested role and I could do that. I mean, I must have married this guy for a reason.

She hurried a hug before slipping out. Oddly, it was a very motherly hug and it brought a smile to my face. Moments later, a bellowing voice cleared the silence.

"You're awake, Madeline." He dropped a dozen long stem roses at the foot of the bed. "How are you?"

I took a second to drink the man in. He was elegant in his suit, an obvious show stealer. It was easily apparent he was used to commanding the room. There wasn't a hair out of place or a wrinkle in his shirt. I'm sure the beautiful bouquet of flowers was more for the attention than for me. He was charming, refined, and carried Pierre Cardin cologne rather well. The only problem, he wasn't exactly the man forcing his way into my memories. Those fragments had come from somebody else.

"Madeline? I'm talking to you. Are you alright?"

"Sure. I'm feeling a lot better. I mean I'm still a little shaken, but—"

"Shaken, why? Are these people dropping the ball here?"

"No! The nurses and doctors are doing a wonderful job of taking care of me. It's just that I've been through so—"

"Then it's settled." He looked to the nurse's station and back to me. "You're coming home. This is a hospital. They have food I wouldn't feed to the neighbour's dog."

"But my ribs, my leg, they need to monitor—"

"Nonsense. Your place is at home." The corner of his mouth hinted a smile. "This will only take a second."

He left my side and I looked down at the roses. They were lovely, but I honestly preferred carnations.

Chapter Four

I could see the nurse's station from my bed. They had all been looking my way as they hid behind mugs of lukewarm coffee. As Lawrence headed their way it quickly became time to scatter. Cups were abruptly set down and the disappearing acts began.

"Stop Lawrence. I'm not sure I should—"

"What? Wait? Your eyes are open, and you've got your colour back. You'd be better off at home. I mean sure you're a little bruised up, bad knock to the head and all, but I can help around the house. You've been gone long enough, and I miss you."

My husband missed me. It was nice. How do I argue with that?

He started down the hallway after a little blonde nurse. She had left the station last. "Hey Nurse. Nurse!"

My mother had returned to let me know he was coming. She hadn't said much all day, letting Dad do most of the talking. Lawrence's arrival had broken her silence. She'd told me that this man didn't do 'maybe'. Now, he wanted me home and someone stood in the way. It sounded like these were the kind of obstacles he enjoyed taking care of and I had no doubt he was revelling in this.

I could hear the argument from my room. Like a lawyer, Lawrence badgered the young woman. Her approach was a lot more practical—I was still on the mend. She kept telling him that it was in my best interest to get my rest and heal, and that the doctor was the only one who could release me. I was glad for that. Lawrence soon tired of her and went on a hunt for the doctor. My nurse came in and gave me a paper cup with an interesting collection of pills along with a glass of water. I remained silent while she obliged a sympathetic gaze. She deserved an apology and with my eyes I gave it to her.

Within minutes Lawrence returned with the doctor. The man grabbed my chart and left for the nurse's station. Lawrence smiled and tossed me a casual wink as he followed. An argument ensued, and it was short lived. The doctor signed the release and the nurses were given their orders.

Nicolas, a small brown paper bag of belongings, and a wheelchair were brought to me. I trembled as I let the two nurses help me turn my hospital gown into something more suitable for leaving. Then they sat me down in the wheelchair. A blank stare, more a grimace than anything, defined my mood as I clutched my baby. I was wheeled out to the car where I looked back at the hospital and silently said goodbye to my sanctuary. I just hoped Lawrence could cook.

In the Mercedes I obediently sat with my child, a newly found fear for the man I had married, and the prayers of every nurse on the floor. Lawrence sat smugly behind the wheel wallowing in his conquest like a schoolboy with all the other kid's lunch money.

I studied him as he started the car. He was handsome in a powerful kind of way. And in some ways, he was right. Leaving this place wouldn't kill me, and staying wouldn't bring my memories back. Maybe this man did know best. At home I could start rebuilding my life.

"I know you're worried Madeline, but I've got this." He patted my leg. "I have a surprise to help you recover."

"A surprise?"

The house wasn't far. Tucked amongst some of the largest trees in Paris, was a two-story Brownstone. The trees looked familiar, comforting, like I'd maybe climbed them as a child. Much like many of the houses in the city, it looked a little out of place amongst all the apartments. We even had a driveway.

I couldn't wait to get out of this car and see my surprise. I'm not sure what I was expecting. His mother greeted us at the door and I was informed that she would be staying. As my surprise, she would be helping with Nicolas. Help I could use so I didn't complain.

The woman, frail and easily in her sixties, was civil enough. Maybe passive would better describe her. Lawrence's father, close to seventy and nowhere near as robust as his son, was already into the sauce brandishing a spare scotch for his boy. They retired to the study in a bluish-grey haze of wine-dipped cigar smoke. His mother took Nicolas to the kitchen for a bedtime snack. I used my cane to follow her.

"Thank you." Walking canes, snacks, and toddlers would be a tough combination over the next few days.

She reached for a wood-panelled door and opened it to reveal a fridge. I opened the other large panel while she grabbed the cheese. It was the rest of the fridge.

"They say you can't remember anything, Madeline."

"I'm afraid not." I looked over her shoulder and couldn't help but notice all the cheeses, sliced meats and every kind of fruit and vegetable imaginable. It was like a mini grocery store. Then I noticed the island. It was massive. The plates were stored in a stand-up rack and I grabbed one for her. Before handing it over, I flipped it to see the back. Our daily dishes were bone china.

My trance was broken as she took the plate from me. "This must be so hard for you."

"Was I happy here?"

Ugh, what a stupid question for my husband's mother.

"I'm sorry, my brain and mouth aren't in sync yet. I don't mean anything by that. I'm sure I was. I'm just trying to piece it all together. Everything's so vague, and Lawrence seems so…"

"My son isn't going to win any awards for his charm, but he does love you. He's like his father in the sense that he takes his place in life very seriously. It's just the way they are." She rubbed her hands and played with her wedding band as if it was starting to burn her finger. "These men of ours need their space. If we give it to them they'll take good care of us. If we don't, they fight back and believe me, they can outlast their strongest adversary."

I let my brain collect and compartmentalise her every word. The woman's trust was appreciated. It was easy to tell by his conduct in the hospital that he was a man that wouldn't back down. That mental note had been underlined an hour ago. We continued to gab about nothing and once Nicolas's eyes started to droop we took him upstairs to bed. I sat in the chair by his dresser while Lawrence's mother sat at the foot of the bed. Our chat had been exhausting, but I wanted to know everything. There was so much to learn. It was all the stuff that I'd once taken for granted.

"Do I do a lot of cooking?" I looked around. The kitchen, this room, hell, the whole house was impeccable. "And do I usually keep the house this clean?"

She smiled. I had noticed the high standards, and this was a good thing. Life would be easier that way. "Just remember, above all, he likes to be right. I know it makes him sound pompous, but he's a good provider." She took my hand in a sympathetic gesture. "I never really knew your sister, but I'm truly sorry to hear about her passing."

I wished for my eyes to well up. They didn't. I'm sure, as her twin, there was some spiritual connection floating around in my head. I just hadn't found it yet.

I'd been so consumed by my child and husband that I'd all but forgotten about her. In fairness, it hadn't really hit me that I'd lost a sister. I tried to remember her, but there was still the brain-gravy keeping me from remembering this stranger that I'd known since birth. My parents had talked to me about her. They told such surreal stories. Maybe if I had gone to her funeral. I should bring flowers to her grave. I was sure my parents would take me if I asked.

Lawrence's mother watched as my emotions stirred. With any luck they'd help me find my life. Her son needed a wife and her grandson, a mother. She left me with a gentle hug and I thanked her, for everything.

With Nicolas asleep in his room I decided to head to my room for a nap. Outside his door I looked left and then right. Uncertain, I chose right. It would give me a chance to see the rest of the house. The downstairs had revealed a beautifully modern floor plan with a kitchen, dinning room, living room and study. Some of the walls were panelled with a dark cherry wood while the others had toffee-coloured wallpaper. It was embossed with a paisley print and was easy on the eyes. There was a fireplace and the living room shared it with Lawrence's study. How cool was that?

I also loved how the floors creaked as I shuffled along with my cane. At the end of the hallway I glanced at an antique mirror that hung above a small table. The woman was bruised and deflated. Her hair was tied back and needed a good brushing. She was frightening so I turned my back to her and stepped through the doorway on my left. It was the master bedroom. Seeing it didn't jar any memories.

There was a third bedroom, but I didn't bother with it. I'm sure his mother had taken that one. In my room I could see a corner tub the size of a swimming pool and it was inviting me to fill it with bubbles and climb in. I passed. Instead I took a seat at the foot of the bed on a chest that held more mystery. Over the next few days I'd get nosy and try to find my life. For now, I had the pictures.

Alone again, I pulled out the envelope. There was a forth photo. It was when Rebecca and I were young. It was my sister and I amongst trees dressed in all the colours of autumn. Those distant days seemed closer to me than any of those moments leading up to the accident. Like a puzzle with the border complete, the pieces started to fall slowly into place. This picture was taken just before we moved. It looked like we were about nine, although I couldn't be sure.

The two of us were sitting at the edge of our pond, trying to convince each other that things were going to be okay.

If only we knew.

Chapter Five

Memories are funny things. I have amnesia and yet all those moments of my life, good and bad, exist somewhere. Most memories sit like photos in a dusty box, waiting for their chance to be pulled out and remembered. The unforgettable ones get frames and earn the coveted spots on the walls or on the top of dressers. The rest get sorted and tucked away in the corner of the attic for later. For the memory of these two little girls in the forest, later had arrived and the box had been opened.

It was the summer of sixty-six. That would make my sister and I nine. I looked closer at the picture, remembering how proud we had been to put our ponytails in ourselves. It was hard to believe two kids could be so innocent.

I let the puzzle pieces lock into place, creating a memory from what started off as images on a piece of photo paper. I found it worked better if I let those moments come to me.

Babbling water from Gopher Creek emptied into the waiting pond of lily pads and bullfrogs. As the currents tumbled and rolled over the rounded rocks, the frail branches of a nearby willow swayed carelessly along the shoreline, their tips stealing a taste of the tranquil water. I'd always felt so safe under that tree, under any tree.

Across the pond and over the adjacent mountain, the sun slowly waned, the day's last reflections filling our eyes. I never felt closer to our little corner of the world than I did that day. My sister and I sat quietly under that willow tree, hoping to freeze time.

"Hey, do you think Dad was serious?"

My sister patiently waited for a 'no' or perhaps an 'I doubt it'. That way, all this could be a bad dream and she'd wake up. I couldn't help her. Instead, I watched the passing clouds, their underbellies glowing with the varied hues of red and orange. I knew that lost and homesick feeling. We were homesick for a house we hadn't even left yet.

"It's Paris," I reminded her. Sure, it wasn't our cosy town in Chilliwack, but how different could it be. Doesn't the sun set there too, and the grass grow green? "Hey, do you think its day or night in France right now?"

"I don't care. I'm not going." My sister's shoulders slumped. "School starts in three weeks. I have Mrs. Anderson as a teacher. She's one of the good ones." She twirled her hair with her finger as she grappled for more reasons, "Uh, and what about our house? There's too much stuff. How will we get it all there? And what about the doorjamb?"

I leaned in and gave her a hug as I imagined Dad carrying her out of the house for the last time. Her arms and legs would be flailing like a cat on its way to a bath. Fingernails would be scratching at doorways, countertops or perhaps latching onto the carpeted stairs or a passing curtain.

The doorjamb that she referred to was the one in the kitchen. At the end of every summer, as long as either of us could remember, we'd back up against that doorway and Dad would get out the ruler and pencil. It had us sprouting at the same pace.

"They have schools in France, you know." What else could I say? I was almost certain of the fact.

She abruptly pulled herself away from me, her eyes shocked by my betrayal. Her words swung at me like a fist. "What about all my stuff?"

Now there was the girl I knew and loved—My stuff. "Well, we obviously can't take it all. I'm sure we'll have to leave some of it behind."

"Like what?" Her mind started contorting as she raced through the inventory of her room. The 'take-with' and 'garage-sale' piles were rapidly forming.

Then my sister got up and looked around as if she'd misplaced her bike. She grabbed a rock as big as a loaf of bread and raised it high above her head. Dirt fell from it, dusting the top of her ponytail. Then she launched into the pond, sending ripples through the picturesque autumn colours of inverted trees.

Alluding to the sudden turmoil, she pointed to the once tranquil scene and screamed. "See! That's us and I'm scared!"

I let out a chuckle, glad that the rock wasn't meant for me. "We'd be crazy not to feel a little scared. Leaving Canada is a big deal. I'd find it weird if we weren't afraid."

"Really?" The ripples in the pond smoothed out as they pushed forward to the opposite shoreline. She quickly sat back down beside me and hooked my pinky finger tightly in hers. "Let's make a pact, that we'll look out for each other, no matter what."

"Sure."

"No. You have to swear!"

"If you say so. Duck crap!" My cheeks tightened as I forced an overly wide smile.

"I'm serious. Pinky Swear that you'll always look out for me."

I tightened my grip on her pinky finger. "I swear to watch out for my sister until the day we die."

Her eyes danced wildly in their sockets, like she wanted to spill blood to seal the deal. "Make it forever." Her eyes had crazed over. "Yeah, make it forever."

I'm sure she saw my eyes roll, but it didn't matter at this point. Sanity had sprouted horse legs and was out of the gate.

She'd be impossible to live with until she heard it. Maybe it would have been better had she dropped the rock on her head. "Okay. I'll look out for you, forever and beyond."

That day my sister squeezed me with enough force to crack ribs. "I swear I'll hold you to this. And don't tell Mom or Dad. I don't want them knowing I'm afraid."

"We'll make it our little secret."

I forced my eyes away from the picture when Lawrence entered the room. He came right over. "Are you okay?" He slipped the picture from my hand and gently rubbed a tear from my cheek. I placed my hand over his.

"Rebecca and I were kids. She was so scared to come out here. She even made me promise to take care of her. I guess I failed."

"You can't change fate. You loved her, and it sounds like she loved you. That's not failure."

"But I…" The words dried up in my throat so I tried again. "I promised her."

"If only life was that easy."

Those weren't the words I wanted to hear. I wanted comfort, hoped for assurance and instead I got that dick comment—not that easy? I shoved him away. "What do you know about easy? One minute I'm a happily married woman with a lovely son, the next I'm living with a stranger and I've got this kid I don't remember having."

"So, I'm a stranger?"

I figured that one might hurt and a part of me wanted it to hurt. "You know what I mean."

"Things have changed. We can't do anything about that, but we can pick up the pieces. Marriages aren't always easy, Madeline."

"But I don't know you. I don't know me. I had to wait for the doctor to say my name. What am I going to do?"

"You start over. See that chair?"

I followed his finger to a tattered old chair in the corner of the room. Much like me, it seemed a little out of place amongst all the newer pieces.

"That was me, years ago. It the first thing I ever bought. It was old and rickety back then, but it was all I could afford. I was scared when I started out, unable to purchase anything except crap like that. Since then I've bought this house and all new furniture. It took time."

"Why don't you throw it out?"

"Stupid thing reminds me of where I came from."

"Don't your parents have money."

"They do, but my father never believed in handing down anything other than advice and encouragement. I had nothing starting out. He always said that nothing ruins a good work ethic like charity."

I took his hand and tucked away another mental note. He had drawn strength from not having a normal relationship with his father. It was a relationship that should have included a pair of baseball gloves, an ice cream cone, or chats about girls.

"Change isn't the enemy, Madeline. Fighting it is." He leaned down and kissed my cheek. "Now you must be tired. You should try and get some sleep."

"I think I want to go to the cemetery tomorrow."

"And I think that's a good idea." Lawrence looked at the picture again and set it down. "Just don't do it right away. You're supposed to be healing, remember."

My head thumped, my heart ached, and my stomach churned. How could I forget?

Chapter Six

I took Lawrence's advice and let a handful of days into this new life pass before making any plans for the cemetery. The time had been nice, but it had only brought more bewilderment. Everything I looked at sparked a question. The daily routine was slowly getting comfortable thanks to all his mother's help. She cooked, cleaned and took care of Nicolas while I sat around and felt obsolete. Even now, as I mustered the strength to get out of bed, I could smell the coffee brewing.

My feet slipped out from beneath the warm duvet and landed softly on the oak floor beside the bed. The day was fresh, and I was determined to make it a cane-free one. I was sick of using it. Lawrence wasn't in the bed or in the room. He must have already left for work.

My husband, who I'd found to be gallant and hard working, had been a big help. He and his mother had seen to my needs and shown great patience with my laziness. However, I could live without his father. He was a drunk of a man, more concerned with hand-rolled Cubans than his grandson. Lawrence was nothing like his father, unless the two were together. On those days the show began, and I felt the need to run for popcorn.

I had been warned by both his mother and mine. I'd started my new life scared. Their advice had been taken to heart, but they didn't see him like I saw him. He was a good man. Years ago, I had seen something in him, something that made me commit my life to him. I was glad I did. I saw the love in his eyes when things were going well, and it was no secret that by well, I meant his way. There was love before the accident and we'd find it again, that I was sure of. He was the father of our child and he was my husband.

"He's my husband, father of my child."

Saying it out loud softened the uneasy feeling in my stomach that had lingered like a ghost in an old abandoned house. I knew that, as badly as I wanted this, he was still a stranger and, like it or not, I had been warned.

So last night I phoned my parents and brought up the cemetery. For them it was a struggle. For me the struggle was remembering that this was hard on them. They'd lost us both. I couldn't help but wonder if they blamed me. It was my car and my driving. A part of me wanted to ask for the details of that day, but what if it was my fault? How could I continue to face them? At least with ignorance I could pretend.

In the middle of the night, in my dreams while I slept, the snow had begun to fall again. It had brought with it the twisted metal and the blood, all the blood. I couldn't see much else other than a second vehicle and the crowd. It was like a snapshot with larger pieces torn away. Only the outcome was certain. I was alive, and my sister was in a cemetery across town. I needed to see her.

I got out of bed, walked over to the wardrobe and swung the doors open in hopes that this would be easier today. It wasn't. What was I thinking when I bought all these pants suits? There must have been one hell of a sale somewhere? My wardrobe consisted of nothing but drab. I have no doubt that Lawrence had a huge say in the conservative attire, but seriously? There were a few nice evening gowns that dazzled, but none of them were cemetery appropriate.

The dresser was next as I rummaged to find a pair of jeans or nice slacks. I found slips, blouses and underwear, mostly in cream and beige. In one drawer there were bathing suits, each of them one pieces. Days ago, I had noticed faded tan lines. They were faint, likely the result of a bikini. I let my curiosity take hold of me for a minute as I tried to find that bikini. It wasn't there.

There had to be a simple explanation. Maybe we had a summer cottage in Milan where I kept it, I had a box in storage marked summer stuff, or perhaps I had left it at, dare I say, my boyfriend's house? Could he be the other man, the one trying to force his way into my memories? Each night I had dreamt of the good-looking stranger. He was also ruggedly handsome, but unlike my husband, who was in his mid thirties, this guy was late twenties. In these flashes he was smitten with me. Lawrence isn't the smitten type. I wish he were.

Even though he had a strong harness on his emotions, Lawrence was still a treat for the eyes. We hadn't been physical yet, which was fine for now, but how often had we made love before? Was I bored and going elsewhere for my primal urges? Even though I couldn't form a solid image, I could almost smell the other man, and he was all man. What if he dropped by the house, wanting to pick up where we had left off? My God, how would I explain that? Hey Lawrence, this is, uh… Then I'd turn to the man and ask his name, a very smooth move for any girl.

But these were merely the thoughts of an emotionally lost housewife, innocent and oddly entertaining. I told myself they weren't my reality. I slid the drawer closed. Later I'd look for a box marked 'summer stuff.' I was sure we had one.

I decided on a pair of black slacks and grabbed a jacket before leaving the house.

* * * * *

At the cemetery, the hills of manicured grass carpeted the ground in all directions. I let Nicolas run ahead of us. Dad was content with chasing him. The aroma of fresh-cut grass filled my lungs. It was so peaceful, and yet so final. I don't remember ever being at a cemetery before. It was bizarre, the idea of such a beautiful park holding so much sadness and death. There were babies, spouses, parents and of course, sisters. I closed my eyes to keep my anticipation from drowning me.

I opened them to see my sister's name set in black-marbled granite. So, there it was. The dark headstone was four inches thick and standing two feet tall. It was curved on the top. The grass was turf and it still had the cut lines showing. There were a few loose bits of gravel lying on the seams. I looked back at her name. The engraving was beautiful.

My mind drifted back to that nine-year old girl throwing the rock into the pond. I had hoped for more, hoped for that woman in the Mercedes. Rebecca was her name and for my parents, her life had ended too soon. For me, it had been her entire existence.

I reached out and gently ran my fingertips along the granite. It was cold. I was hoping for energy that might generate a connection. A jagged edge of the stone bit through the flesh of my finger. I watched as the blood surfaced and wondered if this was some sisterly sign of rebellion. Was my sister a rebel? She sure knew how to ripple a pond.

A drop of blood formed, and it mesmerised me as I watched it swell in size. My parents knelt with Nicolas, their heads down in prayer. Well, my mother prayed. Father looked like he'd been carried off to some far away memory. My son sat watching a ladybug perched on a blade of grass. For me the focus was the blood. Holding my hand up, palm away from me, I let the droplet make its way down my finger to my wedding rings.

It was the sight of the diamond with the sun glistening through it that opened the doors to another memory. My sister and I had been in a little shop with Nicolas. We were clothes shopping. There had been snow, and I had stood there holding Nicolas in my arms while he watched the flakes falling from the sky. Rebecca was off changing or shopping. I was holding my hand up for Nicolas. He had wanted to see the diamond sparkle as the light from the store window gleamed off it. I remember feeling lucky and yet a little jealous. So why was I jealous of my sister? Was I missing something? Maybe it was my lack of freedom, or the world she'd made for herself.

My thoughts shifted to Rebecca's boyfriend and what this must have done to him. Devastated by her death, his life would have been ruined. "Hey Mom. When you saw Johannes at the funeral, how was he?"

She looked away, as if ashamed. "He didn't come, but he left a message on the phone. There was some family emergency. He sent flowers." As if apologising for him she added, "They were nice. We haven't really seen or talked to him since."

"That's so sad. I guess he needed his space."

But this wasn't about space. He would have been angry, not wanting to see the tombstone that read 'Rebecca Harrows, Rest in Peace.' For him that would have ended her life. I read the words 'Rest in Peace' again and wondered if she was. To me she was still no more than that scared little girl. "I think I'm ready to go."

I didn't get two steps before a smell froze me in my tracks. My stomach started to retch instantly. It started in the deepest depths of my gut and twisted its way through my brain like poison in blood, dizzying me to one knee.

A second later, the smell came at me much clearer. It was a scent as familiar as an aged book or a fine wine. A couple, both puffing on cigarettes, walked past me dropping another handful of puzzle pieces.

Chapter Seven

Back at the cemetery I had to push the scent of the cigarettes away. There was a power in them that I couldn't understand. Dad had helped me up from my knees and I assured him repeatedly that I was fine. I simply hadn't been eating properly. It wasn't a lie. There was no fever to speak of, just a little come-and-go nausea and headaches. It might have even been the concussion or a bug that I'd picked up at the hospital.

Mom had invited me back to their apartment and offered me a bowl of soup. Father praised her chicken soup and claimed it was a cure-all. It couldn't hurt.

I noticed a table on the balcony. It looked charming enough, so that was the direction I headed. The sky was blue and the air was scented with the neighbour's potted lilacs. I pulled a chair back for Nicolas and watched as he bolted for the kitchen. "Nicolas, come back here."

"Ah, let him go. Gramma loves it when he helps." Dad grabbed two glasses and pulled a Gewürztraminer off the shelf. "It's 5:00 pm somewhere. Gewurzt is okay, isn't it?"

I smiled politely and took a seat. The outdoor patio of my parent's apartment was a beautiful spot to take in Paris. It was spacious, quiet and I sensed I used to like it here. The apartment, albeit small, had three closet sized bedrooms. It felt familiar, but it didn't trigger any memories. No, the patio was the place to be.

"Everything okay?" My father asked as he started to pour the wine. "You scared me, back at the cemetery. Hey, are you allowed to have wine?"

I gave him a playful I-dare-you look as I grabbed for my glass. "I'm fine, Dad, and this is a medicinal wine." I pulled my eyes away from him as I took a sip. The doctor had told us it was best to talk about my past. You never knew what might trigger a memory. "Hey, have I ever smoked?"

"Smoked? Not as far as I know. That being said, we had found cigarettes hidden in the barn once, before we left Chilliwack. You girls were young and I was ready to kill one of you, but which one? I never found out. You two were thick as thieves."

"We were? How about as adults, the smoking that is."

"Yes and no."

"Huh?"

"No, I never caught either of you smoking since and yes, you two were always thick as thieves."

I looked over to see Mom and Nicolas in the kitchen. She was spoiling him with cookies. So much for him having soup, but that was okay. Dad and I were six stories up and I had just noticed the magnificent view of Sacré-Cœur. You would think I'd have remembered a view like that. I also noticed the haywire holding the railing to the building. I had to believe there was a story somewhere in the cluttered attic of my brain, but it was faint. "What happened with the railing?"

"Are you kidding me?" He set his wine down as he leaned forward and transformed into story mode. "That crazy sister of yours almost killed herself."

My last mouthful of wine found the wrong pipe and I coughed it back up. So, there *was* a railing story. "What are you talking about?"

"I came out here to find your sister hanging sixty feet above the sidewalk, arm stuck through the railing. It had come loose and swung out like a door on a hinge. She must have fallen forward when it swung out and grabbed for it."

I could picture her toes on the balcony, her hands stretched out to the railing. "Gee, Dad. What happened?"

"She let go with one hand and reached back for me. I grabbed her wrist to pull her back in."

I cleared the last of the wine from my throat. "You saved her?"

"I thought so, but then the balcony broke away completely and she went over. It was stuck to her sleeve, dangling off her arm like the pendulum of an old grandfather clock. Below, the people scurried by, oblivious to it all. A sudden downpour had popped their umbrellas open and put a jump in their step. Your sister tried to pull her arm free from the railing while I held on to her for dear life, but she couldn't. It clattered against the side of the building as it held on to her."

"Oh my God."

"I struggled to keep my footing on the wet cement as I shuffled closer to the edge. There wasn't much real estate to work with. The rain was pelting down. It was going to drag us both over the edge if something didn't happen soon. I yelled at her to shake the railing free. Well, she shrugged and shook her arm, but with each movement, the railing held on. I was losing my grip on to her."

I sat on the edge of my seat. I had almost lost my sister earlier. It was like fate was after her. "So, what happened?"

He continued, "I gave the poor girl's wrist a bone-crushing squeeze and jerked her upward as hard as I could. I'm sure there was a short-lived moment when her shoulder considered leaving its socket. I'm sure it hurt like hell. With that final surge the seam of the sleeve tore, peeling the fabric from her arm. Damn thing started its decent down to the sidewalk, the black sleeve trailing behind it like a kite-tail."

I looked back at the railing and this time I noticed the extra marks in it. These dents and slight twists would have been from the impact. It would have left quite a mark in the sidewalk.

"The rain continued to fall. She was trembling so hard."

"Nobody was hurt?"

"No, but Rebecca was pretty upset." He paused and let his eyes find the haywire. "Poor thing."

I surprised both of us by getting up and giving him a hug. "Thanks, Dad. I don't think a girl could ask for a better father."

"Awe, thanks, Madeline." He added one last trinket to the story. "It was the night you met Lawrence. Rebecca probably told you this story. I remember her waiting up for you."

"Really?" My chest began to tighten—thick as thieves. Even they knew my sister and I were close. So much had been taken from them. "I really am sorry, for everything."

"Don't be." His eyes never left the railing. "I just bought her a little more time. That's all."

Mom and Nicolas stepped out onto the patio. "The soup is ready. I could use a hand setting the table and dishing up."

I started to get up, but she stopped me with a hand on my shoulder. "That's okay, Madeline. You should rest. We've got it."

Dad took Nicolas's hand. "Want to help me set the table, Tiger? I'll put you in charge of spoons."

Nicolas nodded, took his hand and they slowly shuffled off.

At the hospital my mother's eyes had shown hints of what I thought was blame, but now I wasn't so sure. Meanwhile, my father's eyes suppressed the hurt. Was there a hint of blame in those eyes? Should I ask him? If I were smart I'd come out and ask them if Rebecca's death was my fault. How could I? Instead I watched my mother as she made her way back to the kitchen. She knew more than she was letting on. I'd have to be careful with her.

I set my wine down. It wasn't sitting well in my stomach. Then I noticed the metal ladder attached to the wall beside the patio doors. It led to the rooftop. It was off-white like the wall and yet it stood out like it wanted to be found.

It acted like it had a secret and was willing to share.

Chapter Eight

I left my purse at the table and headed over to the ladder. It took a bit to clamber the eight feet to the rooftop. My leg wasn't exactly one hundred percent yet. Once atop, I saw a sanctuary where, hidden by vent boxes and chimney pipes, a forgotten seclusion awaited. There was even a wooden crate. I took a seat on it and leaned back against the plaster wall. It was a lot to take in. "Breathe, Madeline."

From this spot I could see the creamy domes of Sacré-Cœur as if I were sitting on a mountaintop. Its splendour sat perched in the distance and that was when I got it. For someone, this was an escape from the daily tribulations. But was this Rebecca's getaway or mine?

I nosed around and found a coffee can behind the crate. It was quickly opened. The contents revealed a few half-smoked butts that were pink-ended by lipstick, a pack of Camel Cigarettes, and some matches from La Maison Blanche. La Maison Blanche sounded like a nice place. I'd have to ask Lawrence if he ever took me there. Wait, maybe not. What if the man who took me there wasn't Lawrence? What if he was the man with my bikini in his dresser drawer? Ugg. More doubt.

What if Lawrence's control issues drove me into another man's arms? Why would I have married him then? Stop it, Madeline. You're being ridiculous. Lawrence is a good catch. He's a kind man and I'm sure if I asked him, he would tell me all about the night he took me to that restaurant. I'd bet I wore one of those elegant evening gowns. No doubt he was a gentleman and held my chair. We probably drank expensive wine and I had a great time. I wasn't about to ask though.

Playing with the pack of smokes, I shook one out and slid it back in. At this point I was sure these were my secret-stash smokes. I smoked and because there were no cigarettes back home, I'm sure my husband didn't know about it. He would never approve. This was why I had them stashed, why I had to sneak off to have one. Did I have smokes stashed back home? Had Lawrence ever found them?

My nausea returned a little stronger, likely from all the stress. Was I cheating, was I smoking, was I responsible for Rebecca's death? Did she know about my affair? What if she was going to tell Lawrence? Were we arguing when we crashed? Was she the kind of sister that would tell? No, because we were thick as thieves. These thoughts were quickly becoming a one-way ticket to Crazy-town. I had to reel them in.

I pulled one of the cigarettes out and put it in my mouth. I imagined the glow of the first red embers as I took that first drag. It would taste like it always had, angry and unfair. How did I know that was the taste? My memories, that was how. This hadn't been my first smoke, yet I hated the damn things. So why didn't I stop?

I fumbled a match from the jacket and thought about striking it. I knew the cigarette, if smoked, would get tossed in the rusted can that sat beside the crate. It would take its place with the rest of those secrets. They were strangely comforting. So why did I hate each and every one of them? Were they clues to my life?

If I smoked one, would it trigger more memories? I lit the match and watched as it flared. With it, my nausea also flared.

The screen door to the patio opened. "Madeline, soup's ready. Madeline?"

I stuffed the Camels and matches in my pocket as I tossed the burnt match into the can and hobbled over to the ladder. "Coming Dad."

"What are you doing up there?"

I shrugged as I carefully started down the ladder. "Just chasing squirrels."

He scratched his head. "We've got squirrels?"

Chapter Nine

Soup at the parents was amazing, So was the excuse I ended up giving my father for being up on the rooftop. Those cigarettes had intrigued me and since Lawrence's mother had left this morning to go home to her husband, I felt the need to satisfy a strange curiosity. Was I crazy?

I tried so hard to resist my curiosity, but being alone with Nicolas wasn't much of a deterrent. The idea of having a smoke was getting the better of me, and the stars were aligned. My boy had started his afternoon nap and Lawrence would be at the office for a couple more hours. With the roast in the oven, I slipped a cigarette out of the pack and headed for the back terrace. In the far corner of our cosy yard the neighbour's tree grew over the fence. It would hide me from any nosy onlookers.

The match flared when I struck it and it magically burned as I held it out in front of my face. The sulphur smell waned as the heat closed in on my fingers. Did I really want to do this? If Lawrence came home and smelt this on me, it could cause trouble. Was my smoking ever an issue? But I smoked, maybe, and I didn't do it in front of him for a reason.

I leaned into the match and let the last flicker of flame jump to the tobacco. It took three quick puffs to get the cigarette burning properly. Soon, the cherry had a glow. Now to take a drag and inhale. I did just that.

It hit my lungs and burnt like I knew it would. I was dizzied as I exhaled. The feeling was strangely liberating. Don't ask me why I thought I had to make my second drag a long lung-filling one, but I did. The ensuing cough choked the life out of me and dropped me to the ground. Nausea quickly replaced the fuzzy light-headed feeling. This all resulted in my mother's soup becoming a multicoloured puddle.

By the time I composed myself, I'd lost the smoke somewhere in the leaves, leaves as grey as my skin. I eventually found it and took it inside to flush. The rest of the vile habit got stashed in the closet. My chest ached, my head ached, and now I reeked like I'd spent the night on the town. I needed a bath.

I ran the water extra hot and leaned back and placed the warm wet cloth over my forehead. What was I thinking? What was I looking to find? I needed to stop taking stock of my life and just enjoy my child and my husband. I let my eyes close. They quickly popped open when the front door slammed.

"Hello Madeline?"

"Crap." I scrambled to get up. "Just getting out of the tub, Dear. I'll be out in a minute." What time was it?

Wrapped in my robe, I walked into the living room to see Lawrence and Nicolas sitting on the couch. My son giggled while my husband read Chicken Little to him. They laughed for a few minutes before noticing me.

"Oops." Lawrence said to Nicolas. "I think Mommy caught us."

He closed the book and set on the coffee table. Then he picked up Nicolas, shot me a wink, and carried the boy upstairs to his room. I quickly checked on dinner before heading to my bedroom. I had a few tangles to comb out.

A minute later, Lawrence met me by the bed. His suit was still on and he had a drink poured. He noticed my tub-wrinkled hands. "You fell asleep in there? Good thing I came home when I did."

"Um, it was just for a minute."

"Nicolas was awake when I got home. He was scared."

"I'm sorry. I didn't think I'd fall…"

"That's okay. You've been through a lot lately. I get that."

"Thanks for understanding. You know, I had the strangest dream."

"In the tub?" His casual must-be-nice look caught me off guard.

"I was modelling clothes." I dared the next question. "Did I ever do anything like that? I mean, I know Rebecca did some."

"Again, with the modelling?"

I didn't see them, but I swear his eyes had just rolled. "Pardon me?"

"It's just that we've had this talk so many times, Madeline." Then he remembered, I wasn't the Madeline with the memories. "Look, you've always been a little jealous of your sister's modelling career. I swear there's a side of you that wants that excitement, that attention."

"And that's a bad thing? Didn't my sister do well for herself?"

"I'm sure she did." He laughed and shook his head in disbelief. "You know you're far too beautiful, and classy, for that. You not only have the beauty, but you have the confidence to accept your beauty without all that drama. Your sister didn't."

"Uh, thank you?" I think that was a compliment. "It's just that the dream was so real, so—"

"You were probably reliving one of your sister's stories. In her own half-twisted way, she liked to brag about her photo sessions. You always hung on her every word like it was the most glamorous occupation."

That had to be where my jealousy came from. "It wasn't glamorous?"

"It's a fairly embarrassing life, don't you think? I mean, here we are doing everything right and making a name for ourselves. Then there's your sister, plastered across every magazine, near naked. They slap her on billboards, posters, you name it. Did you know I saw her on a billboard out by the airport? It might as well have read 'Welcome to Paris, where virtues are optional.' It gets to be a bit much after a while."

I'd seen a few of her photos. "But her pictures are so pretty."

"I'm not talking about this any more."

"I'm sorry." Could this dream have come from the stories she had told me? Everything was so vivid. "Did Nicolas fall back asleep?"

"He's playing in his room," Lawrence answered.

"Have I ever worked?"

"You don't need to. Taking care of Nicolas is your job."

That was true. I was a wife, a cook, the cleaner and a mother. I braved another topic. "You're home early. Not that I'm not glad to see you, but I didn't expect you for another hour. Is everything okay?"

"Do I answer to you now?"

"No, of course not."

"Good." Lawrence walked over to his dresser, pulled a small bottle of whiskey out of his sock drawer and topped up his drink. The cap hit the floor and what didn't fit in the glass was poured straight down his throat. "How about you drop the robe and get in bed. I've been extremely patient and I'm a tad overdue."

"Overdue?"

My look must have been both horror and disgust when he grabbed me and pressed his drunken lips against mine. I choked on the over-powering fumes. He locked his hands onto my biceps and threw me back onto the bed. Then he started to undo his belt. "Very overdue."

His knees pried mine apart as he climbed on top of me. He shoved me back and the pain in my shoulder brought a tear to my eye. At that point, he held me down and informed me that this was going to happen. Oddly, I had hoped it would. This moment had been in my thoughts all week and watching him read to Nicolas had strangely turned me on. I had wanted this, wanted to feel his passion. I hoped it would bring us closer. But now the stranger had returned.

He slapped me with the back of his hand hard enough to let me know that he wasn't playing around. Thing is, I had already figured that out. My hands came up in self-defence and I tried to dig my nails into his chest. They were grabbed and pinned to the bed. All I had managed was to tear his shirt open.

"Get off me, Lawrence!"

"I deserve what every husband deserves."

But what he wanted wasn't what every husband got. He wanted sex, rough and forced. I had wanted to make love, tender, burning, a moment to remember. For that, I was as ready as I'd ever be. For me there was no past. This would be our first time. "No Lawrence, not like this."

I'd wanted to be held and kissed with a passionate mix of hunger and a gentle heart. Lawrence's touch was drunken and authoritative. It was about my understanding that he was in charge. I couldn't let him have me this way. We'd both regret it.

The weight of him kept me from getting away and in seconds he was forcing his way inside me. With each thrust he drained any of the love I might have felt for him. The man had become a monster. I'd been warned.

I managed to bring my right knee up and wedged it between him and my chest. This time his hand found my jaw. He squeezed for all he was worth. It brought the taste of blood as he held my mouth. "Lawrence, no…"

I bit down. My teeth found the fleshy web of skin between his fingers and thumb. It made him smile. He pushed down harder against my face and I couldn't breathe. I almost didn't care. My teeth remained tight on his skin.

Then the lamp fell from the nightstand and shattered on the floor. In the next room Nicolas started to cry. It was his sobbing that gave me the strength to surrender.

"Lawrence please. Let me go take care of our son."

He pulled my body straight and placed his lips on my left breast. It was a delicate kiss at first and then he bit down. His teeth clamped onto my nipple and he pulled back.

I screamed. "Fuck, Lawrence! Stop!"

He tugged harder before letting go. The suffering fed his anger. I closed my eyes. I couldn't give him that. He got between my legs again and I let him finish without a fight.

The man was expectantly quick. That was the only part of this that was tolerable. He rolled off me and I remained motionless. If this was how he loved, how he would love in the future? Had this happened before? Should I get used to it? I'd have to. There was no way I'd be able to care for Nicolas from an emergency ward. A while ago his mother had told me that although he didn't always show it, he did love me. This was a twisted and perverse affection.

Getting to his feet, he hiked up his pants. I could see the shame in his movements. His eyes, although softened by the guilt of his actions, remained threatening. It was hard to place where or when, but I had seen that look before.

I looked away only because it was expected. After a couple minutes, I got out of bed and cleaned myself up. I did this before running to take care of Nicolas. As I passed by Lawrence I noticed his eyes again. This time they were cold and contemptible, the guilt had subsided. Still, amongst the bitterness, I saw what looked like fear. Minutes later he grabbed his car keys and headed down the stairs.

As I rocked my child, the memory of his eyes came back to me—not the eyes that belonged to the Lawrence who had just raped me. These were from the Lawrence that had taken my sister and me to Versailles. That was where I had seen them before.

We had just started dating and he had given my ass a playful slap, except his hand did more than slap. It was a cupping grab and made me feel like he was checking me out. I turned to reprimand him, but his stare had stopped me. Those baleful eyes knew I'd say nothing. I had studied them briefly before conceding.

The man had it all figured out. Responding to my snarl, he had returned a wink. It was a game and he played wilfully. I'd let him have that one. He probably had most of them. I continued to rock Nicolas as I gazed out the window.

In the distance the clouds had begun to thicken. Their darkness set an emphatic gloom over the land. They knew I'd made a huge mistake the day I had married him. Why didn't I see it at the time? Was it his money? My only comfort, like these clouds, this relationship could only storm up for so long. Eventually there'd be blue skies again. Couples called it complacency and it calmed things. At least, I hoped that was how it worked.

I placed Nicolas down by his toy box and watched as the lid was pulled open and toys made their way from box to floor. He could have supper later. My face and arms ached and although there wasn't enough water to cleanse me, I had to try. I held my stomach as I sat on the floor of the shower. The steaming water cascaded over me, carrying my sorrow down the drain. I could have stayed in that shower for an eternity, but within minutes I was scrambling on my hands and knees across the bathroom floor toward the toilet.

The headache and my nausea had returned.

Chapter Ten

My mother met me at a little coffee shop across the street from Notre Dame. I'd arrived there earlier and managed a bit of sight seeing. For me it was like seeing Paris for the first time. What I liked the most about this part of the city was the smell of the Seine River. It wasn't a fresh smell, and I'm not sure why I liked it, other than its odd informality. The only way to describe it was 'Paris in the afternoon.' It relaxed me. I needed that because my mother and I needed to talk.

"So, Lawrence and I had sex last night, sort of."

She took a sip of her coffee and looked up at me. "Why are you telling me this, Madeline?"

"I'm sorry. I'm guessing we never talked about sex or my relationship?"

"We did that talk a while ago." Her lips pursed as she attempted a smile.

"You did that talk. I didn't. Besides, I've got a problem with it. I just thought we could... I mean I don't really have any girlfriends to share things with. I just thought..."

She set her coffee down. "I'm sorry. It's easy to forget that this is all new to you. From my end, we've had this talk and you've already asked your questions. We've talked them all out."

I took a second to look around for the cream and there wasn't any. "Maybe we should talk about something else then."

"What are you looking for?"

"Cream."

"I don't see any. You can take it black."

"But I like it with cream."

"Forget the cream." She shook her head. "So, how was this sex of yours? Please, no details."

"I don't drink it black?" I scouted a second time for the cream and not finding any, I decided to try and flag down a waitress. "The man raped me."

She grabbed a menu, opened it and started to browse the lunch menu. I grabbed mine and did the same. This must have been how we communicated. The daily soup was beef barley. It was rare for a country that doesn't cook anything without cheese. I might order that with the toast if I ever see a waitress. When I put the menu down my mother had already dropped hers and was staring at me.

"Okay, Mom. What did I do now?"

"I didn't say anything."

"Exactly. I just told you my husband raped me, and you say nothing."

"He didn't rape you, and stop using that word. It sounds terrible."

"I was there, and he did. And it's a terrible word because it's a terrible thing to do to somebody." I looked around again. "Where is our waitress?"

"He's your husband Madeline. Husbands don't do that to their wives."

"He hit me. He forced himself on me. That's rape."

She put a finger to her lips. "Shush. Stop saying that word. This is hard on him too. He thought he lost you. The man works all the time and it's not an easy life. I'm not saying he's right, but the man's French and he was brought up differently than us. Aggression is a culture thing. He's been a good man otherwise, right?"

"He is. I'm just…"

"I hate to tell you this, Madeline, but we've also had this talk before. It was two months into your relationship. French men are aggressive. You will get used to it. Some women even like it."

"It sounds like I'm supposed to put up with it?"

"A happy husband is an attentive one. Take away his stresses at home and he'll come around."

My hand went up when the waitress appeared. "Let me get this straight. You're saying that last night was my fault."

The oblivious waitress started wrapping a handful of silverware in napkins. I watched as she ignored me. I snapped at her. "Seriously?"

At that point my mother got up, grabbed the cream container from the next table and slammed it down in front of me. "There is no fault here. You're married. Cook him a nice supper, take care of his son and keep the damn house tidy. Everything will be fine."

I poured the cream into my coffee and let the white and brown swirl as I stirred. The sight of it turned my stomach. "Let me make sure I understand this. Cooking a pot roast and vacuuming is going to save my jaw from being knocked off my face. I can't believe that's how marriage works these days?"

"Don't do this, Madeline. Clean the house and put on something nice. I guarantee you he'll be a new person when his home becomes his sanctuary again."

I took a minute to let it sink in. Had I over reacted? I replayed the sex over in my head. It always ended the same with him hitting me and me lying helpless and waiting for the filth to end. "I don't know."

"Cook him supper. You won't regret it."

I pushed the coffee away as the headache returned. I should have had it black.

"I hope you're right."

Chapter Eleven

Cream in my coffee, no cream in my coffee, I think either choice turned my stomach. Maybe I was meant to be a tea person. I grabbed a basket as I entered the corner grocery store. In my mind I made a list of the items my husband would like, and the ones I figured I could cook. The man was a meat and potatoes kind of guy, so I'd start with pot roast and potatoes. But did he like asparagus, cauliflower, or carrots. And what was his favourite salad? Hold it. Not once did I see his mother make a salad. That helped.

"Madeline? Madeline Trembley?"

I turned to see a beautiful leggy blonde standing there. Her long blonde locks hung in loose curls and she had a smile that left me spellbound. Heck, the dress she was wearing left me spellbound. It was obvious that she knew me. I wish I felt the same.

"Hi, uh?"

She stopped and eyed me from my Prada slingbacks to my Dior shades. "Don't you look good."

I was wearing beige. It was high-end couture, but it was still beige. If I ever wanted to disappear, I'd just have to find a beach. Still, it was nice of her to say. "Um, thanks?"

She quickly realised I wasn't on the same page. "Oh, sorry. I guess it's been a while. I'm Rebecca's friend, Ingrid."

"Ah, Ingrid." I tried to look all astute and everything, but who the hell was that? "So how have you been keeping?"

She wasn't buying it. "Is everything okay, Madeline?"

"I'm right as rain." I gave myself a rap on the head with my knuckles. "Except for the amnesia."

"Amnesia. That would make sense." She held out her hand. "Let me introduce myself. My name is Ingrid Beauchamp and I knew your sister very well. I kinda knew you too."

"You knew me? How?"

"Drinking, dancing, a night out with the boys." She shot me a wink. "It was one heck of a night."

"Do you…" I stopped.

"You want to hear the story, don't you?"

"I remember so little of my life, and none of hers. I'd honestly take anything."

"Oh, this wasn't just anything, trust me." She grabbed a bottle of wine off the shelf and set it in her basket. "And it's a story for a luncheon, not a casual passing in a grocery store."

"Do you want to…"

"I have to be somewhere in an hour." She pulled out a business card and a pen. She circled the one phone number. "That's my personal number. You want the story, you call that number."

"Are you asking me out for lunch, because if you are, the answer is yes."

"It's not fair that you don't get to know your life, or that crazy sister's life. I could do an afternoon coffee tomorrow. I have a friend staying with me, but I know he won't mind if I have a guest over."

"So you knew my sister?"

"The good, the bad and the ugly. We were best friends." She took my hand. "And how are you holding up?"

"I'm okay. Lots of surprises. Lots of sitting around and wondering, like about my sister. It's hard to miss someone you never knew. Hell, I'm just getting to know myself. I mean right now I'm shopping for dinner. I kinda had the crazy idea that if I came here the meal would just jump in my basket. What the hell does my husband like?"

"He's French. He'll like beef, scalloped potatoes with loads of cheese and broccoli, again with loads of cheese. Trust me, when in doubt add a cheese sauce."

"I never thought of broccoli."

She grabbed a box of pastries and gently dropped them in my basket along with a bottle of Merlot. "And never cook without these staples. Dinner isn't the same without them."

"Good point."

"Well, I should get going. It was nice running into you, and I'll set tomorrow afternoon aside. It really is a good story."

"I'll call you."

"Do that. I'll give you directions to my place when you do."

I watched her leave and for the first time since the accident, I felt perfectly comfortable talking to someone. She wasn't judging, oozing with sympathy, or treating me like I was breakable. I liked her.

I brushed a tear from the corner of my eye and whispered, "I will."

Tears were stupid. God, I needed to find the handle on all these damn emotions. Could Ingrid be the solution? Could she give me the answers to my sister and this life I was trying so hard to be a part of, and should I tell Lawrence about this?

I grabbed the broccoli and an extra bottle of wine before heading for the cashier.

The second bottle was solely for me.

Chapter Twelve

A day after Lawrence had forced himself on me, flowers were sent to the house. They came with the most beautiful card, which I tore up without reading. It was dropped in the trash. Lawrence ran across it while I was putting supper on the table and pretended not to notice.

Instead he took a seat at the table and loaded his plate. "Scalloped potatoes, broccoli? I love broccoli."

Again, I ignored him and dished up. A part of me wanted to unload a barrage of curse words on him while the rest of me wanted to cower like I'd done last night.

"So how was your day, Madeline?"

I gave him silence.

"Did Nicolas already eat?"

I looked up at him, letting my fork full of potatoes cool inches away from my mouth. "He did."

He took a drink of his water and set it down. "I think we need to talk?"

I let my silence linger.

"I want to apologise." He waited, briefly. "It wasn't right, and I know it."

"Well, as long as you know it, I guess we're good." I put the potatoes in my mouth and stabbed a piece of roast before sliding it through the gravy.

"I know that an apology isn't enough. I need to make it up to you."

"There was a card and flowers. We're good."

He looked down. "I deserved that."

"Damn it, Lawrence. I wanted our first time to be special. I wanted it to mean something."

"Our first time? Our first time was in that park down by the Seine. You know the one, out by the Eiffel. We hid in the bushes when that couple came by. We almost got caught." He added, "That was a special day, one I'll never forget."

"Sounds nice. I wish I could have been there."

"You were…" The bulb went off. He got it, the fact that I didn't remember him, the sex, or the couple that wandered by. Last night's romp had been my only measure of his love, and it hadn't been the stuff of fairy tales.

"What can I do to make this up to you?"

"For starters, promise me you'll never do it again."

"Done."

"And…"

"Whatever it is, you've got it."

"I want to know why. Surely that's not how we normally do it."

"No." He took a minute. "Look Madeline, I'm not a patient man. You know that."

"The old Madeline might have known that."

"You're right. I wasn't like this at first. I was gentler. Work changed me."

"And I got used to it, how?"

The smile he passed me was an impish one. "I bought a lot of flowers, and a lot of cards."

"And that worked?"

"Surprisingly yes, but this time I took it too far. That's why I've rented a room at one of the nicest hotels in Paris for this Friday. We'll have a wonderful dinner, see a play, and afterwards, go for a moonlit walk."

"That doesn't take this away."

"Nothing can. I want to show you the other side of me, the rose pedals on the sheets, the champagne, the bubble bath." His eyes softened. "I once promised you the world. Just give me another chance to deliver it."

"No sex?" I asked.

"Not unless you want to."

"And Nicolas can stay with my parents?"

"Of course. There's one more thing."

"What's that?"

"It seems like we're starting a lot of our marriage on different pages. I mean, where as I'm in a relationship that has spanned a couple of years and brought us a child, you're still in the early dating part. Maybe I need to retell you something."

"What's that, Lawrence?"

He paused. "I lost my parents when I was very young. It's no excuse to be an asshole, but it does play a role."

"Who are the Trembleys then?"

"He was my first boss. The man mentored me. He liked what he saw, and eventually brought me into the fold. Since they never had children of their own, and he wanted to carry on the family name, the decision was made to adopt me. I was twenty-two."

"When did you lose your parents?"

"They both died when I was a baby. I've had different *adoptifs* all my life. Those people put a roof over my head and food in my belly, but none of them ever cared."

"I'm sorry, I never knew."

"You did though. We had this talk a year and a half ago."

"What else do I need to know?"

"Let's just say that work brings out the worst in me. Over the years you've learned to deal with my moods. Sadly, that only enabled me to become more of an asshole." He got up from his chair to give me a hug. "But that changes today. I'll work on leaving my anger at the office. Okay?"

"I'd like that."

I let him hold me. His confession was a reminder that this wasn't all about me. Sure, I'd lost my sister, my memories, and my marriage, but I wasn't the only one suffering. Lawrence had lost a wife. It sounded like we'd worked hard at what we had. The fact that he trusted me enough to open his heart like this meant a lot and I needed to be supportive.

A feather-light kiss landed on my forehead. "I'm going to read Nicolas a story, maybe do a tea party with him and his teddy bears. Care to join us?"

"I think I'll pass. These supper dishes need washing."

"Meet you in the bedroom in a couple hours?"

"No sex. Are you going to put him to bed?"

"No sex, and yes, I will."

"Then I'll see you in a couple hours."

We talked, we cuddled, and twice we made love. It was tame, respectful, and loving. He held me afterward, his touch as gentle as a spring breeze. The man hadn't seen an easy life, explaining the moods. I tried to imagine him bouncing around stranger's homes, trying to fit in while staying out of everyone's way. That I understood.

And here I thought my mother was crazy, but she was right. Men were somewhat complex.

The next morning I'd find out that I was equally complex.

Chapter Thirteen

Knuckles, suddenly rapping on the front door, rescued me from my thoughts and pulled me away from feeding Nicolas an early lunch. Had Lawrence lost his keys, or left them at the office? How would he have driven his car home? I swung the door open to see a man, well dressed, handsome, and by no means shy. He wasted no time entering our home as he politely forced his way past me.

"Hello, Maddy. It's been a while. So how have you been keeping? I heard about the accident. It must have been terrible."

"It's been a struggle for sure." I stood in the doorway and let my eyes chase him across the room. "Do I know you?"

"And a hello to you, little Nicky." He walked over to my son and took a spot at the table. Nicolas seemed comfortable with him. "It's great to see you again my little minion. You've grown an inch, I swear."

His accent wasn't French. It was more Italian, but that didn't help. "Excuse me. How do I know you?"

He cocked his head and gave me a dip of his brow. "Very funny, Maddy."

I returned a polite smile, as if sharing a joke with the family priest. Was this man an old friend? Was he one of Lawrence's old friends, or a work associate? Could this man be family?

"So how have you been feeling lately? I had heard something about you losing your mind. Maybe it was your memory. So hard to believe." He glanced over at me. It made me want to cross my arms over my chest. "You do remember me though, right? I mean I am a touch unforgettable, no?"

"No, I mean yes. I mean I'm sorry but I—"

"Don't you dare finish that sentence." He waved his arms as if acting out a scene in Macbeth or Othello. "I could not bear to think that you would not remember me, no matter what the circumstances." He walked over to Lawrence's bar and poured himself a glass of vodka. "I take care of business for your husband."

"You work with him?"

"I would rather slice my wrists than spend time with that anthropoid."

"Uh, so you're family?"

He paused for a second before letting out a laugh. "Why Maddy. You surprise me with your candour. No, I am not family."

"Can I have a clue?"

"Stories." He took a sip. "I have heard all the stories."

There were stories? That sparked my interest. My husband wasn't perfect, and he had a temper. I had learned from his moods, and from my mother, to keep him happy. A happy Lawrence was a husband that I could handle. A happy Lawrence was a decent guy. Still, there was always something lying in the folds of that man's mind that kept me on edge. It was a darkness that demanded its distance, even when his charm was stirring the emotions inside me.

"You have me at a disadvantage." I kept my eyes focused, trying to burn him for any sign. "You see if I admit I don't know you, I risk not hearing these stories. If I lie, or try and bluff my way along, I will most certainly stumble into my own web."

"Smart girl. I've always loved that about you." His smile sharpened. "You want the stories?"

"Yes."

"I don't know. What's in it for me? Perhaps the usual fee." His eyes started the undressing.

I'd met people, lots of people, over the last few weeks. They'd become family and friends, once people from a past life. I had been nothing but cordial to these strangers, until now. "Okay, cut to the chase asshole. How do you know my husband?"

"Sorry, Maddy. It's just that you've heard these stories before."

"Look, I'm suffering from amnesia so spill your guts or get the hell out."

"My mistake. You see, you were the one who told them to me." He grabbed me by the arms and pulled me in for a hug. His arms wrapped around me like a Christmas bow. "You usually told them to me after we…"

His kiss was everything that passion cast fire to. It was enchanting, burning, and hungry. I'd never felt this with Lawrence, my husband. I wanted to pull away. I should have pulled away. I was a married woman. Somehow, I couldn't. Instead I let him whisk my mind into a land of fantasy and lust.

It was a child's spoon dropping to the floor that brought me back.

"Stop it!" I placed my hands on his chest, a chest as chiselled as a marble statue, and pushed myself away. He wasn't familiar, but this passion was. "Who the heck are you?"

"Why, I'm your Ricardo. You and I have been lovers for the last six months, less the time you were in your coma, of course."

"Of course." He tried to reel me back in and I pulled away. "Stop it! I'm a married woman."

"Have you not been paying attention? This man of yours is the Beelzebub, himself."

"Beelzewho?" I had no idea what this Beelzebub was, but neither he nor Ricardo was my husband, the man I had made my vows to. "You should leave before he gets home."

"Tell me our kiss didn't remind you of all those precious evenings we shared, nights when our passions left you too exhausted to move. You said you never wanted this to end, yet here you are, acting like it never happened."

"I don't remember any of this."

"Spend the next few hours with me." He took my hand and tried to pull me upstairs to the bedroom. First the bar and now the bedroom, he had definitely spent time here. "We will make love for hours and you will understand the magic. You need to feel it again."

"Again?" I pulled free and headed over to the table where I picked up Nicolas's spoon from the floor. "Look, I'm flattered, and I'm sure whatever we had was nice. I don't doubt I even needed it at the time, but consider this over. I have no desire to crawl into bed with you. I think you should leave!"

"But I don't want to leave, and you don't want me to leave."

"Guess again." I backed away from him. "If you touch me, I'll tell my husband and he'll take care of you."

"You'll never tell him. He would kill you first. Think hard, Maddy. We spent a weekend in Naples just two months ago, when Lawrence was in England."

I didn't remember the trip, but I did remember seeing the tan lines when I had come out of my coma, tan lines made by a bikini. I had looked for that bikini. All I found were drab one-piece bathing suits. Perhaps I needed to look in Naples. "Please, you have to leave. I'm—"

"You are afraid. I get that. You were afraid when we first found each other as well. But it was also exciting back then, hiding in shadows, sneaking around like teenagers. We can have that again, but I see you are not ready yet. I am willing to wait."

He started for the door and I was happy to see him out. "Soon Maddy, you will want me again and we will find our way back to stolen kisses and plush hotel rooms."

At that point he took my hand, placed a gentle kiss on the back of my knuckle, and grabbed me for one last kiss. His brute strength and overpowering cologne weakened me into submission. I gave him his kiss, willingly, earnestly. Then, trying to hide my schoolgirl grin, I closed the door behind him.

I stood in the doorway, watching him through the peephole.

Seconds later the stranger was gone. I honestly hoped that I'd never see him again, but I knew better.

Chapter Fourteen

My husband had raped me, apologised, and since that day had made love to me like the man I hoped I'd married. Still, there had been a need for a lover. Why did I need a Ricardo in my life? It wasn't like Lawrence was lacking. He was handsome, wealthy and he had his moments when he made me feel special. Sure, there was the temper. Was that reason for me to run out and find the arms of another? But I had once wanted this life and Ricardo was no accident, he had been a choice.

I reached for the phone and dialled my parents. Dad answered and told me they would love it if Nicolas and I swung by for lunch. There was always something special about hearing that. An enormous part of me wanted to confess my infidelity with my mother, but as I got closer to their apartment the reality returned. Our last talk hadn't gone that well and what would I share? What would it prove? I'd put them both through so much. No, this was my marriage, and Ricardo was my mess.

At la République Metro Station, Nicolas and I got off the train, made our way through the tiled corridors, and climbed the stairs that led to the streets. Since I'd smashed up my car weeks ago, we were all trains and feet. It wasn't the best way for Nicolas and I to get around, but it worked. These closed in streets were a comfort to me. Rue de Malte was one of the areas I truly treasured.

I put Nicolas down and took his hand. The air was brimming with sugar-laden delicacies as we made our way through the alley and past the patisserie. This area gave me a few simple memories. I remembered waiting to make a purchase at the patisserie's day's-end window, but what was it that I always ordered. I loved sweets so maybe it was the chocolate cake. I would have also liked anything with cherries.

These were the memories that didn't matter. What I liked to eat, or what my favourite colour was, wasn't important anymore. My pallet had been cleansed. I could relearn my favourites, find new preferences. Maybe my tastes had changed. Where I might have been a strawberry tart girl, I was a chocolate brownie person this point forward. I'd be okay with that. Change wasn't the enemy, fighting it was. Lawrence was right.

"Rebecca!"

The man's befuddled slur of my sister's name startled me. I grabbed Nicolas's hand tighter and pulled him close. "I'm sorry, and you are?"

"Rebecca, it's me." The man sat on the sidewalk, his coat tattered and his hair uncombed. In his hand was a stained coffee cup with a chip in the rim. Beside him there was a rolled up sleeping bag in a small cardboard box. I had to believe that box held all his belongings.

"I beg your pardon."

"I'm Dougie."

Dougie? The name was curiously familiar. "I'm sorry, but have we met?"

From his childlike excitement, came an unsettling sadness. "Aren't you my friend, Rebecca?"

How was it possible that this man could have known my sister? This man was homeless. He owned nothing, except for a box of God-only-knows-what and the stench of the street. "Rebecca is my sister."

"Don't do this to an old man. Are you trying to kill me?"

"What?"

"Don't lie to me after all we've been through, Rebecca."

"Who's lying? I'm not…" I had to stop. Did I really want to have this argument with an old man?

His lashing out wasn't anger. He was scared. His wrinkled face was hoping this was a joke. And how could I tell him the truth?

"You used to eat with me. I haven't seen you in a while." He dropped his eyes to the ground. "You helped me stop drinking. Don't you remember?"

My eyes followed his to the ground. There I saw the shoes without laces and the feet without socks. She must have adopted this man—a sister with a gentle heart. The thought put a smile on my face. Then I looked back at the frail old man's face. He reminded me of a lost little puppy.

"I'm sorry that I don't remember you. You see, I was in a car accident." I waited for him to look back up at me. When he did I added, "And I'm sorry I didn't come around sooner."

His smile returned. "I'm glad you're okay."

"I'm not fully okay. I have amnesia. Do you know what that is?"

"I'm a doctor. I know."

"A doctor?" I doubted that. The man was old. What would it hurt to play along with him? I took his hand and it was cold and weak. "I've lost my memories. It kinda sucks." I dropped my head and gave him a minute.

He looked up at me. "You don't remember me?"

I had to give him something, for Rebecca. That way I could keep her alive for this old guy. "A few recollections, nothing major."

His eyes trailed off to Nicolas. "Who's the kid?"

"Oh, he's my…" Damn, lies were complex. "He's my sister's boy. This is Nicolas."

"Why doesn't she have him?"

God, did I really want to play this game? "She, uh…" It was easier than telling him the truth. And I guess it didn't hurt anybody, quite the opposite in fact. "She's off getting her hair done."

He pulled his hand away and rubbed the back of it. "You're a good person, Rebecca."

"Thank you. You are too, but I really should go."

"It was good to see you again."

"I'll see you around." Why did I just say that? I didn't have time for this. I chuckled inside at the idea of having him over for supper. Lawrence would freak out, especially if I dressed the old guy up in a suit and said he was a doctor.

And with that I lifted Nicolas to my arms and left the man with his thoughts. But I couldn't leave our visit like this. Instead we bought a bag of croquettes at the patisserie and I set them in his hands.

He stared at it.

"It's okay, there's still twelve in there."

He looked up to me and smiled. "You usually keep a couple for yourself."

"To be honest I thought about it, but I've been fighting this bug. I didn't think you'd want my germs."

"But I touched your hand a minute ago. I never felt a fever."

"I know. It's just a nausea thing, stomach flu I'm thinking. I was getting headaches from a concussion, but they've stopped."

"You'd have a fever if it was a flu." Then he added, "it's not a bug."

"Oh, that's right. You're a doctor."

"Don't be like that."

"Sorry." From the worn shoes to the hair-lick protruding from the back of his head, there was nothing screaming he was much of an authority on anything. "Tell the toilet it's not the flu. It might disagree."

"I think it's something else."

"Okay." I thought of the accident and wondered if it was related, a concussion, a neck out of whack. But I felt good, other than the bowl hugging. "I'm sorry. I don't mean to—"

He scratched at the scruff of hair on his head. "I just want you to go get checked out."

"I will." I looked around at the other people living on the street. It was like seeing them for the first time. Each person was a somebody, or wanted to be a somebody. My sister figured that out and good for her. "If it's not the flu, then what's the diagnosis? And let's not make this anything fatal. I don't have time for that."

"Go get checked out."

I took another look at the old guy playing the part of a doctor, instead of the drunk? Granted it didn't hurt anybody, but I had to go. "I'm sorry, Dougie, but my parents are waiting."

He patted my hand with his. "Be patient with your memories. The past is never gone, merely misplaced."

Chapter Fifteen

U p at the apartment, Mom was getting lunch ready for us. She'd poured me a coffee and I took a quick sip. The visit with Dougie had left me rattled and I needed to settle my nerves. It tasted good.

"You forgot the cream, Madeline." Dad slid the porcelain black and white cow over to me and I reluctantly took it.

"Right." I poured the cream into my cup and watched as it folded like clouds on a blustery day. My stomach began to spasm at the sight of it. Again, I'd been given a preference. This one had changed with the amnesia. It was crazy to take cream when it made me ill, but Dad needed this.

I noticed the magazine tucked away with some unopened mail. It was the one with my Rebecca on the cover. Dad must have had it out. The walls of my heart stiffened as I reached for it. On one dog-eared page there was a beautiful young model looking incredible in a designer body suit. It had sparkles. There was a second dog-eared page. In this shot my sister was half-naked with a scarf drawn through a brass buckle on her left hip. It drew my eyes straight to the smoothness of her curves. It didn't jog me into any homesick feeling for her. The woman remained a stranger, but I remembered seeing this shot. It was in my dream.

I closed the magazine. "Dad?"

"Yes, Madeline."

"What do you know about an old man named Dougie?"

"Dougie?" He looked up, giving me his undivided attention. "I haven't heard that name since…"

"He says he was Rebecca's friend. I met him downstairs. He talks highly of her."

"The man should. She fed him enough donuts." His jealousy was comical. "The old fart had a power over her. I'm afraid your sister was more heart than brain at times."

"He talks about her like she's a Saint."

"Patron Saint of Pastries, perhaps."

"He claims he's a doctor."

"He was, although it's easy to forget. He's been a bum on the corner as long as I can remember."

"He really was a doctor?" The thought rattled me. "Rebecca saw him different than us. Why do you think that was?"

"I'm not sure." A smile widened across his face. "But that's what made her Rebecca."

"Interesting." I'd tossed the magazine face down and just noticed the advertisement on the back-page. There she was again, my sister sitting on a beach in a pair of cut-offs. She'd strategically draped her arm across a bare chest. She looked incredible and I'd be lying if I didn't admit that I was a little bit jealous. It looked like she had an exciting life, one I knew I'd never have. Sure, I had Lawrence and, for the most part, he was a good husband, but was it enough? Who was this sister of mine?

"Hey Mom, do you have anything here of Rebecca's?"

She ignored me. I'm sure she was tired of dealing with my needy quest for my memory. It was a little tiring, even to me. I decided to persist. "Mom?"

The wooden spoon slammed down onto the counter. "What now?"

"Mom please. I'm sorry, I just want to feel something, anything."

"Try to remember our feelings." She stopped for a second. "I'm sorry. I just wish you weren't making this so hard for everyone. You have a life and for some reason it doesn't seem like it's good enough for you. Why can't you just give it a chance? Your life isn't that bad."

"I'm not saying that it is. I'm just trying to see where I fit. Maybe I'll get my answers if I remember my sister."

"You have parents that love you, a child that needs you, and a husband that takes care of you. I'm just saying, most women would be satisfied."

I wanted to correct her. My life consisted of a husband that worked too much and an Italian who I'd once had an affair with. Either way, it wasn't what I'd have expected. "Mom, he drinks a lot and he works too much. I never see him. At first I thought it was normal."

She closed her eyes and held a finger against her lips. "Quiet. Your father doesn't need to know. Nobody said marriage was easy. All marriages have struggles and you have to make this one work, for your son."

I watched her as she got up and stirred the stew. Then she grabbed a broom and started to sweep the floor. She wanted to sit but couldn't as long as I was here. This conversation wasn't what she wanted. I tried to wait her out, but she was good.

"Thanks anyway, Mom." I got up and walked down the hall to my old room. With any luck I'd find a bikini. Heck, I'd settle for anything that still fit that wasn't brown. I browsed through my stuff with no luck.

Rebecca's bedroom door had been closed when I walked past it. I'm guessing that meant off limits. But wasn't she my sister? I get the whole, their daughter thing, but I needed my life back. I'd be discreet.

I tiptoed back down the hall and slipped into her room. Closing the door behind me, I headed for the closet doors. My eyes, if they could have, would have been drooling at the sight. Oh my

God, did this girl have clothes. There were jeans, pink blouses, t-shirts and oh wow, were those hoodies? I had to try one on. It was such a sloth-like comfort.

A jewellery box had been set on top of her dresser. I had to continue my indulgence. I tried a couple of the rings and put one of her necklaces around my neck. I kept the rings on my fingers and then I spotted the photographs.

There were three of them and I grabbed them as I took a seat on the edge of her bed. The top picture was of my casually dressed sister. Could finding her be my way of finding myself? I don't know. She doesn't own anything in light brown. That alone makes her cooler than me. "Who are you Rebecca? You had homeless friends, a modelling career and a life of fun."

The next photo was of a ruggedly handsome and somewhat familiar man. He was damn hot. I couldn't place him, so I flipped it over to see if there was a name. Scribbled on the back was Johannes? Yikes, he was my sister's boyfriend.

"Madeline, what are you doing in here?" That was not my mother's happy voice.

My heart sank. Would I be grounded or have my allowance docked? "I was just…" What was I doing?

"This is your sister's room. You shouldn't be in here."

"I'm not hurting anything." I held up the picture of Johannes. "He's a cute one. This was Rebecca's beau, right?"

"Give me that." She snatched the picture from my hand. "Take those rings off and get out of here."

"What?"

"You shouldn't be in here. Why would you do this?" She grabbed the rings as I took them off and slammed them on the dresser top. "Out!"

I watched her rage continue as she closed the closet doors and took me by the arm. Suddenly I was a six-year old brat about to be stuffed nose first into a corner. "Mom. What are you doing?"

She pushed me out of the room and closed the door behind me. "You have a lot of nerve, young lady."

"Young lady?"

Dad arrived, as confused as I was. "What's going on here?"

"Madeline was just leaving." She stormed off to get Nicolas and in seconds we were standing in the hallway outside their apartment.

Through the door I could hear Dad arguing on my behalf, but she didn't sound like she wanted anything to do with it. I had no idea what had just happened. I did know that Nicolas didn't need to hear any of this. Besides, it was getting late and I still wanted to see Ingrid.

With any luck her story would save the day.

Chapter Sixteen

I arrived at Ingrid Beauchamp's door with my son firmly propped on my right hip. The ride on the Metro was lengthy enough to allow Nicolas a juice box and an orange. It also allowed me enough time to give some serious thought to what my mother had said. I was now certain that she was going crazy. I mean why would she snap like that? Had I really stepped that hard on anybody's toes? I was just trying to find myself.

Ingrid opened the door seconds after my knock. It took that long for me to catch my breath.

"*Bonjour*. Please come in and bring that tiny man of yours. I bought animal crackers yesterday, just for him."

"Thank you, Ingrid." I looked at the opened box on the coffee table. There might have been a giraffe or two missing. "For him?"

"They're *magnifique*. I also picked up a few jars of baby food and those I haven't touched, yet. Does he like peas? I also have banana."

"He's actually eating real food, although I'm sure he'll love it." My breath was caught as I set my son and his bag down by the door. Nicolas grinned before bolting for the cookies. "Nicolas, please."

"Relax, Madeline. *Il est un garçon.*"

And being a boy, he dumped the cookies on the hardwood floor and started to play. Dazed, I stood and took it all in. "I really can't thank you enough for having us. It's awfully generous of you."

"Your sister was a special girl." She pointed to the couch. "Make yourself comfortable and I'll get us some iced tea."

I looked over the apartment while she was gone and cringed at the sight of the marbles in the bowl. I hoped Nicolas didn't spot them.

The room was large, with hardwood floors and glass doors that opened to a patio. It was huge compared to what my parents had. The corner of the living room consisted of a large pile of beanbag chairs, awaiting the next large gathering of friends. It might be a party or a family get-together. Either way she was ready.

Ingrid set a plate of cheeses and crackers down on the couch between us and we started to talk. It didn't take me long to realise this girl was articulate. She made her money modelling, but it was easy to tell that this girl had done a few years of university. There were beautiful paintings, a Lucrezia Borgia and two Albrecht Dürers, all high-quality replicas. They weren't your average wall hangings. I'd have expected a Picasso, Rockwell, or Monet because they were the popular choices.

"Do you have a degree in the arts?" I took a sip of tea. "I mean the Borgia is an amazing piece."

"I do, and *merci*. I love her stuff"

"So, where did you study?"

Ingrid folded one leg under her as she outstretched the other to the coffee table, a pane of glass held up by two over-sized acrylic clear dice. Meanwhile, I sat proper, knees together and back straight, like I'd been taught.

"I have a doctorate from La Sorbonne."

Her accent intrigued me. "You're not German, are you?"

"You're looking at a bit of a mix. I moved to Germany in pursuit of Marcus. I met him at the university and it was love the second I saw him, for me anyway. He was doing the photography scene and I was taking historical arts. We hit it off. After he graduated, the man became a little boy, homesick for his Frankfurt. I followed. He needed a model to get his company started so I helped him."

"Marcus is a boyfriend then?"

"The man is now. He and Johannes, your sister's beau, were childhood friends. They were both born in Bavaria and living in Frankfurt. Your sister and I eventually talked them into moving to Paris." She finished her glass of tea and set it on the coffee table. "*Techniquement*, I'm a Frenchie, born and raised. I speak several languages fluently though."

"So, do Marcus and Johannes live here?"

"*Oui*, but that's not why you're here. You wanted to know more about your sister, so ask away."

Where to start? I wanted to know everything. The more she could tell me, the better the chance I'd find a memory. "She was a model. How'd that happen?"

"That was my fault." She pulled her pant leg up to reveal a four-inch scar. "I broke my ankle on a photo shoot. A word to the wise; never let them tell you stilettos and ladders are a safe combination. Rebecca came to Frankfurt and filled in for me. Marcus loved how the camera saw her and decided to bring her aboard. He was looking to hire an extra model and this way he could hire someone he knew instead of some stranger."

"And she had what it took?"

"Oh, she was shy at first, clumsy as a drunk in a domino factory, but that was just a hiccup. Have you not seen her pictures?"

"One or two."

"People saw her soul in those photos, saw her passion. She was very likeable to the clients."

"Was she a smoker?" The question popped out before I could register it.

"*Pourquoi*? Why would you ask that?"

"Because I've had a crazy week."

"She smoked once and a while, we all did. For her it was more a Friday thing."

"A Friday thing?"

"Our girl was a strange one. Do you remember the night she tried to hook you up."

"Like with a guy?"

"Rebecca really wanted you to ditch Lawrence."

"But, she knew Lawrence and I were serious, right?"

"Crazy sister, huh. She wanted to see you happy. That was the story I wanted to tell you. You want to hear it?"

"Absolutely." I really wanted to hear everything, unless it included a man named Ricardo.

Chapter Seventeen

Ingrid left to refill our ice teas. Nicolas found the marbles. My own marbles started to scatter across the floor as they rolled in every direction. I imagined the pain of stepping on one of them. His bottom lip began to grow as I dropped to my knees and started to round them up. I pointed to the cookies and his grin returned.

Ingrid entered the room and started in on her story as if the marbles had never happened. "Rebecca moved in with me shortly after I broke my ankle. She needed a place to live and I had the extra bedroom. You came for a visit days later."

I set the marbles down as I scanned for strays. It looked safe, so I returned to the couch. "This was in Germany? I'm surprised Lawrence let me go."

"It was, and you didn't tell him. Your head was a mess and you needed a break."

"It was that bad?"

"You were having doubts." She continued, "Rebecca's first week in Germany was a tough one. There was a lot to learn and Marcus had her working quite a few accounts."

On the night you arrived the plan was to go out with the boys and burn up the town. At the very least, she wanted to get your mind off your man. So, after a quick change at the apartment, complete with the tour, we phoned for a limo. We sipped champagne to a night of whatever awaited us."

My doubts were strong, even back then. "Please continue."

"Marcus and Johannes met us downtown, at a little club called *Die Musik-Fabrik*, The Music Factory. It was all disco lights, mirrored walls and they had all the up and coming bands. The odd time they had comedians, good ones, but that night it was a band named Meatloaf. Marcus had done a lot of advertising work for the club over the last few months. We didn't worry about cover charges, waiting in lines, or finding a table."

"Sounds like we had fun."

"You were a tad tipsy from the drive over, and I mean flirting with Johannes tipsy."

"Flirting? Seriously." I remembered the photo and it didn't surprise me. He was a handsome one. "Didn't Rebecca mind?"

"It was playful. Your sister enjoyed watching you with your hair down. You needed this."

"And Johannes was a good sport about it?"

"Please, he's German so it's in his blood to flirt," she laughed. "But he was also a gentleman."

"Did I know they were dating?"

"Like any girl, your sister was playing games with him. Who doesn't? She encouraged the flirting. I asked her about it and she said she just wanted you to have a good time. I had no reason to doubt her, at first."

"At first. That doesn't sound good."

"It wasn't."

"Wait, Rebecca wanted *me* to have him?"

"She did. The nightclub got busier and we couldn't find the waitress. Johannes and Marcus decided to brave the mob and get more drinks. You wanted to powder your nose and I decided to go with you. Rebecca was stuck staying with the table. We'd lose it if she didn't."

"I'm guessing you and I talked in the bathroom?"

"Oh yes. We talked. You drunk-told me she wanted you to take Johannes. She had found him for you. Her plan was for you to drop Lawrence and fall in love with Johannes."

"She was never interested in him?"

"That's what she kept saying. When you and I returned to the table all hell broke loose. I called her out and the truth came out. You were horrified, and Johannes didn't know anything about the switch. He had fallen in love with Rebecca. The man was crushed that your sister didn't have feelings for him.

There was a lot of yelling and a lot of hurt feelings that night. Lawrence was looking pretty good at this point. As fun as this night of dance and drinking may have been, you preferred the stability of your man. The boys ran off and I went with them."

"I can't believe Rebecca did that."

"Oh, she'd planned the exchange from the moment they met. She was stringing him along until the time was right. She figured you needed him more than she did. Rebecca was scared for you."

"If things were that bad, why did I marry him?"

"For that one we need to trade our ice teas for glasses of wine."

Chapter Eighteen

I hadn't done my math. Ingrid handed me a Chardonnay and informed me that I wanted to leave him, but had changed my mind. Days after the whole nightclub fiasco, Rebecca had flown to Paris to see me. We had gone for a bite of lunch and I had told her the truth about some bruises that she had noticed earlier. They were from Lawrence and we'd been working on the anger issues. Ingrid also mentioned that I had told Rebecca that I couldn't leave him because I was pregnant.

"And what about Johannes? They started dating." I asked. "It's a fair guess that he eventually forgave my sister."

"It wasn't easy." Ingrid folded her other leg underneath her as she shifted on the couch and took a sip of wine. "The next day Rebecca arrived at the apartment alone. She'd just dropped you off at the airport. You couldn't wait to get back to Paris. I was sitting at the table with my coffee when she walked through the door. I poured her a cup and told her to have a seat."

"You were still mad at her?"

"Mad, disappointed, more confused than anything. She tried to tell me she was only doing this for Johannes and that all she wanted was to see the two people she cared about happy. Then she lit a cigarette."

"Yes, about that. You said she smoked."

"Yes, your sister smoked. It had a lot to do with her past."

"How?"

"Rebecca was a very broken girl." Ingrid continued, "I asked her if this was about Billy? Her jaw bounced twice off the floor. I wasn't supposed to know about him."

"Billy?" Hearing that name had my jaw hitting the floor. He was a boy we both knew back in Canada. The memories were instant.

"He must have been a pretty important kid. Rebecca had a major crush on this Billy."

I inched forward. "We both did. What did this have to do with the smoking?"

"That, I never found out. I don't think Johannes ever knew either."

"There was a can on the rooftop at my parent's apartment. It was full of cigarette butts. Was it hers?"

"I don't know anything about a can on any rooftop. I just know your sister had a lot of hang-ups over Billy. Johannes had to work hard at knocking down the walls."

"Good for him."

"Rebecca had a huge heart. We had many cries and they were all therapeutic. Shortly after you ran off and became a wife and mother, Rebecca got her own place. After a few sessions of therapy with Cabernet and Merlot, a box of tissues on hand, she and Johannes started dating. Shortly after that we all moved back to Paris."

"Well, some of this makes sense now. Lawrence wasn't somebody I loved with all my heart. He was just the guy that got me pregnant. I'm not a smoker. That was Rebecca."

Ingrid got to her feet and rounded up the glasses. "So, now you know."

I watched as Nicolas ate the last cookie. It was an elephant. I hadn't heard Ricardo's name through any of this and that was good. It was a safe bet that I had grown to need somebody like him. But, that was then. Now I needed to get home and start dinner. I lifted myself off the couch and started to cleanup after my boy. "I can't thank you enough, Ingrid."

"*Avec plaisir.*" She returned from the kitchen with a package. "I've been meaning to drop this in the mail."

I took the parcel from her. "What is it?"

"A few items your sister left at my place. The woman left her crap everywhere." She sighed as she watched me slip it into my purse. "*Elle me manque.*"

That was my cue to go in for a hug. I barely knew Ingrid and yet, I felt we had known each other our whole lives. She was that kind of girl. A few memories had been sparked and even though they were distant, they were mine.

"I miss her too, Ingrid."

Chapter Nineteen

When I got home, there were two cars sitting in the driveway, Lawrence's black Mercedes and a matching grey one. That could only mean one thing, we had company and I hadn't even started dinner. I hurried my pace as I scurried Nicolas through the front door.

"Hi Lawrence. I'm sorry about supper, I'll get started on it right away."

"Never mind. Did you see your present?"

"My present?" Birthday immediately came to mind. I hadn't given it any thought, but I'd have one, just like everyone else. I had no idea what day that was, but I'm thinking I do now. Or was it an anniversary?

He grabbed my hand, led me out the door a stopped beside the grey Mercedes. "You are welcome."

This time I gave the car a second look. I almost lost my lunch when I did. Other than the fact it hadn't rolled through a patio of chairs and tables, it looked just like the car from the accident. My mind hazed over, as my legs turned to tree stumps. What was he thinking?

"What do you think? Go ahead, get in."

But I didn't want to get in it, or even look at it. He opened the door and shoved me twice to get me behind the wheel. "I don't know Lawrence."

"Try it." He reached across my lap and put the keys in the ignition.

I could feel the sweat forming on the nape of my neck. The seat sucked me in like quicksand. Then Lawrence closed the door, trapping me inside. He motioned for me to open the window and I tried the button. It didn't work.

"You have to turn the damn key on, Madeline."

I fumbled with the key, turned it on and pressed the button for the window. "I'm sorry. I, uh…"

"God, I swear this is your first time in a car. Good thing we're not doing this at the dealership. You'd be making asses out of the both of us."

"Again, sorry." I looked on to see Nicolas standing in the doorway of the house. He looked lost and I just wanted to hug him.

"Quit apologising. A Trembley is above that."

"It's just that I haven't been behind the wheel of a car since…"

"Shit Madeline, that happened weeks ago. You need to get over it already."

Shame kept me from saying anything. I had done everything to be the good wife. I'd cooked, cleaned, and put up with his moods. I'd worn beige day after day with a smile. The one thing I couldn't do, was deal with that accident. The images still haunted me. Now, sitting in this car, all I could see was the blood on the leather seats, the matted blonde hair and the lifeless eyes of that woman staring through a shattered windshield. She was my sister. I didn't remember much lately, but those eyes were very real. So was the chill they set in my bones.

"It's not as easy as that, Lawrence."

He took a step back, put a hand on his hip, and shook his head. "Seriously?" When the first tear started down my cheek he slammed his fist on the roof. "Damn it, Madeline. I buy you a fucking car and you turn this into something awful. Can't you just say thank you like other people? Do you have any idea how much this thing cost?"

I kept my eyes forward, looking at my son. He was crying. Lawrence banged the roof again and I fought off any further tears. If he saw them he'd hit me for sure. Then I looked up at the rear-view mirror and I saw her.

A whisper escaped my lips. "I'm so sorry."

"You need to get help." Lawrence put his index finger up to his head and circled his ear twice. Seconds later he was in his Mercedes and tossing gravel at the front of the house as he sped off. Tires bit the pavement and he was gone. It was safe to let the tears fall.

I looked up through my wet eyes and saw my son. He was still standing there. "Damn it. What have I done?" My husband bought me a gift and I had turned it into this. My stupid memories had hurt both him and my son.

I dropped my head and tried to force them away, but in my mind the metal was twisting and the glass was pelting against my face like hailstones. The new car scent was hidden somewhere behind the smell of blood and cigarette smoke. I didn't look up. If I had, I'd see the faceless people standing like statues. I'd see the smoke curling up from their fingers. Lawrence hadn't seen any of this.

He had bought it because it was a safe and practical car. I had to make this up to him.

I wiped my eyes, grabbed Nicolas and buckled him in. Then I started the car and backed it onto the street. We did two laps around the block and one lap around the park. Nicolas had stopped crying. After sitting in the driveway with the engine off, I unbuckled my boy, took him in the house and headed straight for the bathroom.

My stomach wretched for close to twenty minutes as I curled up on the bathroom floor beside the toilet.

There, that wasn't so hard.

Chapter Twenty

I saw Lawrence off to work the next morning with a coffee and the most sincere apology a wife could muster. The car was a gift and although the sight of the damn thing scared the shit out of me, it was meant as a nice gesture. This was how my husband reasoned things out, a sensible and secure car for the ones he cared about. I should have seen it. Nicolas and I had survived the crash. Call it luck or practical, this car was proven.

After Nicolas finished his toast and egg, I washed him up and loaded him in the car. He was buckled in with a teddy bear and an unopened drink box. By the time I grabbed my purse and got in the driver's seat, the drink box was open and it was half-emptied all over the seat. In hindsight I shouldn't have given it to him until he needed it. In hindsight, I shouldn't have taken my eyes off him yesterday with a bowl of marbles in the same room. No one had left the brochure on child-raising with me after the accident. Did I have one before it?

After a quick clean up we were off. The juice box incident turned out to be a welcome distraction. Shaken by that screw up, I wasn't thinking so much about the driving. It was a nice car. Everything was automatic, the windows, the seats, and the side mirrors. My old car didn't have those things, at least I don't think it did.

"So where are we going, Tiger?"

Nicolas looked at me and answered, "Home, tub." He held up his hands. They were still a little sticky. "Home, tub."

"No way, Kiddo. Those dirty paws are your fault." I thought for a second. "Hey, wanna go see Ingrid, or Gamma and Grampa?"

Nicolas's eyes lit up. "Ingrid."

"Good choice." The woman had a way with the men, no matter what the age. "Ingrid's it is then."

I didn't know if she'd be home, but we had a full tank of gas and the whole day ahead of us. Getting out and not having to deal with the Metro was even better.

Ingrid's apartment was a fifteen-minute drive and I handled it like a pro. This car handled it like a pro. I really shouldn't have reacted the way I did.

We parked and quickly found our way to her apartment. I knocked and was about to give her a big hello until the door opened. It wasn't Ingrid. It was the guy from the photo. It was Johannes. He looked a lot taller than the photo.

"Hello, I uh…"

Johannes reaction was equally as suave. He stood there staring with his mouth slightly open.

From the kitchen Ingrid called out, "*Qu'est-ce*, Johannes?"

When he didn't say anything, I answered. "It's me, Ingrid, Madeline. I brought the marble monster."

With that Johannes broke his silence. "I'm so sorry, Madeline. You look so much like her. I…"

"Rebecca and Madeline were twins Johannes," Ingrid reminded him as she joined us.

"I know that." He shook his head and stepped back. "Please, come in."

Ingrid gave Johannes a shove toward the doorway. "You are going to be late if you don't get moving."

"Yes, I uh, it was nice to see you again, Madeline." He stepped through the doorway, stopped, and turned back to me. He thought of saying something, closed his mouth and walked away.

I watched him leave before turning to Ingrid. "What's with him? Did I do something wrong?"

"You do look a lot like her. I think he forgot how much." She took Nicolas's hand and led him toward the kitchen. "Do you think he'd like a drink box?"

"Don't get me started." I waved my comment off. "It's your home, but the little monster dumped one in my new car earlier."

"You have a car? I thought you were a Metro girl."

"Lawrence got it for me. It freaked me out at first and I over reacted. I'm good now."

"Why did it freak you out?"

"It's the same car. He shoved me behind the wheel and I froze. I don't know why I did that. It was stupid. It's a wonderful, and very safe, car."

"Is that how you got the bruise?"

I followed her eyes to my wrist, where Lawrence had grabbed me. My cuff had ridden up a bit and you could see the blues and greens. I quickly pulled the cuff back down.

"Well I guess that answers that question."

"I pissed him off a couple days ago, forgot to iron his shirts. Then he…" I twirled my finger around my ear, "said I needed help."

"I don't mean to judge, but that's not right, Sweetie." She waited for a second and added, "Rebecca used to worry about his temper. She said you'd been roughed up once or twice before. We French have a saying, *seul un fou cache la vérité d'un fou*, only a fool hides the truth of a fool."

"This isn't something new for me, is it?"

"I'm afraid not, and your man is right. You do need help."

"You're taking his side?"

"Not a chance. I mean you need an ear to bend. Get it off your chest." She put her hand on my shoulder. "Good thing for you I took a semester of psychology. I will be that ear."

My cheeks tightened as a smile stretched across my face. "So, if I were to hire you Doc, how would you fix this?"

Ingrid kept her eyes fixed on mine as the bubbly persona sobered. "Sorry, but you'd be leaving him."

"Whoa." I pulled away from her. "He's not that bad. I just need to pay attention. He's under a lot of pressure with work and think about what he's been through. He also thought he lost me. It overwhelms him at times. That's all."

"I don't doubt that life is tough for him, but it's also tough for you. Don't forget that."

"I know what you're thinking, but he's not like that."

She put her hand back on my shoulder. "Relax, Madeline. You don't need to convince me. He's your husband and I'll always respect that."

"I know. I've put him through quite a bit over the last few weeks. We just need to settle back in on each other."

"True enough. Hey, how would you like to help me plan a dinner for Marcus? The man thinks he's got a woman who can cook. He's such a silly boy, but silly me if I can't."

Lawrence really wasn't that bad. "I can give you an excellent recipe for cheesy scalloped potatoes. It worked for me."

She handed me a pen and paper and I started to jot the ingredients down. As I wrote the cooking instructions a question came to me. I wrote the last line, took a deep breath, and then spit it out. "What do I do about my mother?"

"What do you mean?"

I explained how I had gone through Rebecca's room, and how she'd reacted when she caught me. It was quite the blind side. Seeing the room, the clothing, and her photos, I'd started to feel something. My mother had squashed that like a bug under her foot. I needed to know why.

"Are you asking Ingrid or the doctor? Because the Doc doesn't sugar-coat anything, whereas Ingrid might."

I thought about it for a second. "The doctor."

"Talk to her."

"Bad advice, Doc. She'll just blow up at me again."

"Let her, and when she's finished, blow up back at her."

"But, she's my mother."

"Exactly. She's your mother, just like you're Nicolas's mother. Like it or not, you're all stuck with one another. You should be able to bring up anything, argue about anything, and get answers on anything."

"Stuck with one another? I like that." I put the pen down and remembered the spilt juice box. I was upset, but I still loved the little imp. I couldn't imagine him doing anything that would change that.

"You're hired, Doc."

Chapter Twenty-one

My father was the one who greeted me at the door. In his face I could see that my mother hadn't recovered from my snooping. I'm sure my eyes held the same contempt. He quickly poured me a glass of wine. "It's…"

"I know, Dad. Five somewhere."

He handed me the glass and pointed to his chair in the living room. "I'm just..."

I gave him my son and a nose scrunch. Then I turned to my mother. She was sitting in the kitchen. "Hey, Mom."

The glance was curt. "Madeline."

Dad and the boy quickly scurried from the room. Was it that obvious. I swear even Nicolas had an idea as to what was going to happen.

I started. "I'm sorry I went through her stuff."

She waved it off but didn't look up at me.

Ouch. "Tell me, Mom, why does it bother you so much?"

"I just don't think it helps. You need to find your life, not hers." She grabbed a photo album from a drawer in the china cabinet and brought it over to me. "Sit. This is what you need to be focusing on."

Dad and Nicolas re-entered the kitchen for a plate of cookies that they had no intention of sharing with us. He saw the photo album and shook his head. From the first pictures of decorating the hall to the last ones where there were toasts and kisses, Lawrence's family stood out while mine seemed absent.

She flipped the page to one of me standing alone by a bunch of flowers. "You were such a beautiful bride that day."

"Really? I think I looked lost, scared, or like I didn't want to be there." I took the album from her and closed it. "What happened that day?"

"You tell us." Dad grabbed the invitation from the back of the album and handed it to me. "All I know is that the invitation said Sunday and the decorating was Saturday. That wasn't what happened."

I looked at the card and read it, a wedding Sunday and decorating Saturday. "Can we pretend I wasn't there for a second, because these pictures don't do anything for me. Tell me what you know and hopefully I can fill in the blanks. Why would I have had a wedding on a Sunday?"

Dad broke an Oreo in half and tossed one of the pieces in his mouth. "That's the thing, you didn't. The wedding was Saturday."

"But the invitation said…"

Dad cut me off. "I know what the invitation said. I also remember the phone call we got at ten in the morning. We'd just finished breakfast and were getting ready to head out. To us it was the decorating day. Imagine our surprise when you called and told us that Saturday was the wedding day, and that everyone was waiting for us."

Mom patted my leg. "It was just a mistake. Maybe the printers got it…"

"The printers didn't get it wrong, Dear," Dad snapped. "And we didn't get it wrong. We were lied to."

Lied to? Those were strong words. "I'm really sorry."

"We were too. You're our little girl." He dropped the other half of the cookie back onto the dish. "We walked in late, holding up your day. The ceremony started forty-five minutes late because of us. Hell, half our family didn't even get there in time. They had Saturday flights, from Canada."

"Oh my God. I didn't know."

"You didn't know you were getting married Saturday? Didn't you find it odd when we didn't show up to decorate on Friday?"

"I uh…."

"Well, not having your family show up to decorate should have put up a few red flags. I don't believe this was any damn misunderstanding."

My mother jumped to my defence. "How can you blame her. She has amnesia."

"She didn't have amnesia when it happened." He turned to me. "Look, I know this is Lawrence's doing, but you should have stood up to him."

"That's not fair." Mom threw her tea towel down on the table. It didn't hold the dramatic effect that she'd hoped for. "Lawrence is her husband, the father of her child."

"And what are we, chopped liver? We're her family too, grandparents to that child."

"Both of you stop it. Nicolas doesn't need to hear this." I grabbed a cookie off the plate and handed it to him. "I don't know what happened, but I can assure you I never meant to hurt anybody. I don't remember plotting anything with Lawrence, but it doesn't surprise me that he might have pulled something like this. I'd ask him, but I've got my hands full with this whole trying to figure out my life thing."

"Forget it," Dad chuffed. "The damage is done. It is what it is, but you need to get a handle on this guy. He's always thought he was too good for us and on that day, he made it clear to everyone. If he had his way, you wouldn't have anything to do with us."

"Again, Dad. I'm so sorry. I won't let that happen."

"You won't have a choice." He grabbed the album and slid it back in with the others. "And I'm sorry too. The more I look at that damn thing, the angrier I get."

Mom snatched the plate and walked it over to the sink. I gave one last apologetic grimace, grabbed my keys, and decided our visit had reached a point of no return. My quota of damage had been reached for the day. They hadn't even asked why I had keys. I gave a quick round of hugs and made an abrupt exit.

One of the pictures from the album kept burrowing its way into my head as I drove home. It was a candid, and in it I could see bruising covered by make-up. This time it wasn't on my arms or wrists. It was up by my hairline.

What had I done?

Chapter Twenty-two

With Lawrence fed and off to work, I started my day clearing the breakfast dishes. I dusted the dining room table and took a minute to admire the vase of fresh roses. Then I moved on to the front entranceway. For the life of me I'll never understand why men leave their shoes where they fall off their feet.

A cream-coloured blazer hung off the chair by the door. I grabbed it to put it away. Before doing so, I emptied the pockets. If important items were lost I'd be blamed and I didn't need that. The first pocket had a few coins and a bent paper clip. The other had an empty gum wrapper.

I slipped my hand down the inside pocket and found a mid-morning surprise. It was a piece of paper, folded in half twice. I quickly unfolded it. About the size of a playing card, it held the number of someone named Scarlett. It was written in the same colour lipstick that I'd seen smeared on the collar of one of his shirts. I had found that shirt scrunched up in the hamper earlier.

My knees buckled, forcing me to take a seat on the floor. I leaned back against the door and let my mind fog over. This stung like the slap I wanted to land on this pretty little whore's face. Lawrence wasn't the best husband, but he was still my husband.

I put the note up to my nose. It smelled like the shirt, not like any of the perfumes on my dresser. This was cheap stuff, the kind you'd find at a corner store. She was young, opportunistic.

Looking again at her name, I had to wonder how cute she was, how firm her body might be. Did she have the body of a woman who had borne children? What had she done to lure him away? I tossed the paper into the corner with the shoes. And so what if she was young and cute. I was young and cute. Tears welled, were pushed back, blinked away, and then returned again.

As a wife, I had somehow failed him. Sure, I could cook, and no one keeps a cleaner house, except for his mother, but Scarlett had nothing. That being said, she was a newer model. She was the wild filly you had to chase. I was the mare, trained with a harness around its neck. Beaten and broken, I had been the filly once.

And who was I to talk? Although I couldn't remember the intimacy of Ricardo, my needs had also caused me to stray. So, what was this then?

There was no need to continue my fight with the tears. I let them flow. Who had been the first to stray? Was Ricardo my retaliation for Scarlett, or had Lawrence grabbed this girl to get even with me? I doubt I'd be alive today if he ever found out about the Italian whatever-he-was. Regardless, Lawrence had been spending long evenings at work. If I had to wager a guess, work wasn't the real reason.

The bruise on my wrist caused me to think about all the pictures in the wedding album. Had he struck me in the face? It was possible. It was safe to say that he'd screwed my family over. It made me wonder if I shouldn't be thanking this little hussy.

No longer needed, I brushed the last of the tears away as I dried my cheeks with my sleeve. Then I got to my feet and smoothed out my skirt. Engaging in adultery is illegal and although I wasn't perfect, I wasn't doing anything wrong, now. If I could prove his infidelity, it would be reason enough to end the marriage. With a good enough lawyer, I could keep custody of Nicolas.

What was I thinking? Was I saying I didn't want to live with him any longer? Granted he's brought the not-so-lovable Lawrence home from work on more than one occasion, but leaving him? Shit Madeline, he's Nicolas's father. That little guy needs him. Hell, I could do worse. "Shit, Lawrence. Why would you do this to us?"

I copied the number and slipped the note back where I'd found it. Was it possible I was wrong and there was a simpler explanation? That wasn't likely.

I put his coat up to my nose and inhaled deeply. What I smelt was a woman falling for someone's husband. I watched as Nicolas tore his toy box apart. Soon the floor would be a sea of teddy bears, fire trucks and plastic bowling pins. A lone last tear fell, leaving a clearer image. I'd never see Lawrence the same again.

"Come Nicolas, and leave the toys. Mommy needs to go see the doctor." I grabbed the keys. "Let's hope she's got wine."

Chapter Twenty-three

I looked up to the heavens with gratitude when the door opened. I don't know what I would have done had Ingrid not been home. It took me a half an hour of small talk and two glasses of wine before I could spill my problem. My husband had a number, written in lipstick, in his pocket. Did that mean what I thought it meant, or was I being absurd?

"Tell me it's nothing, Ingrid."

Ingrid got up and wrapped me up in a hug. She held me, knowing I would cry. I'd go to pieces while my world crumbled. As a friend, it was her job to help me pick up the pieces. Then we would eat a tub of ice cream and start talking options.

But, I wasn't in the mood to cry and after a minute, she let me go. "*Pourquoi ne pleurez-vous?*"

"I know he's my husband and I should be all choked up, but he was nothing more than a stranger weeks ago. What do I do about this woman?"

"I don't understand, Madeline."

"She's sleeping with my husband. And I don't think this is the first time this has happened." I wanted to mention Ricardo and that I'd gone else where for my primal releases, but I didn't.

"You need to deal with this properly. Do you have any money?"

"What for?"

"You need to hire a private investigator. I know one. He's good, cheap, and works fast. And I want to meet this Lawrence."

"Why?"

"It's hard for me to give decent advice, when I've never met him."

"I don't know. I don't think he wants me socialising."

"Call it group therapy. I need to meet him, Madeline. Think of me as your doctor and I need to know all the symptoms before prescribing you options. Options are wonderful things, and you never know when you're going to need them. But they come in many forms; forgiveness, freedom, and in the mask that gives you hope. The latter is always a Trojan horse."

"You think I need options?"

"Right now, you have no idea what you're a part of. As you figure everything out you'll decide what's beneficial, tolerable, or unbearable. For the unbearable, you'll need to be prepared."

I nodded. This wasn't the answer I had wanted. What I had wanted to hear was no, he's not cheating. French men always have notes in their pockets, and they're almost always written in lipstick. That was what I wanted. Now I needed to start skimming from the grocery money to buy options.

"Madeline?"

I turned to see Johannes standing at the front door. "Hi."

He walked over. Again his mouth was hanging partially open. It looked a little weird. Ingrid watched while he tried to choose his words. He chose poorly. "You look great."

"Pardon me?" The comment wasn't a terrible thing under normal circumstances, but considering the fact he was looking at me like I was my sister, it wasn't good.

"It's good to see you," he added.

"Same." I walked over to him and held out my hand. He looked at it for a second before reaching out and giving it a gentle shake.

He held my hand and pulled it forward. "What happened to you?"

"What's…" I followed his eyes to my wrist.

"How'd you get that bruise?"

"I uh…"

Ingrid quickly came to my rescue. "She was changing a light bulb and fell off a stool. She was lucky she didn't break anything."

I pulled my hand back and rubbed the bruise. "Yes, stupid stool, shot out like it had a mind of its own."

"Next time call me. I'd be happy to come over and help." Again, his eyes fell on mine.

Didn't he know I was married, and that I wasn't her? I looked over to Ingrid and she was on the same page. This was going a little left of normal.

Ingrid stepped between us. "How about I walk you to your car."

"You don't have to leave, do you?" Johannes asked.

"I do. Thank you, Ingrid. You can come down and see my new wheels?" I pulled my son from the marble bowl. I turned back to Johannes. "It was nice to see you again."

Ingrid took Nicolas's hand as we made our way to the Mercedes. "*Belle voiture.*"

"It's just like the one from the accident." I shrugged. "I'm getting used to it."

"Do you have time to take me for a quick *essai routier*?"

"Sure." I motioned back to the apartment with an open hand. "Is he okay?"

"I'd say no." She hopped in the passenger side with Nicolas. "I have a few things to pick up at Haute Couture. It's just a couple blocks away." She pointed up the road. "It's a few outfits for Marcus's next shoot. They were brought in from a designer in Turkey."

"Really? The place sounds expensive."

"Expensive, exotic and very fashionable, hence the name."

Nicolas climbed up on her lap and I got behind the wheel. "Could we come in? I mean, all I have is beige, off white, cream, tan, and ochre. I'd love to try a splash of any other colour."

"Definitely." She spun Nicolas around, so he could see outside. "So, you'll talk to your husband about dinner? I really want to meet this guy. That way when we talk about him, I can paint a better picture."

I dropped the shifter into drive. "Are you telling me you never met Lawrence?"

"Rebecca barely knew him."

"But she was my sister."

"I know, and that's what scares me about him."

"Sounds like you knew him pretty good."

"Trust me. I only knew what Rebecca told me and her opinions were tainted."

Nicolas found that word interesting and started to chirp. "Tainted, tainted, tainted."

Ingrid tousled his hair with her fingers. "I guess we should watch what we say around parrot-boy."

My eyes widened. The words had come out of his mouth so clearly. Had he ever heard Ricardo's name? I didn't need that name being repeated. Then Ingrid opened her purse and handed me a business card.

"What's this?"

"That's the number for the private investigator," Ingrid answered. "Give him a call and remember, it's an investment in options."

"I will, and I'll ask Lawrence about dinner."

"Do that. Tell him it'll be fun."

That was what scared me.

After a handful of turns Ingrid pointed to a shop just off on our right. "That's the place."

I found a spot in front of the store and the three of us made our way inside. I stopped in the doorway. I didn't doubt I looked like a child walking into a candy factory. And here I had wanted a splash of colour. Inside there was colour, texture, plunging necklines and outfits that would make a call-girl blush. I immediately started touching, smelling, and imagining what my closet could look like.

"Hey, Ingrid."

"Yes?"

"Where are the price tags?"

"They have a motto, *si vous devez demander*."

"*If you have to ask.* I get it." There was a dress that would have hugged my curves, moulded to my butt and showed off my legs like no other. Surprise, surprise, it was tan. I put it back on the rack. "How much are the scarves?"

She saw me grabbing for one loaded with greens, blues, and purples. "Cute choice. Let me buy that one on Marcus's account and you can borrow it. It might be too much for your hubby. If he runs across it, you can say it's mine. Tell him you haven't returned it yet. Not a lie."

"Not a lie." I smiled at the idea of having a friend and borrowing clothes. "*Merci*, Ingrid."

"*Avec plaisir.*" Her eyes darted left to a doorway that opened to another room. "You should go in there. It was your sister's favourite place in the whole world."

"Really?"

"Go in and see why. I'll keep an eye on the little one."

I did as she said and let the elegance entomb me. It was the smell of the leather, the dazzle of the sequins and the idea of designers pouring their hearts into each piece. This room was a cathedral of fabric and I was drowned in tactile love. My fingertips darted from leathers to silks to the various furs.

One dress, covered entirely with aged copper sequins, looked like a greenish brown dragon. It had to weigh a good fifty or sixty pounds, and damn it was cool. Another dress was knit with wool from alpaca and mohair. I wanted to try it, but it was brown.

Then I saw a rack of dresses that buckled my knees and brought a flash of a memory. A black sequin dress reminded me of the accident. It was the same cut, same length. I remembered picking it up on that snowy day. I had tried it on, brushed my hips with my hands and modelled it for my sister. Her eyes had lit up with jealousy. I remembered loving that look on her. Minutes later, the dress was soaked with my blood.

The mental image made me wretch.

I ran through the store, desperate to get outside. I really hoped that the fresh air would help with the nausea. It didn't.

Ingrid put a hand on my back. "Are you okay?"

"I'm beginning to really hate this amnesia. The memories come back hard."

"A bad one?"

"No. That's the thing. This was a good one at first." I wiped my mouth with as much lady-like poise as I could. "I don't get it."

"This is how we heal."

I let my body lean against hers as Nicolas dropped rocks down a sewer drain. "Healing sucks."

Chapter Twenty-four

L awrence's drink was ready and waiting for him when he walked in the door. I'd heard him drive up and had the glass and ice at the ready. I'd also taken the liberty of putting a chicken in the oven and dressing Nicolas in nice slacks and a button-down shirt. I'd learned you need to give a little to get a little.

"Thank you, Madeline." He took the drink and returned a hug.

My nose went into bloodhound mode as I tried to find that hussy's scent. It wasn't there. "I'll be taking supper out of the oven in five. So how was your day?"

A cigar was lit as he took his place at the dinning room table. I grabbed an ashtray for him and let him start his daily rant.

"I'll be glad when the renovations are done. We've been working around ladders and drywall for what seems like forever."

"You're getting the office redone?"

"Oh, that's right, you have the whole broken brain thing." He went to spin his finger around his ear again but caught himself.

"The guy that owns the building's doing it. Next thing he's gonna up the rent, but I'm working on that one."

"How is the place looking?"

"Place looks great, and speaking of great, how's that car working out? I see you're driving it."

"You were right. That car is amazing. It has power everything."

"Only the best for my family."

"Did you notice how I didn't apologise for my behaviour?"

"I did." He smiled as he blew out a mouthful of smoke.

"That's because I'm a Trembley." I waited to see if there was any guilt in his eyes. Was his recent interest a Trembley? No. Did she cook him meals or raise his son? Again, that was a no. And did she listen to him go on about work, the primates he worked with, or how the world was out to get him? She did not.

"Yes you are, now go get dinner. I'm starved."

So much for being a loyal wife. I started for the kitchen and stopped. "I ran into an old friend today."

"Funny, I didn't see any new dents on the car."

I looked back to see him smiling. This was rare to see him joke around like that. Under different circumstances, I might have found it funny. "Nope, car's okay. Do you remember Ingrid?"

"Who?"

"She was Rebecca's best friend."

"Rebecca as in your sister? We barely saw her, let alone any of her friends."

"I'd like to have her over for a meal some day."

"That sounds okay. Just let me know what day works for you and I'll make a point of working late."

"What, no. I want her to meet you, Darling." I would have thought that was understood. I should have known he'd want no part of it. "Come on. It'll be nice to have someone over. We never entertain."

"Look, I deal with people all day long. The last thing I want is a stranger in my house. The only thing worse is me having to deal with them."

"I'll do the cooking, the talking, and I know she won't stay late. I promise."

"No later than nine."

I wasn't planning on dinner until seven, but I could push that up and fast track dessert. It could work. "Nine is fine."

I'm sure he hoped his glare would back me down, but I ignored it and ran off to get his supper plate made up. I set it down in front of him and got Nicolas to the table beside him. His plate had cooled so I handed him a spoon. I took a seat beside him to give him a hand when he needed it. I patiently gave Lawrence the time he needed to absorb the idea of having Ingrid over.

Nothing was said while we ate. Even Nicolas knew better than to cackle his usual gibberish. Worried about any new words Nicolas might have learned, I was happy with his silence. I'd given a lot of thought to the what-ifs. If the name were mentioned then Ricardo would become the guy at the grocery store, or perhaps the man behind the counter at the pharmacy. Could I sell that, or would it put the red flags in place?

In the one wedding photo there was the hint of a bruise. I had been struck hard in the face. My mother had noticed it and said nothing. I needed to believe she was only looking out for me when she told me to be that good wife. It was what he expected, and what kept me from having to use make-up to hide my mistakes.

I looked over to Lawrence. The man had a bit of a temper, but I didn't see him as the crazy violent type. He was more the 'rough em up to keep em in line' type. I let the last bite of food enter his mouth. He chewed, swallowed, and was done eating.

"So, is it okay to have Ingrid over?"

"Are we still on that?"

"No later than nine, I promise."

He set his cutlery down, finished his drink and pushed himself away from the table. "This is a one-time thing. You know this city has a coffee shop on every corner. It's okay to meet up with her at those places too, you know."

"She wanted to meet you."

He got up, grabbed his jacket, and started for the door. "One time, no later than nine."

"Where are you…"

He turned and dared me to finish that question.

I didn't.

Chapter Twenty-five

Morning came shining through the dining room windows as I wiped the breakfast crumbs from the table. Normally the sight of sunshine cheered me up, but today, all I could see was the dust. It was everywhere. It was even where I'd already dusted. Nobody said this would be easy. I grabbed a coffee before starting the re-dust.

I couldn't stop thinking about what my mother had said—focus on me, not my sister. A part of me agreed to put my sister's life aside. It wasn't going to help me find myself. My sister was gone and today I was jealous of that fact. She didn't need to worry about my husband's house, she didn't have to drive cars that reminded her of the accident, and she didn't have to worry about parrot-boy.

And what was Nicolas doing? He was running around with something. I squinted to see what he had. It was the package that Ingrid had given me. He wasn't about to hand it over either, so the chase was on. It was a chase that didn't last long. With my leg still sore from the accident, I decided on the next best thing. I pulled out my secret weapon.

I had found a little thing called Play-Doh while I was out shopping. All he needed was my cookie cutters, a small rolling pin, and a clean section of floor. I even rolled out the first bit of dough for him. My mother didn't want me delving into my sister's life, but her concerns were shoved aside as I slid my finger through the taped part of the package. I was about to do just that.

These were her belongings and although they were nice to have, nothing jumped out at me right away. There were pictures of Rhommer Square and the Opera House. There was a lovely set of opal earrings that I remembered wearing once, no doubt something I'd borrowed at some point. More likely, they were mine and she had them on a permanent loan program. Were we like that?

There was a picture of Johannes. He was a photogenic man and his smile brought the picture to life. I stared for a bit, wondering what their lives might have been like had there been no accident. Then I thought about how he looked at me back at Ingrid's apartment and put the picture face down on the table. Ingrid had promised to talk to him about that.

I was putting everything back in the envelope when I spotted a receipt. It was a woman's curiosity to read it. It was for clothing—not a surprise. An eerie cold settled over me and wove its way into my bones. "Oh my God."

The receipt and remaining photos slipped from my fingers. They landed on the floor at my feet. The fog from the accident was lifting, freeing my thoughts. Suddenly I could smell the cigarettes. I could smell the blood. Nicolas was still elbow deep in the assorted colours of dough, so I quickly ran up to the bedroom.

I started at the drawers, pulling them out, emptying the contents on the floor. The first was underwear, then slips. Soon nylons were dumped on the floor and bras were scattered about the room. "Where the hell are you?"

I had nine drawers to go through—nothing. I turned to the wardrobe and started rifling through the boxes on the floor. I dumped hats, shoes, and belts, and again, I found nothing.

"Think, damn it. Where the hell did you put it?"

On a shelf above the hangers, my sweaters were all neatly folded. That didn't last long. It had to be here somewhere. It wasn't. "Shit."

There was a storage room downstairs on the main floor. That made sense because the accident had happened in April. Nicolas was stacking his multicoloured cookies as I rambled past him. He was oblivious to the fact that mommy was tearing the house apart.

The storage room was a narrow one, four feet wide and twelve feet deep. Most of it was stuff that should have found a yard sale. There was also a bicycle, more books, and all of Nicolas's summer toys. I opened the first box, looked inside, and set it aside. With the next one I swore before I tossed it aside. The third landed on top of the first box.

"Where the hell would I have put it?"

I broke a mean sweat on the ninth box and fell on top of the bicycle as I tried to wheel it through the doorway. The sprocket scraped my leg and tore my slacks. Like everything else I owned, they were beige, so I did not care.

The bicycle fell against the side of the couch and I went back in for more. The twelfth and thirteenth boxes were disappointments and the fourteenth slipped out of my hands and dumped upside down. It spilled old movies and magazines onto the floor.

I straddled the mess. There was one box left. I flipped the tabs open and started to root through it finding stuffed animals and kid's games. There was a mousetrap, a couple of mothballs and tin full of buttons. At that point I let my body fall back against the wall and I slid to the floor.

"Mommy hurt."

I looked over to see Nicolas standing in the doorway. "Hi kiddo. Mommy's fine."

His little arm extended, his finger pointing to my leg. The blood had soaked through the torn fabric and dribbled down to my ankle. It wasn't a bad bleed, but he had noticed it.

My mind had clouded with the need to find one item. And attached to that one item was the truth, and my sanity. But that damn item wasn't here. "Go get your coat Nicolas."

His eyes lit up. "Ingrid, Ingrid."

"Sorry, kiddo. Not Ingrid."

Chapter Twenty-six

I tried to reel in my sanity, without any luck. A part of me wanted to take care of my leg, but I was on a mission. Nicolas fumbled with his coat while I found the keys and made my way to the front door. His Play-Doh was left out, which the package claims you should never do if you plan to leave it for more than fifteen minutes. Sadly, it was about to dry out.

There was a piece of paper that I had guarded with my life. On it was an address that I never thought I'd visit. It was a ten-minute drive, but the traffic was light. We'd be there in seven. Nicolas was holding back tears, and I was doing my best to convince him that things were okay. It was hard to sell when I didn't believe it myself.

Then I remembered the cookies in the glove compartment. A good mother had stashes everywhere. I pulled them out and opened the box. "See if you can find Mommy a giraffe."

Looking for it relaxed him instantly. I wish life for adults could be as easy as finding a cookie. After three minutes, Nicolas had eaten two elephants and found my giraffe. I took it and shot him a wink. Then I asked for a monkey. That should keep him busy. These cookies didn't have monkeys.

The address was a townhouse and my heart began to beat out of my chest as I pulled into the stall in front of number 114. I told Nicolas to stay put and locked him in the car before starting for the building.

The first knock was a pounding of my fist. There was no second knock. I swung the door open and walked in. The place smelled like bachelor. The greasy food stench masked the lack of cleaning. I left the front door open to air the place out. "Ricardo!"

There was no answer, just a shuffling in the next room. Panicked voices were coming from the other side of the door. I headed straight for them. "Ricardo. Where the hell are you?"

I swung the door open to see his bedroom. He wasn't alone. She was dark-haired, in her thirties, and pinned underneath him. Ricardo rolled off the woman taking most of the blankets with him. "Madeline! What are you doing here?"

I continued to stare at her, seeing part of one leg, breasts covered by her arm and eyelashes that were as big as butterfly wings. Her eyes were beautiful, a deep brown. They feared this crazed blonde that had just interrupted them. "Who is this woman, Ricardo?"

"Oh, don't pay me any mind. I'm looking for something." I walked over to his closet and started pulling out clothes and dropping them on the floor.

The woman tried to steal some of the covers back. "Ricardo, talk to me. What is she doing?"

"She...uh...she is just a friend."

I stopped and turned to him. "Just a friend, seriously?" I left the closet and started going through his drawers. "That's not what you told me." I continued to empty the dresser as I fumed. "Come away with me, Maddy. Let's have sex, Maddy. Any of that sound familiar?"

"Maddy, please." Then he noticed my leg. "You're bleeding."

"Bleeding? My bloody leg is pretty minor right now. My sanity is what I'm more worried about." I pulled one of the drawers out too far and it fell to the floor and broke. "Shit, sorry."

"What are you looking for?"

"I'm looking for my shit. Where do you keep it?"

"I don't have anything of yours. This is all my stuff." He wanted to leave the bed, grab me, and stop me from trashing his room. She wasn't about to let him have the sheets and he wasn't leaving the bed without them.

I looked over my shoulder to see the slender woman put one leg on the floor. Ricardo grabbed her by the hand. "Where are you going, Maria?"

"Three's a crowd, Ricardo."

"Crap." I had pulled another drawer out too far. "Don't mind me, Maria. I'm almost finished here. He doesn't have what I'm looking for."

"Maddy, you can't go. You're hurt."

Maria quietly uttered, "Yes she can, Ricardo. She's crazy."

I shoved him back down as he tried to get up. "This is a me thing. You two go back to your thing. Sorry to have bothered you."

"Hey, Maddy. All this craziness aside, is everything okay?"

"That depends on your definition of okay."

Back at the car, Nicolas was crying. The cookies were gone, and Mommy was missing. "It's okay Tiger. Wanna go see Gramma?"

That calmed the tears. His boyish grin returned as Mommy made the tires howl on the cobblestones. We were on our way to Gramma and Grampa's house.

They'd be my next victims.

Chapter Twenty-seven

My Dad buzzed me in over the intercom and, carrying Nicolas on my hip, I took the stairs two at a time all the way to the top. Adrenaline had taken over. I handed Nicolas off to my father and without saying a word, went straight down to my room.

The rampage continued.

When Dad walked in, I was sitting on the edge of the bed fighting back the tears.

"What's wrong, Madeline?"

"I'm losing my mind. Where's Mom?"

"She needed a few groceries. She's down at the MonoPrix." He stepped aside as I headed for the door. "Are you staying for supper?"

"I can't, Dad."

"If it's about that photo album, I was just in a mood. Your mother and I have been working through a few things. That's all."

"I know, and honestly, I'm sorry for everything I've put you through. I'd give anything to take that damn day back." I wanted to give him more, but I couldn't. "Can you watch Nicky? Mom and I need to talk."

"Sure. We'll be right here when you..."

Anything he said after the word 'Sure' trailed behind me like the contrails of a jet plane. I was already down one flight of stairs before the sentence was finished. There had to be a simple explanation as to why she'd do this, although I couldn't imagine what that would be.

I was practically sprinting by the time I got there. My leg was starting to cramp. The aged glass door slid open when I stepped on the worn mat and I limped inside. I looked around the store but didn't see her. "Mom!"

A few people in the produce section looked over, saw me, and scooted in opposite directions.

"Mom!"

A head popped out from behind a tower built out of paper towel rolls.

"Madeline?"

I hobbled toward her. "You and I need to talk."

"What are you talking about? Oh my, your leg."

"Forget the leg." As I said that it buckled. I grabbed onto the display, toppling the paper towel tower. "You and I need to talk."

"Talk! You can barely walk." Embarrassed, she started to pick up rolls of paper towel.

"What are you doing? We need to talk."

She grabbed two more rolls and stacked them with the others. A stock boy stood off in the distance. He looked like he wanted to help, but wasn't sure.

I stretched my arms out and swept the remaining rolls onto the floor. They scattered down the isle and into the produce area. "Screw the mess, Mom."

"You're not right. Stay here and I'll run home and get the car. Where's Nicolas?"

"Forget the car!" It came out louder than I meant it to. "Do I take my coffee black or with cream."

"What?"

"With or without, Mom. It's an easy question."

"Uh, you've always taken it with cream."

"Wrong. Madeline always took her coffee with cream. I take mine black."

"That makes no sense, Darling. I need to get you to a hospital." She looked around. "And lower your voice. People are staring."

"I don't care."

She tried to get past me, hoping to leave me behind. I stepped in front of her. "Dad's the one who thinks I'm Madeline. He always offers me cream for my coffee. I don't like it, but I take it, for him. He doesn't know any better, and until now, neither did I. When you and I went out, I wanted my cream, more out of habit than anything, and you said I didn't need it. You even got upset when I kept trying to find some. That's because you knew I didn't need the cream."

"This is about cream? I'll get you cream next time." Again, she tried to get past me and I stopped her.

"When did you know I wasn't Madeline?"

"What?"

"I mean I just found out, but you've known for a while, haven't you?"

"Madeline, please."

"Don't call me that!" I held my hand up. "Don't you ever call me that."

"This is crazy. You're making a scene."

"Today I was going over a few things that I got from Ingrid. Do you remember her?"

"Rebecca's friend?"

"No Mom, *my* friend. My fucking friend! She's *my* friend."

"Calm down."

"She gave me a package of belongings. There were pictures, a set of earrings and a receipt for a black dress. It was the same black dress I was wearing when we got in that accident. I remembered the blood pouring out of me, staining that dress. It was an expensive dress, the kind that Madeline would wear, but the receipt wasn't in her name. It was in mine. That triggered a flood of memories. I remembered the day I picked it up.

We were in a child's clothing store. The snow had begun to fall. I remembered having to duck out to get my dress. It looked great on me. Madeline was holding Nicolas up on her shoulder. She spun around so he could see me. That caused Nicolas to vomit down her back."

"I don't…"

"No, Mom. Let me finish. My sister needed to change because she was covered with puke." I remembered the stench of the curdled milk. It filled the air, filled my nostrils. "I had just changed into the dress. My jeans and t-shirt were in a bag. I offered them. She had no choice. Nicolas didn't get any on himself, so I took him."

The memories had flooded in, the vomit, the dress, and the sticky sweet smell of blood from the accident. It was like watching a movie, one that I'd forgot I'd seen. I remembered as the frames rolled.

"Why were you driving the Mercedes, wearing the wedding rings?" she asked.

"She handed me her rings so that she could wipe the vomit off her hands. Nicolas and I went back to the window to see the snow while she cleaned herself up. I was holding her rings and curiosity got the better of me. I slipped them on. I was admiring them when I heard her coming. She grabbed Nicolas and was out to the car before I could say anything or get them off. I was still wearing the rings when I opened the passenger door. That was when she slipped past me and got in. She wasn't about to put him down and I ended up driving."

"That's why you were driving?"

"I had to, and we were doing okay until the truck hit us."

"The man had slid through a stop sign."

"I remember that, now. I also remembered that two police officers dropped off the contents of the car after I got home from the hospital. A bag of clothes was amongst the belongings. It was a disgusting mess and I threw it out. One of my many beige outfits would never be worn again, except it wasn't my outfit. Besides, why would I want it when all I really wanted was my bikini."

"You have a bikini?"

"I'm glad you asked. You see I had faint tan lines after the accident. They were from a bikini. Funny thing, I couldn't find that bikini anywhere, and trust me, I've destroyed the house looking for it. Tell me Mom, why do you think I couldn't find it?"

She dropped her eyes down to the floor. "Your sister never owned one."

"My sister never owned one. Thank you, Mother." That statement was a confession, her admission that I wasn't Madeline. "So how long have you known?"

Chapter Twenty-eight

First of all, I want to say you've done a remarkable job. Nicolas is such a lucky boy to have you in his life. I can't imagine what would have happened to that poor child had you not stepped in."

No one ever starts a sentence with 'first of all' unless there's a confession, or an excuse. It seemed a little moot, but I still wanted to know. "It wasn't like I had a choice. Why, Mom?"

"Nicolas needed a mother. Don't tell me you regret being there for him. I won't believe you."

"Nicolas is a wonderful kid, and in a way, he's become my Maddie. Today, when I started to figure everything out, it was chaotic, yet I felt whole. So much made sense. Like I've always loved Nicolas's smile. Now I know why. It's my sister's smile."

There was a short-lived silence and then she opened up. "I wasn't sure who you were when I identified you."

"Then what possessed you to say I was her? I mean, I could have woken up, less the amnesia, and said you were crazy. You'd have looked pretty bad."

"You could have, except I heard one of the paramedics say you had a head injury, and that you couldn't remember your name."

"I was Madeline, regardless, wasn't I?"

"No, you were Nicolas's mother, regardless. The doctors had already jumped to the conclusion, seeing the wedding rings. You were driving the Mercedes. Madeline didn't own a pair of jeans. They asked for confirmation, I gave it to them."

"But she'd had a baby."

"It had been almost two years. Her body had bounced back weeks after having him. Nicolas wasn't that big when he was born, so there were no stretch marks. Neither of you had any birthmarks. You wore that beautiful dress, she was in those jeans, and then there were the rings. It was an easy sell, to everyone."

"And you say you didn't know?"

"Honestly, I wasn't sure at first. You were banged up and fighting for your life. I knew that if you survived, no matter which one you were you'd have to take care of Nicolas. That boy couldn't be left alone with that man."

"That's why you got so upset when I went through her things."

"What if you found something that jarred the memories free?"

"Then I'd get my damn life back."

"I know you can't forgive me, and I'll live with that, but I had to do this for Nicolas. Someday he'll be a loving man with a wife and kids of his own. He'll be a good man and a good father, and you'll be the one to thank for that. I just hope that in time, you'll see why I did this and forgive me."

"But here's the thing. I'm not Madeline, and I'm not going to stay with Lawrence. The man is cheating on me."

"No! You can't. Nicolas needs you."

"I know. I just need to find a way to trap him into letting me leave with my son. And he *is* my son."

"Honey, he's more your son than anyone knows. You have given up so much, which is what a mother does. You've done a wonderful job and I'm so proud."

She was proud of me. This was some messed up logic. "Damn it, Mom."

"Are you're going to stay with him?"

"No longer than I have to."

She placed a hand on mine. "Are we're okay?"

"No." I pulled my hand away. "It was never my imagination that you preferred Madeline over me. I can't help but wonder if this was some twisted way of keeping her alive?"

"It's not like that. I just—"

"Stop it." I stepped around the kid that had braved the crazy women, arguing with her mother. He was trying to clean up the display. "Up until now you've managed to keep her alive, but it stops now. I'm telling Dad. He has a right to know."

"No! Please don't, not yet."

Who was the crazy one now? "What? And why not? He deserves to know."

"Your father isn't the kind to keep secrets. Imagine him blurting out Rebecca's name the next time we see Lawrence."

"He would never do that, and when was the last time you saw that man, at the wedding?"

"Nobody would say anything intentionally. But your father doesn't have it in him to lie. Lawrence would see it in his eyes."

"But he deserves…"

"I agree, and we will tell him, just not yet. Do it for him. Do it for Nicolas."

I thought about the lipstick note and the man who was cheating on me. I knew I wouldn't be living with him long. Dad could do it. "I'm telling him."

I started for the door. My mother stood there amongst the spilled rolls of paper towels, willing me to stop. When I didn't, she hurried to catch up.

Back at the apartment my father was reading to Nicolas in the kitchen. He stopped and got up to pour a couple of coffees. "Is everything alright. You left in such a state."

"Mom, can you take Nicolas into the other room and let me talk to Dad."

"No."

He looked at her and then my leg. "My God Madeline, you're bleeding."

I looked down at the leg of my pants. The blood had dried and darkened. "I think I'm done leaking. Sit. We need to talk."

"Sure, Dear. What's going on?"

Mom handed Nicolas a colouring book and crayons before taking a seat herself. Dad set the coffees down and slid the cream over. I blinked back a tear as I stared at it. "I have to tell you something, Dad. I..."

He broke my train of thought as he slid the cream closer.

"Dad, I'm..." I looked over to my mother who was sitting with her eyes closed. No doubt she'd give anything to God, if her daughter would just shut up.

"You're..." The smile withered as he waited. "What's this all about?"

I thought about what Mom had said. Dad would botch things up for sure. He'd never mean it, but she was right. He was a lousy liar. And it wasn't him telling Lawrence that was the issue. It was his calling me Rebecca in front of Nicolas. It wouldn't be long before parrot-boy was calling me that at home?

Hearing the silence, my mother's eyes opened.

"Uh, something's been making me crazy lately. I've wanted to tell you for some time now. I take my coffee black. I have for days. I hate cream."

"Why didn't you tell me sooner. It's not that big a deal, Madeline."

I held a firm grip on my emotions as I looked up at him. "It's bigger than you think."

Chapter Twenty-nine

A sour churning took over my stomach as Nicolas and I drove home. The out-of-control flood of my life, spilling its banks and unable to get to me quick enough, was wreaking mayhem. Being twins, I could see how the mistakes were made. I was in my new dress, the elegant kind that Madeline might wear to a fancy dinner. She was in my faded blue jeans. They were the ones she always said she'd never be caught dead in. I was wearing her rings and driving her car. It had seemed obvious.

There had been snippets of modelling in my dreams and now, I vividly remembered hiding behind an antique dresser as I changed at Marcus's studio. It was into a black bikini with a buckle on the hip. I also remembered the snowflakes falling the day of the accident, the day I met Ingrid, and drinking endless cups of black coffee with her.

I remembered falling in love with Johannes. What he must be thinking. I hoped Ingrid's talk wasn't too harsh. Had he seen me when he looked into my eyes?

This clarity was too much. I hadn't remembered giving birth to Nicolas, screwing around with Ricardo or loving Lawrence. Now I knew why. I looked over to Nicolas. I had never carried him, but now I loved him as if I had. He was all that I had left of my sister.

I remembered the day he made his big debut. Madeline had brought him into this world while I was downstairs in the waiting room, babysitting his drunken father and the lushes that he called friends. I had watched him hit on a young girl with a broken leg while his wife was upstairs screaming in pain. The girl had a beautiful head of thick auburn hair.

The breeze from the open car window caressed my face as I tried to pull myself together. My mind kept drifting to Johannes. He was a beautiful man. Had I been too hard on him? Then, as my stomach lurched, my thoughts turned to Dougie. Somehow, he had known, just like somehow I'd known to play along. I owed him a slice of cake.

But first, I had to get busy on dinner. Ingrid was coming over tonight. Lawrence said I'd owe him for this. I just prayed it wasn't anything sexual. He could never be allowed to touch me again. And now that I knew, would I be able to hide this news from Ingrid? Should I?

God, I had slept with Lawrence. It hit me like a baseball bat to the back of my head. Again, my stomach lurched.

I pulled into the driveway as the tears returned. I couldn't shake the thought that I had slept with my sister's husband. Sure, it had been a rape the first time, but not the other times. I had enjoyed his touch. Hell, at times I had wanted it, like a wife should.

Jamming the shifter into park, I opened my door and fell out the driver's side onto the gravel. I crawled to the edge of the driveway. I had let that man inside me, wanted him inside me, and even climbed on top of him to.... My stomach emptied.

I kneeled looking up at the sky. "Forgive me Madeline, I never knew."

Chapter Thirty

I sat at the dinning room table with a black coffee while I waited to see who would arrive to this dinner party first. Would it be Ingrid or my sister's husband? I poured myself a coffee, extra strong, no cream, because that was the way I liked it. I'd have to find an excuse for drinking it this way, like Ingrid was a bad influence on me.

While the lasagne baked, I had repacked the boxes and stacked them back in the storage room along with the bicycle. Supper, now out of the oven, was starting to set. If I had to find a silver lining in all this, it was that I'd learned how to cook.

With Nicolas snuggling a teddy bear on the couch, I took a moment to let more of my memories surface. Since waking from the coma I'd felt uprooted, unable to find my memories. I had been that stunted little pine tree, the one that clung to the ledge of the cliff with no dirt, no future. In the distance the others stood tall. Not knowing any better, I had begged for dirt, the proof of my existence, and any amount would have done. Who could have imagined the dump truck waiting around the corner? There it was, smothering me with the truth.

The day of the accident kept playing over and over in my mind. It made me want to go back to the cemetery. That damn headstone had my name on it. It should have Madeline's name. Out of respect, she should be the one remembered. I wanted to take a spray can and paint her name over mine, or scratch it into the stone with a knife. I will do that some day, and soon. I'll put it there just for us, maybe etched into the granite somewhere unseen. It would be our secret until I could make things right.

I took one last scan of the living room and saw the picture of Madeline and Lawrence on their wedding day. I hadn't said 'I do' that day. I would rather have jumped naked onto a hill of fire ants. No, I remembered having eggs and bacon with my parents. I especially remembered the bacon. Dad had a connection back in the Fraser Valley. The man kept him supplied with some of the best maple smoked bacon in the world. That was the day we were supposed to decorate the hall, but it hadn't worked out that way. Madeline had mixed the days up on our invitation. We almost missed her wedding. Her life was spinning, faster and faster out of control.

Madeline even had a Ricardo. How sad that she didn't feel she could tell me about him. I would have given her a high-five. I slipped the wedding photo into a drawer as the front door opened.

Lawrence walked in and filled his lungs with the aroma from supper. Then he flipped his shoes off by the door. One landed upside down, the other against the wall. "Where is she?"

He was feeling cocky. Tonight, would be a win, win, for him. With any luck she wouldn't show, or she'd be late. Win—my guest was standing me up. I could learn from this. Win—this would soon be over, and I could forget about asking again. What did my sister see in him?

"I'm sure she's on her way." I continued to set the table.

Lawrence opened a new bottle of scotch and let the amber elixir slither over the ice in his glass. It would help him find his tolerance. He walked over to the study and returned with a cigar. A blue haze wafted behind him, competing with my lasagne. I pretended not to care, but everything he did irritated the shit out of me.

Ingrid loved anything pasta. I changed up the lasagne recipe a bit with pricier cheeses and adding eggplant. I had made it for her several times and needed it to taste more like something Madeline might make. The aroma was incredible.

I rolled my eyes as Lawrence walked past. He didn't notice. I grabbed a bottle of red from the wine rack. It was the perfect Merlot. I opened it to let it breathe, albeit from the noxious cloud of smoke. There was still the garlic bread, but I'd wait on that until my guest arrived.

The wait was a short one. Nicolas was dressed in his Sunday best and ran for the door when he heard the knocking. He fumbled at the handle until I helped him open it. Ingrid came in first followed by Johannes, and he had a gift. I wanted to die when I saw him. Nicolas's eyes were like saucers as he ran the package over to the table where he carefully started on the tearing.

Johannes watched Nicolas while I stared at Ingrid. She looked over and I mouthed the words 'What are you thinking, bringing him?' She mouthed back, 'I'm sorry. He was very instinctive." Thinking about it, she may have mouthed the word 'insistent'. My next word was easy for her to read, 'Shit'.

The gift was a book of fairy tales, complete with pictures and a leather cover. Behind me I heard Lawrence mutter that the gift was inappropriate, and that Nicolas better not start expecting a gift from every stranger that came over.

"What do you say, Nicolas?" I asked.

"Thanky." He held it up to me. "What, Mom?"

"It's some new bedtime tales, Nicolas. I'll read you one tonight." He hugged the book as if it were a favourite teddy bear. There was nothing better than a good bedtime story. It was a thoughtful and much-needed gift. Goldilocks and the Three Bears could only be told so many times. He ran off to put his new book in his room, staggering side to side from its weight.

"Thanks Johannes," I offered. "That was very nice of you."

"Please, call me Jon. I know you prefer it."

I turned to a less impressed Lawrence. Had he caught the way I looked at him? I didn't mean to let my eyes linger. Hopefully he didn't make too much out of the 'Jon' comment—Madeline had preferred Jon. Am I insane or what? I cleared the thoughts. "Lawrence, this is my friend Ingrid and her friend Jon Weisman."

He extended his arm and Johannes shook it. Ingrid stayed a step back. I broke the silence. "I hope you all like lasagne. Why don't you all take a seat while I put the garlic bread in the oven."

Lawrence held his drink with the same hand that held his cigar. He took a sip and held it in his mouth for a second before swallowing. "What do you do in Paris, Jon?"

"Normally I'm a contractor. I've taken a break to go on a quest."

"A quest?"

I swore I could hear Lawrence rolling his eyes from the kitchen. I waited for the click, click, click and then the sound of nickels pouring out of his mouth.

"Yes. I recently got some interesting news. My parents died a few months back and, in the will, they mentioned a brother. I'm taking some time off to go look for him."

"Really?" Lawrence failed miserably at acting interested. If the topic wasn't about money, stocks, or real estate, it wasn't worth wasting the time on. He turned to the bar. "Want a drink?"

When I returned with the bread I was met with another awkward silence. There would have been a salad, but Lawrence lived by the motto that salad was for the ones that couldn't afford the meat and potatoes. Not being shy, he scooped the largest piece to his plate. The rest of us followed and I cut Nicolas's up into smaller pieces. He puckered up and started to blow on them.

Johannes took a bite and wiped his mouth with the napkin. "This is delicious, Madeline."

"Thanks Jon."

The compliment hung in the room like a bad smell. I would have preferred he not say anything. We all felt the uneasiness.

"That means you're looking for a brother. And what happens if you find him?" Lawrence asked. He wanted to move the evening along. Eat, talk, and then everybody could get the hell out.

"Well, I hope to get to know him. But I also want to share our inheritance with him." He shrugged. "It's more than I need, and you never know, this guy might need a break. Maybe he's not doing so well."

Lawrence stopped chewing. I could see the steam leaving his ears. Had he heard that right, that some schmuck, who couldn't hold his own, would get rewarded with free money? To him this was ludicrous. "Are you serious?"

"He's my brother."

"This guy got a name?"

"Yes, and it's being run through the library of adoptions. We're running it through the Mac Noble's Agency tomorrow."

"Mac Noble?" This sparked Lawrence's interest. "I didn't realise that agency was still around?"

His knowing of this place caught me off guard. "You've heard of them?" It wasn't like Lawrence to give a damn about anything that didn't involve him. Had he looked at investing in it? Nah, where was the profit in helping others?

"Madeline, you know it was the Mac Noble Agency that handled my adoption."

"Oh, right. I must have forgotten, with the accident and all." This could only be a blessing. He could help Johannes find his brother. If anybody could get things done it was Lawrence, that is, if he wanted to.

Lawrence turned back to Johannes. "So what name are we working with? Weisman?"

Johannes stopped eating and let hope widen his eyes. "I can give you the name, but he wasn't born here, or in Frankfurt. I think he was born in Koblenz. He's also not a Weisman. He's a Falkman."

Lawrence traded the fork in his hand for his drink. He knew something. "Falkman?"

"Yes, Georg Falkman."

"Really?" Lawrence pushed his half-eaten plate of food away as he slumped back in his chair.

He knew something. This was the first time I'd ever seen the man stop eating before he was finished. His thoughts, now in overload, could only mean that he knew this Georg guy. I wanted to ask, but what if there was hatred, or this guy died? Lawrence didn't bother to hide the fact that he was shaken.

"Are you okay?" I asked. Whatever this was, it was big. "Do you know that name, Lawrence?"

"Oh, I know this Georg guy alright." He held his drink in front of him, mesmerised as the cubes clinked against the edge of the glass.

We all sat dazed by his reaction.

Jon put his fork down as he leaned forward. "How do you know him?"

Lawrence downed his glass of scotch, bringing him back to us. "Georg Falkman was my name before I was adopted."

Chapter Thirty-one

Ingrid cleared the dishes while Johannes and Lawrence talked about the past. I was stunned as I leaned against the doorway of the kitchen. Ingrid quickly gave up on the dishes and joined me.

"There are subtle similarities," I whispered. "The shape of the eyes, they're kind of the same. They both have a rugged nose. There's the hair colour and jaw line."

Ingrid put her hands on my back. "*Qu'est-ce que c'est*, Madeline. You're shaking. Talk to me."

I said nothing as I continued to gawk. How could I tell her? These two men could be brothers, and if that were true, this was a disaster. The last thing I wanted, or needed, was Johannes becoming a part of my family, especially *this* way.

"Well," Ingrid conceded, "tell me when you're ready."

"I will."

The two men talked with smiles on their faces and drinks in their hands. Where Lawrence wanted, and sorted through the facts, Johannes searched for that bond. Ingrid and I rushed through the dishes so that we could join them. In the five minutes, while we were away, the worst had happened. Lawrence had found out how much money was at stake. He was formulating an investment plan and it wasn't just his share of the inheritance on the line. He'd managed to involve Johannes's part as well.

Johannes, high on the spoils of finding his brother, looked blissfully overwhelmed. He mirrored Lawrence with a scotch in his hand and a cigar in his mouth. I wanted to shake him, pull him aside and knock some sense into that thick German skull of his. Instead, a handshake cemented the two brother's investment strategy. The chequebook might as well have been out with Lawrence's pen at the ready. I was about to say something when Lawrence cut me off.

"This is family business you two. Could you give us a minute?" His smirk dared me to intercede. Ingrid saw it too and although I'm sure she wanted to go toe to toe with him, she respected the fact that I still had to live with the man.

"I suppose we could get Nicolas ready for bed."

"That's a great idea," Johannes added as he took a wine-dipped puff.

He was filling a void, created by the loss of his parents. Why was I so darn worried? Lawrence had always done well, and they were family. Ingrid tucked Nicolas in after reading him one of the stories. I sat and stewed.

The night rolled well past nine before we exchanged our good-bye hugs. Promises had been made and the damage was done. I let my heart ache as I closed the door behind them. Then I slowly turned to my sister's baneful husband.

My words were sharp. "What just happened here?"

"I have a brother, and he wants to be on a winning team. I think this night has tuned out better than I could have wished, and I have you to thank for that." He headed for the study. "Good idea on the dinner tonight, Darling."

"About tonight." I followed him, unsure how to word my next question. I just blurted it out. "Do you think it's clever to invest all of his inheritance? I mean he just—"

"What are you saying?" He set the glass down on his desk and pulled out the chair. "Are you questioning my ability to invest this guy's money? Remember, I'm investing too."

"No, I never said that." Yet, that was exactly what I meant.

"You never had to. He's my brother, for God's sake. Do you think I'm out to steal his money?" Sitting at his desk the way he was, he looked like a man who would do just that.

"I'm sorry. I didn't mean to imply anything of the sort." I took a step back. "I just think it all happened so fast."

He picked up his drink and downed it before tossing me the glass. "I think you need to focus on your own responsibilities and leave me to mine. Look around. I think I've done a damn good job. You're not lacking, and you've got me to thank for that. Don't you forget it." He pointed to the glass. "Are you going to fill that thing?"

I turned without saying another word. Anything I might add would only sink me deeper.

"Don't take forever getting it back to me, either."

I brought him the drink and made myself scarce. Later, after he'd gone to bed and fallen asleep, I slid under the covers and quietly rested my head on the pillow. I was mad as hell because I *didn't* trust him.

Why was I upset? He hadn't given me any reason to think he'd make a bad investment, and it wasn't in him to throw away money. But it wasn't in him to help others either. Was it possible I had issues with him getting too close to Johannes?

Hell, yes.

Chapter Thirty-two

At the corner of Quai Branly and the Avenue de Suffren, there was a little bistro. Close to twenty wrought-iron tables littered the front patio, along with planters full of purple pansies and red geraniums. I've never eaten there, but I've walked by it a hundred times. Close to the Eiffel Tower and the office of Pierre Stoltz, it was the perfect spot for a bite of lunch. It had been a week since that fateful supper and eight days since I made the call to Ingrid's private investigator.

Soon a man with an envelope would hand me back my life. There'd be no talking, no exchange of pleasantries. He was merely a messenger and discretion in front of my son was paramount. The nearby park, a distraction full of ducks and ponds, would allow me to go over the photos and see what kind of options I'd purchased.

I settled Nicolas in his seat. Then I hung my jacket on the back of my chair and sat down. The top of the Eiffel Tower peeked out from behind a clump of trees that were full of newly sprouted leaves. The sight of the structure amongst such nature made me smile. It always did.

Could these photos free me? Over the phone, Monsieur Stoltz had assured me that on more than one occasion Lawrence had been caught taking a young redhead into different hotels. He had documented photos of them freely kissing. There were times, places, room numbers, and copies of receipts that were bought with bribe money, again, my extorted grocery money. Soon these pictures would be mine.

A young man's voice startled me from my thoughts. "May I have your autograph, Mademoiselle?"

He set a magazine and pen down on the table. Open to one of the ads, a beautiful woman donned an elegant dress. She also wore quite the necklace. I took a moment to study her, remembering the day I did this shoot. I was so scared.

My hand reached for the pen and then I stopped. I looked up at the man, his eyes star-struck. "I'm sorry, but this was my sister."

"Really. You look so much like her."

I wanted to sign the magazine, grab my life back, but this wasn't the time. Rebecca would have to remain dead and I'd have to stay strong. What if this was a trap, Lawrence's attempt to flush me out? Had he figured things out? It seemed impossible. He didn't know Madeline, let alone Rebecca. I picked up the book. "My sister died a while ago."

I'm not sure when the man left, too embarrassed to ask for his magazine back. I kept it. It carried me back to that day when Johannes had called. Ingrid had broken an ankle. Johannes had assured me there was no reason to be afraid. That should have raised a flag. Instead I blindly got on a plane and raced off to Frankfurt. It changed my life.

He had picked me up at the airport. In minutes we were pulling up to a warehouse and I was meeting Marcus. A dress was handed to me and before I knew it, flashes were blinding me. Two photo shoots later, I was modelling for one of the advertisements in this magazine. I remembered the butterflies, the fancy clothing, and how I marvelled at seeing myself on the photo layouts. A proof magazine came in the mail in a large manila envelope. As much as I didn't want to be doing this, it was sick-to-my-stomach exciting.

Then there was the magazine at my parent's house. I remembered it now. The girl sprawled across the front cover wore a black bikini with a brass buckle on her hip. I was that girl, and this was my lost bikini. I had to wear it for days while I sat out in the sun. I needed colour before Marcus could start snapping.

This was a huge part of my life and it was gone.

Monsieur Stoltz had better have the damning evidence he promised. I hadn't realised it until now, but Rebecca's life, my life, was a treasure.

I wanted it back.

Chapter Thirty-three

Nicolas and I both decided on the crêpes. Okay, I made the choice, but I knew he'd love it. Nicolas had Nutella, whipped cream, and a few strawberries while I opted for the banana, Nutella, and light drizzle of Grand Marnier. I watched as my son worked away at his meal. He was methodical, like every bite was consequential. My little man eats like he's going to be a big boy, and he's forever smiling. Madeline had to be cheating on Lawrence.

I ate slowly as my mind flirted with the magazine that I'd so desperately wanted to sign. A chair scuffed against the cements as it was pulled from the table. I looked up, expecting to see some scrawny courier or overweight detective, balding and too cheap to hire a messenger. I was wrong.

"Good morning my Maddy." He turned to Nicolas. "Hello, Tiger."

I leaned forward while my heart froze in my chest. "What the hell are you doing here?"

"I saw you sitting and thought I'd come over. Is there a problem?" The man had a smile as if he knew what I was up to.

"Shit, Ricardo." I tried to keep my voice down, as I tucked the magazine in my purse. "What if Lawrence sees you?"

"How exciting. Is he here?"

"You can't be taking chances like this. He has friends, family, and co-workers. They can't be seeing us together."

"The man is always at work. Besides Maddy, after what happened the other day, you owe me."

"Owe you? Answer me this. Why me?"

"You're a beautiful girl. We have chemistry."

"You're a beautiful boy and there are many other beautiful girls with chemistry, like the one in your bed the last time I saw you. So what? This thing we had, it's over."

"You need me. You're still the passionate housewife, lost in a world where only the dreams can satisfy you. I want to be the dream that satisfies you."

"I see. This isn't about love, leaving Lawrence, or us riding off into the sunset."

"Pardon me? No, this is about us having fun. Why, do you want more?"

"What?" I choked.

"Has my beautiful flower fallen in love?" he asked. "I should have seen this coming."

I looked over his shoulder to see a man coming up the sidewalk. He was carrying an envelope and he would be looking for a woman, alone with a child. "Quick. You have to leave."

He looked around not seeing what I was seeing. "Why? Is your   husband—"

"Go, and I'll catch up with you later, at the Concorde."

"Promise?"

"Go!"

He quickly fled, looking at no one, making eye contact with no one. I watched as he scurried off like a rat with a piece of cheese. The man wasn't the swiftest current in the creek.

An envelope, dropped on the table, brought my eyes around. "*Vous-etes Madame Trembley?*"

I looked up to see the scrawny young man, clean cut and in his late twenties. His eyes caught the faint bruising on my wrist as I reached for it. The expression didn't change when he looked back to me.

"Yes, yes I am."

He slid the envelope closer. "*Je suis vraiment désolé ...*"

I held up my hand to stop his consoling words. We both knew what was in the envelope. "*Merci.*" I hoped he wasn't waiting for the tears. This day was all about hope and the envelope, my key to that passage.

He ruffled Nicolas' hair. "*Enfant mignon.*"

Then the man turned and disappeared into a crowd that had just surfaced from the Metro Station. I stared at the envelope while Nicolas, my *cute child*, worked on his crêpe. When he was finished, I took a cleansing breath and we went for a walk.

I needed to find a secluded spot. With acres of gardens, pathways, and park benches, it wouldn't be hard. The Champ de Mars is one of many wonderful places to go if you want to fade from the crowd. There were shrubs, trees, and acres of groomed lawns. I let Nicolas pick the spot. He chose a pond with ducks.

Me, I grabbed a nearby bench and let the sun's rays warm my body. Since the accident, I'd been prone to getting chilled. For that reason, I seldom sat in the shade and usually had a blanket or a wrap close by. If it were up to me, I'd live in front of a warm fireplace. It was something Madeline always loved.

Nicolas, on the other hand, didn't care about shade or sun. He didn't care if he was wet or dry. If he found a puddle, he'd stomp in it. I couldn't keep him dry, so I did the next best thing by always carrying a change of clothes.

I looked over to see him knee deep in the pond looking back at me as if to ask if it was okay to get wet. The pond was only a foot deep at its centre and he already had water spilling into his gumboots. I smiled back to him, which was the green light to have fun.

The boy would stay put as long as the pond didn't dry up. The ducks didn't mind his company, although they weren't sure about the leaves he was trying to feed them.

I reached into my purse and retrieved the envelope. This was Pandora's Box and once opened, I'd have no choice but to play this game to a checkmate, or an execution.

I tried to imagine Lawrence's reaction. He'd deny it until seeing the photos. Then he would lose his mind. He'd try to scare me and there was no doubt he'd hit me, but I didn't belong in this life.

The pictures slid out of the envelope and I gasped as I put a hand up to my mouth. I thought I knew what to expect, thought I knew the man better than this, even in the short time that I had been his wife. I was wrong. The girl, a darling little red head, was just that, a girl. I thumbed through all the pictures before deciding that this child, trying to look twenty-something, couldn't have been a day over seventeen. She carried textbooks in the one shot as they entered the hotel. It sickened me that he'd crawled into a bed with this girl.

Nicolas continued to play in the water. The sun's rays found their way through the trees and shimmered off him like he was an angel, my angel. I looked back at the pictures. This young girl should have been doing her homework, or talking on the phone with her girlfriend about Bobby, some boy that sat in front of her in math class.

I continued to torture myself with the photos, trying to remember what I was doing at that age? My sister and I were likely giggling about boys or running off to the Louvre. Madeline initially hated going to museums. After a while, she learned to love the arts, but never had time to go unless I dragged her out. Like me, she had an eye for the good stuff. And like me, she gravitated to the Flemish painters.

One painting always stood out to us. It was a bowl of fruit. We found it fascinating that it had ants, flies and a slice of cantaloupe that looked like it was spoiling. It was so real. This young girl should have been looking at those paintings, or awkwardly gawking at marble statues of men, not hanging out in some seedy hotel room.

I was sliding the pictures back into my purse when a familiar voice eased its way back into my life. I almost dropped them.

"Madeline? It's nice to see you, again."

I looked up to see Johannes, backlit by the sun.

Chapter Thirty-four

Johannes stood in front of me, his silhouetted body looking all rugged and manly. This wasn't Johannes, my husband's brother. This was Johannes, the man I loved.

I quickly got to my feet and let him slip his arms around me as my legs turned to cooked spaghetti. The man smelt like he had all those nights in our bed. I think my heart had just performed its first back flip, and then he pecked me on each cheek. My mother was right. This man was a dangerous fantasy.

"Hi, Johannes."

"You can call me Jon. I know you prefer it."

But I didn't. Madeline did. I had always loved how it rolled off the tongue.

The strength of his hug squeezed the memories out of the most carnal folds of my mind like toothpaste. I tried to fight them at first, but soon gave in. Each one stirred the already dangerous cauldron of feelings.

The sight of his silhouette floated me back to the day he had stepped into my life. My university classes had ended for another term and I made my way down la Rue Dauphine. As I did, I turned my attention up to the sky where my mind had drifted from the challenge of mathematics and grammar, to the wads of fluffy cotton that floated high above.

I had grabbed a baguette, full of the various meats and cheeses, and headed down the weathered steps to a large weeping willow that sat on the edge of the walkway along the water's edge. That tree was like home to me and if I was a couple years younger, I might have climbed it. To my right the Louvre sprawled several city blocks, the Institute de France on the left. People strolled along the banks, oblivious to all the eyes peering through the gaps between the strands of leaves.

The sun dared an appearance from behind a cloud as two white swans, as large as any I'd ever seen, made their way toward me. The small white pieces of bread from my sandwich fell like snowflakes, lucky to hit the water before being gobbled up.

I remembered setting my sandwich down and later reaching for it, but instead of bread I found shoelaces and a foot. They were attached to a man. The uneven cobblestones kept him from realising that he had part of my baguette under his shoe.

That was such a wonderful day.

I had to catch myself from falling when Johannes ended the hug. "Please sit back down, Madeline."

He held my hand as I took my place back on the bench. It was a gentlemanly gesture, my knight in shining armour. Then he took the spot beside me. We were sitting close enough to touch.

"How amazing is this. I was walking from the train, looking for a place to get a bite to eat, and something told me to walk through the park."

"That is pretty amazing, Jon."

"Hey, I'm sorry about the weirdness a week ago. Ingrid talked to me about that."

"No. I think I was being overly snotty that day. I know I look a lot like her. Sometimes I forget."

"Still. I don't know you and I seem to forget that when I see you."

"Really, it's okay."

I wanted to tell him he knew me better than he thought. Again, my mind drifted to the day we met. He had thought the swans I was feeding were ducks. It didn't matter to me what he called them. He sat beside me and we fed the squashed baguette to them while he tried to talk me into joining him for dinner. He called it an apology. I had called it an opportunity.

This guy was charming, built like a tank, and drop-dead gorgeous. I saw a prince, but not for myself. At the time, I had wanted him for my sister. Lawrence was a stump of a man and this would be one kick-ass upgrade.

Again, Johannes pulled me from my trance. "I want to thank you again for dinner the other night. It was amazing, a life changer. Isn't Lawrence a great guy?"

"He's, uh, good." But to me, Johannes was the amazing one. I was rapidly getting lost in his eyes and becoming that bored housewife that Ricardo had so badly wanted. For Johannes I could be that woman. Our rendezvous would take place at some secluded spot in a park. We'd start by catching up on each other's lives, like we were doing right now. Soon we wouldn't be able to contain ourselves. Hungers would have to be fed and I was a damn good cook. A gentle kiss would rage into a sweaty whirlwind of passion. Hidden behind the shrubs, rolling around on the grass, leaves in our hair, I'd let him devour me.

How pathetic was I? "It's nice to see you, but I should get going."

"What's wrong, Madeline."

"Nothing. I'm just a little tired." What could I say? I wasn't Madeline and this was way too hard on me?

I also felt an odd guilt, sitting with Johannes. This was Rebecca's man, and she was dead. What would people think? Hell, overnight Johannes had become ... and that was when it hit me— Johannes had become my brother. There shouldn't be any harm in sitting with him, my brother-in-law, unless I did something stupid.

I took a long deep breath and leaned back. I wasn't doing anything wrong and I shouldn't feel guilty about this. Forget about all those thoughts swirling in my head like snowflakes in a prairie blizzard.

"Johannes, Lawrence told me you two had a meeting yesterday."

"Yes, about that." He reached into his pocket.

Chapter Thirty-five

Johannes pulled a folded piece of paper out of his pocket and handed it to me. His accompanying smile reminded me that there was a little child in everybody, no matter what the age. I unfolded the paper to see a copy of Lawrence's original birth certificate. The man really was a Georg before becoming a Lawrence.

"He's my brother, Madeline, or should I call you sister."

I cringed and forced a smile. Johannes's dream was my disaster. The man I loved was the brother of the man I was pretending to be married to. I had every hope of crushing Lawrence so that I could be free. I even had the damning evidence in my purse. Where would this leave Johannes?

"He's working on an investment strategy."

How could I show my concern without sounding like one of those people? "Are you sure about all this?" It came out poorly.

"Don't worry, Madeline. I've got a good feeling about this. Why do you ask?"

"No reason." Suddenly my chest hurt. I was sure I was coming across as an uncaring wife. I should be supportive.

A chill caught my shoulders as a breeze swept through the park. Maybe it was fear. Our visit had quickly become an emotional hodgepodge of confusion, love, and unspoken passion. The different scenarios took turns torturing me. I only focused on the ones that begged me to run off and recreate a moment from our past. And in my mind, I could justify this. He was my Johannes.

Sadly, I wasn't his Rebecca.

Still, there was an odd curiosity. What did Johannes see when he looked at his girlfriend's sister? We looked and sounded the same. Was he still getting caught up in the similarities like he was a week ago, or was I simply an entirely different person? Did he even remember that drunken girl that had enjoyed being flirted with on the dance floor in Germany, or was I Madeline, the wife of his brother? She was a sister now.

Johannes sensed he was losing me and changed the subject. "Has Nicolas been enjoying his bedtime stories?"

Focus Rebecca, I mean Madeline. "Nicolas doesn't let that book out of his sight when we're at home."

Hearing his name, Nicolas quickly returned and tugged on my pant leg. "Wet."

"Yes you are. Are you done playing?"

"Duckies gone."

"Those silly duckies." I started to dry him off. "Nicolas, do you remember Johannes?"

Nicolas jumped to attention and offered Jon a very rigid hand to shake. It melted Johannes and he shook his little hand with a very adult shake. "Wow, you have a very strong grip."

Nicolas pulled up the sleeve of his t-shirt and made a muscle. Johannes gave it a squeeze and nodded his approval. I broke up their bonding moment to slip a wet shirt off and a dry one on. "Now scoot the pants, mister." Nicolas shed the trousers and as soon as the underwear came off, he started to run.

I got up and gave chase. "What possesses little boys to run around as soon as they're naked?"

Johannes laughed as he joined me in the pursuit. "It's just what we do."

We managed to corral him back to the bench. I got him in his fresh clothes and combed his hair. He looked surprisingly good for a little pond rat.

"What is Marcus up to?"

"He's decided to take some time off. He and Ingrid can't handle any more clients. Rebecca and Ingrid gave his company quite a reputation. He has to turn people away now that it's just Ingrid. They're getting burnt out."

I sat back down thinking of those days. I'd be able to help if I ever freed myself from the entanglement of this horrible life. This was my briar patch. My own father still thought I was Madeline. I hadn't even told my best friend, Ingrid. To her I was dead. But in my purse, there were pictures that might prune those thorns and bring me back. And how would Johannes see me once I'd destroyed his brother?

Could this get any worse?

"Madeline?" The voice behind me sounded Italian. It just got worse. "We meet again. How is my favourite person?"

I spun around and leaned in close enough to keep Johannes from hearing me. "Why are you following me?"

"I'm only protecting my interests. Good thing, too." He gave me a peck on the cheek and continued, "who is your friend, Maddie?"

Forced to stay tangled in the thorns, I was still Ricardo's secret romance. Oh, how I wanted to kick him in the groin, dropping the man to his knees. That would wipe that smug little smile off his face. To this bastard, my sweet misguided sister was nothing more than a horny housewife, a play toy. Why didn't she see any of this? Perhaps she did.

I didn't bother trying to hide my disinterest. "Ricardo, this is Johannes."

He held out a hand for Johannes to take. When Johannes did, Ricardo held it longer than he should, all while making uncomfortable eye contact. "And how do you know Madeline?"

"I used to date her sister."

Ricardo looked back at me stupefied. "You have a sister?"

"Yes. Her name was Rebecca," I answered. "Don't you have somewhere to be?"

His eyes undressed me, no doubt thinking *ménage à trois*. "In my dreams, I am already there."

I stared him down, tired of his game. "You should probably go and take care of those dreams. I have no doubt you're good at that."

"I'm always around, Maddy. I will see you later."

Johannes sensed the tension. "Nice to meet you, Ricardo." He put a hand on his shoulder and ushered him away.

"He's quite a piece of work, Madeline. So how do you know him?"

"You wouldn't believe me if I told you."

"Okay."

"Honestly, he's a nobody."

Johannes let it go. "How are your parents?"

"Good. They'd love to see you." Why did I just say that?

"That would be nice. I've always liked visiting them. They remind me of my parents."

"I could set something up." Breathe Rebecca, and slow down. "You're probably busy though."

"I do have a lot to do. I'm renovating my apartment, but I can always find time for them, and for you. I'm staying in a hotel." He handed me a card with his room number on it. "Please, don't be a stranger."

"Renovations?" I remembered the little apartment, remembered it well. It was cute and didn't need any work.

"The building had some electrical issues. I'm living at the hotel until we can get things fixed."

"I'll find a time that works for them." My head swirled with all the good times we had at his apartment. There were the beers on the patio, the stolen kisses on the elevator, and all those nights spent curled up in each other's arms.

I flipped the card around in my fingers. Soon he'd be walking away, and this would be good-bye. I didn't want that. I couldn't let him go, not again.

"It was good seeing you again, Madeline." He gave me another hug. This time it was brief and awkward. Confusion danced in his eyes as he peered into mine. Shaking the feeling, he walked away, but I had seen it.

"Good seeing you too, Jon."

He had wanted to see something, hoped it was there. He wanted it there as badly as I did. If only I was her. ""Bye, Madeline. Call me, sometime."

I waited until he was out of sight before I took my next breath. It came out in a whisper. "Definitely."

Chapter Thirty-six

The morning after seeing Johannes, I sat at the kitchen counter with his phone number, the only thing on my mind. Lawrence had left for work and Nicolas was making trips up and down the stairs, dragging stuffed animals into the dining room for a tea party. I had the phone in my hand twice, and both times I dropped it back onto its cradle. What would I say to him?

My nerves hadn't fluttered like this in some time. This schoolgirl crush was euphoric, playful, and oh so foolish. My body trembled with the thought of stealing a kiss. I hungered for a night where we could lay together and talk about…whatever. The sun would break, and we'd watch it climb to the heavens while our love entombed us, keeping us safe.

I picked up the card and studied Johannes's handwriting. There was an artistic flare, the 'J' in his name written so dramatically. Jon was the name he had written on the card. My sister had always preferred calling him that. I was Madeline, but I already knew that. How could I forget? Could he someday fall for a sister? Even though I was sure he could, I doubted he would. The man was not a home-wrecker and he'd forever see Rebecca in my eyes.

But I needed to see him again, steal a hug in a feeble attempt to hold on to what little of Rebecca I had left. Weeks ago, her life was nothing more than a name chiselled into granite. But the memories had returned and Johannes's chance meeting had given her life. She was crazier than I remembered and for that reason I dialled the number.

"Hello." The voice was his and it tickled my brain.

"Hello, Jon. It's Madeline. So how are you doing today?"

"Fine thanks. I'm surprised to hear from you so soon."

Why? Wasn't he feeling the same emotions that were driving me to light-headedness? This was a mistake. I was on the verge of a straight jacket fitting—God, I hope they don't come in beige.

"I just got off the phone with my parents, just touching base with them, and I mentioned that I ran into you. They wanted to hear all about it and I remembered what you said about wanting to see them." I continued to weave the story. "If you're still interested, they can do lunch today."

"I have an appointment at eleven, but it shouldn't be more than an hour. I could shoot for twelve thirty if that works for you."

"That'll work." Of course it would. My parents had no idea I was coming over and no idea I was bringing my sister's old boyfriend. Mother had better play nice. She owed me, that is, if they're even home today. In hindsight, I should have called them first.

The silence soon reached an uncomfortable length while I juggled my thoughts and tried to arrange them in some practical order.

Johannes politely excused himself. "I'll see you around noonish?"

"Noonish sounds good."

There was a click followed by a dial tone. I set the phone in its cradle and pocketed the number. The man was making me insane. Did I really want to go on a lunch date with Johannes, all the while lusting over him in front of my parents? Deep down inside I knew I had a better chance at swimming the Atlantic. This was just an escape, silly daydreams replacing my not-so-perfect reality. In my purse, there were pictures of a teenager with my husband. Lawrence and I deserved each other, and maybe our mess was as close as we'd get to true love.

Whatever.

I loaded up my lashes with mascara and dressed as if I was heading on a date. I made sure I didn't wear any of the jewellery he might recognise. At one point I stopped. Did I really want this man falling for my sister? Then the preening continued. I just wanted to know he could. With Nicolas all spit-shined and his shoes polished, we were off to my parents.

The Mercedes that Lawrence had bought me spooked me every time I got behind the wheel and today was no different. I guess he never saw the connection to the accident, or he did and enjoyed my suffering. I should cut him some slack. It wasn't the Mercedes that had killed Madeline. It was the driver of the truck. The police claimed he had been distracted. The man was sentenced to two years for the accident. He'd likely serve six months. I'd still be trapped in my sister's life.

My Dad answered the apartment buzzer. "Hello?"

Oh, shit. I could tell by the surprise in his voice that I still hadn't called them. They had no idea I was coming over, or that Johannes was going to be a lunch guest. My mind was scrambling for an excuse when I answered. "Hi, Dad, it's Rebecca."

"Madeline?"

Did I just say Rebecca? "Shit." My eyes rolled twice before slamming shut.

"Madeline? Is that you?"

"Uh yes, it's Madeline. Sorry Dad, I'll be right up." What the hell was I thinking? Mom was going to kill me. This might be for the better, just not today.

The door buzzed as the lock released. I smacked my forehead with my hand as Nicolas and I started up the spiral stairs.

There were six flights, plenty of time to start stringing the next part of this damn web of lies. The door was ajar when I reached it.

"Again, sorry Dad. I just ran into Johannes, remember Johannes?" I didn't wait for a response. "We were talking, and he wanted to see you both. I was going to call, but I forgot. Just like me, huh. He'll be here at twelve thirty. Again, I'm sorry for not telling you. I've had Rebecca on my mind all morning and I—"

Dad stopped me with a hug. "Relax sweetheart. Take a deep breath." He gave me that Dad smile, the one that let me know everything was okay. If he only knew how *not* okay things were.

At least he had bought my story, disaster averted, or I'd just set it on a different course. I almost wished he wouldn't have believed me. It was hard lying to him. I took a deep breath as I walked by the tan suede couch. I let my fingers run delicately along the length of the back, something I'd done so many times before.

This time it froze me. Madeline and Lawrence's first date had just jumped into my head.

I remembered walking through the front door to a butter-thick tension and that could only mean one thing, Madeline had a date. Having carried my shoes the last two blocks, all because of a broken heel, I dropped them by the door and entered to find the apartment fully engulfed in yet another Madeline Emergency.

Her stocking feet were stomping heavy on their heels as she made her way down the hallway. Then a door slammed, causing the wrought iron railing on our balcony to tremble like a scared child. A thrill-seeker to the end, I tracked the mayhem to her bedroom.

Inside, Madeline was mopping up an overturned bottle of nail polish with one of our good face cloths. Mascara and foundation sat unopened on the floor, in front of her dresser. A purse, with its contents close to spilling out, hung on one of the opened drawers. Clothes, beige, cream, and tan, were strewn across the floor and blanketed the bed. A slightly damaged closet door hung off its hinges as if drunk. Maybe it was trying to keep the room from falling over.

Madeline tossed the ruby stained face cloth aside when she noticed me in the doorway. Both eyes narrowed to angry slits. "What!"

I had no response except to close the door and retreat. Then I heard a car roll up to the curb outside. It gave an impatient honk making me wonder, was this honk meant for my sister?

I wove through the dining room to get to the balcony. I passed through the glass doors and pressed my hips against the paint-chipped railing. Six floors down, a silver Mercedes waited like Cinderella's fairy tale pumpkin.

I called back for her to bring him up, but all I heard was the clipping of heels as she made her way down the stairs.

The railing creaked and moaned as I leaned out further and waited for her to appear from the front lobby. Flakes of concrete broke away from the bolts that held the railing. Again I yelled at her to bring him up.

Ignoring me, except for the wave of a middle finger, she gingerly shuffled the cobblestones in her stilettos. The car door slammed shut and the Mercedes pulled away from the curb. Mortified, I slammed my fists hard against the railing and the wrought iron abruptly gave way. I was airborne.

"Madeline." My father was used to my drifting off and he walked me into the kitchen and sat me down at the table. It was like I was sleepwalking. "Cookie?"

"No thanks, Dad."

"I meant for Nicolas." He turned and handed the cookie off to the small, outstretched hand. "I'm glad you invited Johannes over, Madeline. It'll be nice to see him again."

Mom worked her last-minute magic in the kitchen, keeping her distance. Dad set the table. My only job was to keep Nicolas from colouring the furniture. The scribble started off with a circle, but soon lost any resemblance to anything other than a rainbow of dust bunnies.

When the phone rang, Dad answered it. "Hello?"

It was Johannes.

"I'll buzz you up, Johannes."

He took a couple minutes to climb the stairs and I anxiously waited for him like a witless teenager.

"Come in Jon." Dad dragged him into the house with a handshake. "Have a seat. Lunch is ready."

Johannes sat across from me. My son sat to my right and my Dad on the end to my left. It was a good visit and the conversation had stayed light until Johannes told my parents about Lawrence. Dad looked over at me, hurt that I hadn't mentioned anything. I could tell that Mom was also shocked. She'd want to talk about it, but I wasn't ready. The idea of him and Lawrence being brothers hadn't fully registered.

The meal of homemade soup and sandwiches hit the spot. The two-hour visit sped past far too quickly. Soon it was time for Johannes to go. Dad grabbed Mom to help with the dishes, leaving me alone to see him to the door.

"You want me to walk you down?" I asked.

"I should be able to find my way."

"I really don't mind. I can work off some of Mom's short rib soup."

"If you want to then." He started down the steps and I trailed closely behind in my stocking feet. There was no further conversation until we had reached the bottom. "So, we should get together for dinner some day."

"That would be terrific." La Maison Blanche quickly came to my mind.

"It's my turn. I can take you and Lawrence out on the town."

Suddenly, I wanted to slap him. Why would he bring up Lawrence? The man was not my husband. I was hoping for a hug and a peck of a kiss.

My insides knotted at the thought and my heart pounding to the tribal beat of a woman that had drank too much of the loco-juice. It was fun. Now, with Lawrence brought up, all I could think about was how rotten a person I was.

He stopped and looked back up at me. "Did I say something wrong?"

"No, I just have to check his calendar. He's a busy man."

"Oh, That's okay. I can check with him."

"I suppose you can." We continued out to the sidewalk and I gave him a very sisterly hug. His car disappeared around the corner and I slowly made my way back up to the apartment.

My mother met me at the door. She looked like she'd just returned from seeing a horror flick, that or a glimpse into my world. "You were gone a long time, Madeline. Is everything okay?"

Chapter Thirty-seven

Dougie lived seven doors down from the patisserie and five doors down from the entrance to my parent's apartment. A covered entrance was what he called home. He would either be there or at the soup kitchen. Today he was in his doorway and I was bearing gifts. "Good afternoon."

"Hello, Mrs. Madeline." Tired eyes looked up to find mine, and a faint smirk found its way through the long stubble. "Were you visiting your parents?"

"I was, Dougie." I handed him an extra cheesy ham croissant. "I owe you an apology."

"I'm not sure I understand." He reached up for the sandwich and immediately took a bite. "What do you mean?"

I briefly put my hands over Nicolas's ears. "You were right about me being *Rebecca*. Quite a few things have jumped out at me since we last talked."

He straightened the blanket on the step, offering Nicolas and I a spot to sit. "I was hoping it was you. So how are you taking it?"

"It's all a little overwhelming. There are two things that you can help me with." I took a second to study his eyes. How could I have ever forgotten my old friend? "First, Dougie, you were so sure about it. How'd you know?"

"That's an easy one. You have a unique quality in your eyes. It's a youthful energy with a hint of respectful sorrow. Most people have to fake these emotions. What you've got is a child's compassion, because children don't fake anything. Even when you thought you were your sister, and I was some crazy old nut-job, you bought me something to eat. You couldn't leave me hungry. Not everybody cares like that. I couldn't be sure, but I hoped it was you."

I remained silent, holding Nicolas's hand and staring at a crack in the sidewalk. The world was full of those lost-in-the-moment flaws, the ones that ground you while the world you're in is travelling a million miles an hour, a million miles away.

"You seem upset." He put his hands over Nicolas's ears. "Why, Rebecca?"

I closed my eyes. How I loved hearing someone call me that again. "Why didn't my mother tell me? She knew the whole time."

He put an arm around my shoulder and gave it a pat. "She had her reasons."

We both looked at Nicolas as I let the first tear find its way to my cheek. It hung there for a second before falling to the ground. "I just don't understand."

"That's because we're complicated. You said there were two things. What's the second?"

"I didn't believe you were a doctor the last time I saw you, but I remember now." I pulled a stethoscope out of my purse. I had bought it earlier. "I can't go to my doctor without my..." The word husband almost left my lips. He didn't need to know. "Let's just say I want to keep this to myself for now. Could you... I mean, I'm still nauseous and it's every day. I thought it was nerves, or a concussion. I'm beginning to wonder."

He took the stethoscope and put it to his ears. Then he warmed up the chest piece. I'd worn a loose coat and let him discreetly place it on three different spots on my belly. He looked up and nodded.

Initially, I had thought my illness had been a result of the accident. I was wrong. My first doubts came at the dress shop. I'd imagined wearing a few of the dresses. I had even smoothed my hand over my flat belly, except it wasn't as flat as it should have been. I couldn't have been gaining weight, not when I hadn't kept a breakfast down in weeks. There had been a thought, but I'd pushed it to the furthest reaches of my mind. Each morning it would wake with me and wane right after I puked. "I've never done this before, uh…"

"What do you want to know?"

Tears were falling in a silent desperation. "I can't change this, can I?"

"Sorry. It doesn't work that way."

"Well that's that then." I took a deep breath and when I exhaled, I startled Nicolas. "So how far along am I?"

He patted my knee and drew me in for a hug. "You need to see a real doctor for that answer. It's safe to say you're at least a couple months along."

I did some quick math. Johannes would be the father. I stood up and dried my cheeks with my sleeve. "This is not what I need right now."

"Reality seldom is."

"Reality?" There was that beast again. "I think this is me being punished."

"You need to see a doctor, and make sure he knows about the accident. They'll want to do an ultrasound. You don't need any complications."

"Of course. You're right." I shook my head as if clearing the dust off my thoughts. Lawrence wasn't the father, so how could I go to his doctor? Was he and Maddy even having sex before the accident? I couldn't take the chance.

A tiny hand pulled away from mine. Nicolas was bored from standing there. He decided it was time to run, except the streets of Paris weren't the place.

"Nicolas, stop!"

I didn't know why I thought yelling at him would work. He darted for a couple parked cars and I dropped my purse and gave chase. I'd read a novel once and in it a boy was struck by a semi-truck and dragged for a city block.

"Nicolas!"

His legs were short, his stride slow. As I ran after him my heel found an uneven section of the sidewalk and it almost tumbled me. I caught myself and grabbed him by the scruff of his coat. "What do you think you're doing?"

It was his turn to cry. I crouched down and wrapped him in my arms. As I did, I looked back to see my heel sitting in the middle of the sidewalk.

Dougie handed me my purse. He also tried to hand back the stethoscope. I didn't take it. "You need it more than I do. Maybe your friends could use a doctor."

He looked around and smiled at the thought of practising again, albeit on his non-paying friends.

I popped off my shoes and picked up the heel. It made me look up to the balcony of my parent's apartment. Days ago, my father had told me how the railing had broken free and crashed down on the sidewalk. Had it caused this chip in the concrete? And why hadn't Dad told me the whole story?

What he'd kept from me, his way of sparing Rebecca's reputation I guess, was that I had tried to wriggle my hand free from his wet grasp. A good part of that was because I didn't want him to fall with me. But was there a part of me that was tired of trying to measure up to my sister? For a brief second, I was ready for that deadly escape. I'm sure he had seen that in my eyes. And in that moment, it was like he didn't even know me. I doubt any of them did.

"I should get going."

"Go see a doctor."

"Mommy, doctor," my parrot repeated.

Chapter Thirty-eight

Today I had my morning coffee in Lawrence's study in front of the fireplace. I continued to reflect on how my world had unravelled into my sister's. Blaming myself was pointless and non-productive. There was no way I could have seen any of this coming. At the hospital I had been told who I was, and I had believed them, all of them. I had found it easier to adjust than to fight any doubts.

But now that I knew, my next moves would have to be chosen carefully. Battlegrounds needed to be peaceful and I had to work my way out of this mess. As Rebecca, I'd have no legal rights to Nicolas and there was no leaving him behind. Until further notice, I was my sister.

There was a silver lining of sorts since Lawrence's romantic desires had shifted. A young girl named Scarlett had become my saviour and although I felt bad for her, I'd get over it. P.I. Pierre Stoltz had received a retainer and he had found enough dirt to give me what I needed, my freedom.

I placed a hand on my belly. I'd have to work fast. A tummy-bump couldn't be hidden forever. So was Lawrence seeing other girls? Could there be others out there? I'd bet his study held the answers. It was his sanctuary of secrets. I had just started jimmying away at the lock to the desk drawer when the phone rang.

It stopped my heart.

Lawrence knew what I was up to. He was calling as a warning, telling me to drop it or I'd get an old fashion lesson on who was in charge. Did I need a reminder as to how these lessons turned out?

The phone rang again and even though I knew it would, I still jumped. "Shit!" I looked around the room to see if I was alone. I expected to see him behind me. How could he know?

I reluctantly picked up the receiver on the third ring. "Hello?"

The silence was eerie. Then I heard the voice. "Madeline, is that you?" A shiver rattled through my bones. "Can we talk?"

My heart had options. It could beat humming bird fast, shut down, or explode. Being preoccupied by the call, I allowed it to choose its own fate. Why was Lawrence calling? I had to hear something else. It wasn't like him to call home.

"Madeline? Are you there?"

It was Johannes. The tightness in my chest loosened as my words continued to fight me. I wanted to tell this man that I still loved him, that I was pregnant, and that he was the father. Then I thought about my funeral, the one I'd be having if Lawrence found out.

"Madeline?"

Why can't I talk to him? Are these pregnancy hormones? I should hang up. Something had to come out of my mouth soon, and it had to sound like Madeline. "I'm here. Sorry, I was just juggling, uh, Nicolas's bottle."

"He's still on the bottle?"

"Pop!"

Good catch. Ugh, no it's not. It's nine in the morning. Who gives their kid pop for breakfast? "I mean he grabbed it out of the fridge and I was getting it away from him. It's a little, um, early…shit."

I could hear his chuckle on the other end of the line. It was the very laugh I used to enjoy over evening beers at Rommer Square. The four of us, Marcus, Ingrid, Johannes, and I often played cribbage at outside tables while the music streamed out from the taverns. Moments like these were starting to claw their way back to me and I couldn't stop them. "What did you call for?"

There was a brief silence before he started to talk. It was his turn to choke on some emotions. "It was nice seeing your parents. I talked to Ingrid. She told me how you're struggling with memories. I know we haven't talked much about that. I'm also struggling with a few."

"The accident made my brain a bit of a clean slate."

"If I can help...I mean if you need to talk..."

"Thank you."

Johannes continued, "The reason I called is because I've always felt bad about something. I never got to see you or your parents after Rebecca died."

"I heard you missed Rebecca's funeral." Did I just blurt that out? I was sure it came out wrong. Did it sound angry? He had missed my funeral, so a little anger was okay. "I mean I heard you didn't go."

"I would have gone, but it was a terrible time. You don't need the details, but I had received a phone call only minutes before your parents called. It was from the hospital in Frankfurt. We'd had snow and the roads were dangerous. It was my parents."

Pain hung on each word as he spoke. "What happened, Johannes?"

He took a deep breath and cleared his throat. "They were returning from Rudesheim when their car slid off the road and into the Rheine. I'm sure Dad had a couple glasses too many. People tried to get them out of the frigid water, but they were too late."

This would have been the same freak storm that killed Madeline. "I'm so sorry, Jon." How could I have been so stupid as to think he didn't care about me?

"I felt guilty missing Rebecca's funeral. I meant to call, but what could I have said to them? Soon I had let it go too long. How could I call them and dredge up such horrific feelings? Then I found out about my brother. Finding him was such a good distraction that I thought I had healed. But seeing you has brought her back."

"Oh Johannes."

"I'm sorry. This must be hard for you."

"Yes, but I don't mind talking about her. Oddly it keeps her alive."

"I'm glad."

"It feels like years, doesn't it?" My words drifted off.

"It does." His words hid the pain poorly. "There are days when time has stalled. Life is not the same without her."

It was nice to hear that the man was still in love. This gave me courage, gave me hope.

"Again, I just wanted to call and tell you how sorry I was about your sister. She was an incredible soul and the world won't be the same without her." There was an awkward silence. "Maybe we can do lunch sometime. I enjoy talking about her."

"I think a lunch would be a good idea, Johannes." I really did prefer Johannes verses Jon and it was nice hearing it leave my lips. For that fleeting breath, I could pretend. I didn't want to hang up.

And that was when a tugging on my pants brought me back. I looked down to see Nicolas and the love in his eyes reminded me that, for now, I was still Madeline. "I have to run, Jon."

There was a click and with it, our connection to the past was gone.

Chapter Thirty-nine

With Johannes deeply embedded in my head, my feelings were as mixed as the coloured pigments in paint. I had been Madeline for weeks, a part of me still was. I had a husband, a child, a home, and I could rule out the flu for the nausea. And although this life hadn't been my choice, it was my current reality. There was guilt, slathered with anger, and none of that was productive.

I picked up the wedding album and took one last look at it before putting it out of sight, forever. The wedding and my need to find any kind of love for Lawrence had ended when I read that dress receipt. And then there were the stories that Ingrid had told me. I had hated Lawrence enough to want to hand Johannes over to my sister.

In the days since Johannes' life-changing dinner, he and I had exchanged phone calls and even did that lunch we talked about. Ricardo, never the one to act the stranger, had found us and briefly joined us. Johannes was his competition and he was still looking to push this new man away. When I told him that Johannes was Lawrence's brother, he excused himself.

I also shared my investment concerns albeit received with deaf ears. He wasn't worried. The rest of our conversations had been about the weather, Nicolas, and how nice my hair looked. Rebecca hadn't been mentioned.

By the end of lunch, things had become awkward. Nicolas, my chaperone, continued to do an excellent job steering me from stupidity. That is until it came to part ways. Johannes held me in an embrace and it lasted longer than it should have. It was a moment, and I think we both were whisked away to the land of what-ifs. I really didn't mean to put him through this. It was irresponsible, selfish, and very risky.

For the third straight morning, Lawrence had informed me his day would be a long one—do not wait up. This has become a trend these last few days. I was okay with that. The weekend was nearing so, as his wife, a deep cleaning of the house was a necessity. One never knew when unannounced company, like his parents, would drop by. Nicolas helped in his own way. Sleeping in, he allowed me to kick-start my morning.

The door to Lawrence's study was open so I wheeled the vacuum in. Running a quick lap around the desk, I stopped to empty his wastebasket. I decided to snoop through his garbage before dumping it. Maybe a certain Scarlett left him another note. I continue to trudge through this minefield hoping for better options.

There was no new incriminating evidence on the fidelity front, but there was a crumpled document. It had Johannes's name on it, hand written with a few investment stocks and a few names listed to the side. This looked like an investment strategy.

I dialled Johannes from the kitchen phone. "Hey, it's me. Is there any chance we can do lunch today?"

"Of course. You know I always enjoy the company of you and Nicolas. When?"

"Can I pick you up in say, half an hour?" A part of me wanted to tell him why, but he'd been closed minded on the topic.

"Sounds serious. Is everything okay?"

It was hard to know without the details of their dealings. "Everything's good."

"See you in half an hour then."

After a short drive, I quickly found a spot at the hotel parking lot. I hurried a frantic Nicolas out of his seat. The boy had to pee. We cruised through the lobby and down the hallway reading the door numbers as we rushed. The place was busy, likely a checkout time. We found the room numbered 107 and knocked. When the door opened, we barged our way past him.

"I'm sorry. Can Nicolas use your bathroom?"

He pointed to a door on the other side of an unmade bed. "Definitely."

I quickly got Nicolas settled on the seat. "You okay, Tiger?" Nicolas nodded so I left him to teeter with his hands propped on the seat behind him. "Give mommy a shout when you're done."

Johannes was buttoned up his shirt when I returned from the bathroom. "Sorry again, Johannes. How are you?"

"I'm good." He stopped three buttons from the top and held his arms out for an innocent hug.

My arms made their way around his waist. My fingers lightly caress every contour of his body. He'd been in the shower and I could smell clean and freshly shaved. I remembered looking forward to that smell when we were together. It was an aphrodisiac, dangerously sexy. I held him close, closed my eyes and soaked him in. I imagined him on top of me, his lips on my neck. Our naked bodies twisted in a passionate embrace. This time the hug lasted far too long.

I knew it was wrong, but I couldn't contain myself. It was as comforting as a child's blanket, and damn if I didn't deserve this. I hadn't been held like this since…

He continued to hold onto me. I opened my eyes and looked up to see him staring down at me. His eyes weren't asking why this crazy woman was still holding him. They were trying to read me, wanting to take a chance. Should he roll the dice and accept the outcome?

My lips met his, or perhaps his lips met mine, it didn't matter. The kiss, the one I'd spent weeks fantasising about, had me wanting to shed my clothes and savagely attack this man. One or both of us might not survive.

His heart was pounding as I mashed my body against his chest. My nails dug into his back as my tongue found his. But the tongue was too much, and he pushed me away.

"What are we doing?"

I stared blankly, my swollen chest fighting against the fabric of my blouse. "I'm sorry, Johannes. This was my fault."

"Mine too. I shouldn't have done this, but you're so damned intoxicating."

Intoxicating? I was in no way sorry now. I wanted to feel him inside me, wanted to feel the sweat from his chest mashed against my bare breasts. Then I saw the hurt in his eyes and I wanted to crawl away and cry. Who was I kidding? He wasn't kissing me. He was kissing my sister. "Don't make it into something terrible, Jon. I see what my sister saw in you. You're a kind and amazing man."

He couldn't look away, more afraid than sorry. He had wanted more and felt horrible for it.

Nicolas emerged from the bathroom and I had to laugh.

"What's so funny?" Johannes took a step away from me as if Nicolas might not approve of us standing so close.

"My chaperone is definitely not getting his ice cream today." I had hoped with that comment Johannes might figure it out, but he didn't. "Why do you think I always keep him close when you're around? I can't trust myself."

"I think lunch is a bad idea."

"This is my fault, Jon." I shrugged and accepted the blame. "I'm an adult and I know better."

"Is there something wrong with you and Lawrence?"

"I can't talk about it. Let's say that Lawrence and I aren't what everybody thinks. He's your brother, so I won't get into it. He has his world and I'm just a wife living in it."

"What are you saying?"

"My husband, my problem, Johannes." I gave him a half-cocked smile.

"You look so much like her, the way she smiles, the way she scrunches her nose when she thinks. It plays on me, makes me believe you are her. I swear I see her in your eyes. Is that crazy?"

"It's not that crazy, and I should leave." I pulled the slip of paper out of my pocket. "I honestly came over because I still don't like the fact that Lawrence is handling your money. I have no reason to believe he's out to get you, but it's all your inheritance and I worry. I found this in the trash. Do you have anybody that could decipher it?"

"There's the guy who was helping me find Georg, I mean Lawrence. He's a whiz with this stuff. I'm not so good at it. That's why I don't mind Lawrence handling our money. Again, Madeline, I'm so sorry about the kiss."

"We all know your brother was never my best choice." I took a deep breath and let it out slowly while I studied his eyes. "Keep me posted on the note."

And with that, Nicolas and I left. I was floating on a cloud for the rest of the day. A sexy bubble bath and a glass of wine would be in order after I got Nicolas to bed.

My plans were shattered around eight o'clock. Lawrence had planned to stay late but came home early. His rage, in the form of a clenched fist, met my face, driving me to the floor.

"You bitch."

Chapter Forty

Hard ow dare you slut around with my brother."
Lawrence stood over me like an animal, ready to
strike again. "Answer me, damn it!"

"I dropped by to say hi. Nicolas was with me, for God's sake. There's nothing going on." I wasn't sure what he knew, but in all honesty, little had happened. "It was just a visit, Lawrence."

He stepped away with his hands on his hips. "How do you think I feel when Rubens tells me he saw you at some hotel? He followed you up to the room and now he thinks my wife's messing around on me. I told him it was just family, but then he asked what family. What do I tell him, Madeline? I can't afford to have these people thinking shit about me."

So, this wasn't about the kiss, or even my being with Johannes. This was about the perceptions of co-workers. I shook the haze from my head and tried to stand. Using the umbrella stand, I got to my feet and rotated my jaw around to make sure it was still attached. "He's your brother, Lawrence."

"Okay, we've established that. Regardless, you don't need to be seeing him anymore. It makes me look bad. These people don't even know I have a brother, they just see you tramping around."

"Tell them." I tried to blink the last of the blurring from my eyes and took a step toward him. "You should be happy to have a brother. Tell them. Hell, tell everyone."

"If only it were that easy. Johannes is neither successful, nor refined. And what would my father think?"

"You haven't told him?"

"Just stay away from Johannes."

"No, the man's family." I knew standing up to him wasn't the smartest move. "You shouldn't let your friends dictate our lives."

I wasn't wrong to think that. I'd been the perfect wife and before me, Madeline had been an even better one. The only return on all that loyalty was this. I'd had enough. "You owe me this. Besides, how do you think I feel when my husband's running around screwing little girls? You don't think that makes me look like an idiot."

That had been blurted out before giving sanity a chance.

Oddly, he wasn't surprised that I knew. Nor was he upset that I'd brought it up. "You've done some snooping I see. I'm impressed, but you only get one warning and this is it."

I'm sure a part of him was glad to see the fight in me. Don't get me wrong, he wasn't happy, but there was a certain level of pride in the fact that his woman had spunk. Sadly, he would have to exterminate that spunk. "She's a good girl and not afraid to be the woman that you're not. Maybe if you were up for it, I wouldn't have to go elsewhere."

I wanted to scream. "When have I ever said no to you?"

"When has your heart ever been in it?"

"Look Lawrence, if you don't want me visiting your brother then you need to stop seeing Scarlett. Otherwise, I'll continue to be his friend."

In hindsight I should have stopped there. I wanted him to see her. I was safe in our bed. Still, I continued, "Shit, Lawrence. What is she, sixteen?"

"And if I don't?" He glared as he grabbed the bottle of scotch and took a swig. "What are you going to do, leave me?"

"Maybe." I couldn't read him at this point. He was calm. Did that mean I had the upper hand or enough dirt to push further? Could I leave him and keep Nicolas? He's a cheater, and with a small child no doubt. I had the proof.

"So, you want to see Johannes?"

"No. I just want to be able to have a coffee with the man. He knew my sister. It's nice to talk about her. And what if he's at Ingrid's place when I go over? Am I expected to leave?"

His smile threw me and as he walked toward me. I returned a tentative smile and held my ground. Madeline should have tried standing up to him more. My hands were shaking so I planted them on my hips. How important was this mistress? I should be able to leverage a friendship with Johannes. It was only a theory.

Again, his rage forced me to the floor, him on top, slapping and punching. The slapping hurt. The punching only surfaced my own rage.

He tried to pin my arms with his knees. I'm sure Madeline would have given in, waiting for it to end. In his twisted mind the hitting should have been teaching me a valuable lesson. It wasn't, because I wasn't Madeline.

My knee connected with his crotch and the pain bought me enough time to crawl out from underneath him. We were both quickly to our feet, but by then I'd put the dining room table between us.

"You bitch." His nostrils flared. He wanted to hit me, get his hands around my throat. He could only stand there, on the opposite side of the table, daring me to bolt for a doorway.

Safety brings false bravery and I thought I was out of harm's way. "You're a stupid ass. You treat me like shit and then you wonder why I want to leave."

"You're not going anywhere."

"You can't stop me."

"You're right." He smiled again. "If you want to go then go, but Nicolas stays. He's my son."

I ran my fingers through my hair and showed him the blood on my fingertips. "I'll get a lawyer. Besides, I have pictures of you tramping around with the redheaded child. She's carrying her fucking schoolbooks in half the shots."

He dodged right and then left, trying to get me to run. My courage was dissolving. I knew I was only safe if I kept the table between us.

"You go. Get out! You don't belong here anyway. But you don't get Nicolas."

Then he downed the last of the scotch and threw the bottle hard against the floor. It shattered, leaving glass all over one of my two escape-routes.

I was trapped.

Kevin Weisbeck

Chapter Forty-one

With Lawrence hovering at one end of the table and a floor full of broken glass at the other, a peace offering was in order. "Okay, I'm not going anywhere, and you can have your mistresses. I was wrong to bring her up." I half-raised my hands and stepped back from the table.

Lawrence also took a couple steps back. "This is out of hand. I don't want to be the enemy here. I'm a man, and Scarlett is just a release so that I don't bring my work home with me. And I can do things with her that I wouldn't do with you. You're my son's mother. I respect that." He slowly made his way over to me. "I don't want to fight."

This wasn't about love, betrayal, or trust. It was about image. That said, we could both agree that the redhead wasn't the problem. I didn't want to know what I was missing out on. Nor did I want to lose Nicolas. "I don't either."

"You know I can't afford to let you leave."

I dropped onto one of the chairs. This was how it worked in his world.

"Tomorrow's Friday and I've put in a lot of hours these last few weeks. They'll have to live without me this weekend. I know a little spot out in the Loire Valley. Get Nicolas packed up for a couple days. I think we need to get away." He gently kissed my forehead. "We'll leave first thing in the morning."

Although I tried, sleep came as nothing more than a series of short catnaps. Because of that, Lawrence and Nicolas awoke to bacon, eggs, and pancakes. Nicolas had brought his book to the table and asked if I could read him a story. I told him that I would in the car. Lawrence quietly worked on his breakfast.

After we ate, I started on the dishes. Lawrence loaded the car. The bags by the door disappeared, one by one. Nicolas made one last bathroom break and we were ready. Lawrence walked Nicolas to the car and buckled him in while I went to the kitchen and grabbed a few bottles of water for the trip. I was putting them in a bag when Lawrence dropped my suitcase at my feet.

I looked down. "What's this?"

"We don't need this." He turned to walk away.

I grabbed him by the arm and spun him back around. "What the hell's going on here?"

"You think it would be so easy to leave. I think you need to see what life would be like without your family." He grabbed the water and started for the door. I followed in disbelief.

"You can't take my son from me."

"He's not your son, he's mine! And as my wife you *will* do as you're told."

I should have let him go, but how could I let him take my Nicolas, even for one night? Nicolas was my world and he expected me to protect him at night. "Please Lawrence, don't do this. Last night we made an agreement."

He stopped and turned back to me. "Agreement? You act like you have a say in this. Let's get one thing straight. As long as I'm paying your way, you do what I tell you. If you leave, it's because I say you can. Oh, and I'll do my little whore whenever I want. As for Nicolas, I'll be the one saying what will or will not happen in his life. Now we're leaving for the weekend and I don't want to hear another word from you."

"You're such an asshole!" I looked for something to throw. On the table by the door, sat a large snow-globe. I imagined myself throwing it at him, smashing it against his skull and splitting him open like an egg. And just like that, I had it in my hand.

I snapped out of it when the bag of water bottles landed on the floor with a shattering crash. He calmly took the globe from me. I watched his lips purse as he cocked his arm. I narrowed my eyes to slits, daring him, knowing he'd back down. The damn thing was a gift from his precious mother. He wouldn't dare.

The globe shattered into a million pieces against my cheek and I landed hard against the floor, my head bouncing off the aged oak. I could only watch as he kicked the bag of broken bottles out of the way and closed the door behind him. The car started, and I could hear the tires on the gravel as he drove away. In my mind I could hear Nicolas asking about Mommy. Where was she? Was she coming? He would ask again and again. Eventually he'd start crying.

The foyer was blurring into an abyss as I tried to clear my sight. I saw the white snowflakes from the globe as they swam around in an ocean of bloodied water. The chunks of broken glass sat on the floor looking like tiny icebergs.

I tried to focus on them, but my eyelids were heavy. The fight in me was exhausted and they closed.

Chapter Forty-two

A knocking on the door drew me out of the abyss. It was polite at first, soon becoming heavy and frantic. Sunlight was forcing its way through the dinning room windows. That meant it was still day but, from that angle, now well into afternoon.

I got to my knees, placed a hand on the wall and slowly rose to my feet. Through the sight glass I could see it was Johannes. My legs buckled and dropped me against the door. I was on my knees again.

A muffled voice called out, "Madeline? Is everything okay?"

I used the doorknob to pull myself back up before fumbling with the lock. The door threw me off balance and I was dropping fast. Johannes swept in and caught me. He quickly dragged me over to the table and sat me in a chair.

"What the hell happened to you? Did somebody break in? I'm going to call the police."

"Don't" I tried to smile while I rubbed the cheek that Lawrence had struck. Crusts of blood flaked from my skin. "He took Nicolas."

"Who?"

"Lawrence."

"Lawrence did this?"

"The man has my son."

"But…"

"He's nothing like you… Actually, you really should go. He could come back. I'll be fine."

Johannes grabbed a napkin and placed it on my cheek. "Does he do this often?"

His innocence was sweet. "What made you come here?"

"I hoped to talk to Lawrence, but that's not important now."

I rolled my jaw and neck, working the kinks out. My eyes didn't fall out of my head when I blinked. That was good, so I blinked twice more to focus. It helped. "How bad do I look?"

"I think you need stitches." He put his arm around me. "I'll get you to a hospital. Can you walk?"

"You really shouldn't get involved. He's your brother."

"It's a little late for that."

Johannes drove me to the emergency ward and it was nice having him there. He held my hand as we waited. A nurse whose nametag read Brianne eventually came by and pulled my hand away from my cheek. She shook her head and grabbed a pen. My name wasn't asked. We watched as she casually filled out the form like we were two friends getting together over coffee. How many forms had she filled out for Madeline? After completing the form, a second nurse took me to a bed and started the prep work.

An hour later, I was back in the waiting room. The local freezing had started to wear off and my head was throbbing. Johannes, waiting like an expectant father, took me in his arms. The nurse smiled at the sight. There was hope for me.

"What's going on Madeline? They all act like they know you."

"It's happened before."

"And what is this?" He placed a hand on the bandage. "What happened?"

I needed to play this down. "Lawrence took Nicolas away for the weekend. I thought I was going, but it turns out he's teaching me a lesson. Too bad I'm a lousy study." I wanted to laugh, but my skin was tight from the swelling.

He continued to hold me in his arms. "You're safe now."

"Safe?" It was a hug like back at his hotel, yet it was anything but safe. I dropped my head to his chest and let him hold me. I was tired of fighting everything, including him. Eventually I pushed myself away. "I'd be safer if I just learned to shut my mouth. This only happens when I provoke him."

"Provoked or not, it's not right."

And wasn't it cute that he figured I needed to be told that. His chivalry was refreshing and very foreign to this world. "I know how it's supposed to work. So, you never told me why you were looking for Lawrence?"

"That friend of mine looked at that crumpled document. He's not sure what it means, but he did say some of the numbers didn't add up. He asked me a couple questions about the guy who sold us the building."

"You bought a building?"

"We did. There were money troubles and we got a deal. It sounds like a few of the tenants were holding back funds. I wanted to ask Lawrence about them."

"I'm not an investor type, but I'm guessing that can't be good."

I thanked Brianne one last time as she handed me a bottle of painkillers. Then I shuffled Johannes away from the gawking nurses. There were too many eyes wondering about my Mr. Charming.

He felt it too. "Should I take you home? Is it safe there?"

"Do you mind if we go to your place?" The idea of being back in that house sent a shudder through me. "I just need a few hours to regroup."

"Yes." He walked me to the car. Then he surprised me with a kiss on my good cheek. It was warm, loving, and it made me feel special under the gauze, stitches, and strips of tape. After the kiss he held my jaw in his hands and locked his eyes onto mine. Again, there was a kiss, this time on the lips and it was brief, but tender.

I was smiling when he pulled away.

"I'm sorry Madeline. I… this… It's wrong. Damn it, you're her sister."

My eyes danced back and forth, trying to fix on both of his eyes at once. "It's okay."

He shook his head. I watched as his eyes welled up. "No. I honestly love Rebecca. I think I want her back so bad that I'm wishing to see her in you. I see her fire, her passion, and her tenderness. I see our memories in your eyes. To me, you might as well be Rebecca and that's not fair to either of us."

I dropped my head back down on his chest. The man was still in love.

And then there was Nicolas. Did I have the right to want him? He was more Lawrence's than he was mine. That was why the courts see it that way. Courts don't see the abusive husband, or the horrible role model. He was a father. I was just the aunt.

Johannes started to talk again. I wished he would stop. I didn't want to hear any of this.

"What do I do, Madeline?"

He waited until I brought my head back up. I knew what was coming so I closed my eyes. A silent prayer tried to stop him. It didn't.

"Madeline, I'm falling in love with you."

"Don't say that."

"But I am."

"Damn you. We need to get out of here, and we need to talk."

Chapter Forty-three

My confession stunned Johannes as he sat on the end of his bed. I told him about the accident, the amnesia, and the enlightening dress receipt. He had no words and after finishing the story, neither did I. A huge part of me had hoped he'd want to shout from the rooftops. He had his Rebecca back.

The man remained silent.

"I'm not with Lawrence because I love him."

"But you're with him."

"Not by choice."

"You were intimate with him."

"When I thought I was Madeline, I tried to wrap my head around the emotional closeness. He was my husband and that meant for better or worse. As hard as I tried, the sex was never more than a wife's duty. My heart beat for the first time in months when I realised who I was. At that point I could only think of you."

"You should have told me."

"I'm telling you now." I kept my eyes on his. "My parents were strangers in the beginning. My brain was cookie dough and because of that, my life became whatever they put in it. They could have added anything, what foods I liked, where I went to school, if I went to school. I wouldn't have known any different. It wasn't until seeing that dress receipt that I figured things out. By then Rebecca was gone and Madeline had taken over."

"You could have left him when you realised."

"I could have, but then Nicolas would grow up without a mother. He'd be raised by a man who treats women like this. In time, he'd become a monster himself. Nicolas was Madeline's son and I owed her."

His eyes didn't leave mine. They were not only hurting, but they were hoping I'd come to my senses and hurdle myself back into his life. We could go back to the life of love and happiness, back to the days of drinking beers. It made sense. I knew it made good sense to me, if it weren't for Nicolas. "I can't."

"I never got over you Rebecca. Your kiss has stirred so many emotions."

"I'm sorry. They've stirred mine too."

He sat, unable to see anything but the betrayal. "I think you should leave."

I didn't see that coming. It was a two by four to the back of the head. "Do you mean leave Lawrence or..."

He looked toward the door.

"But I don't want to lose you again, Johannes. I can't..."

"Think about what you're asking. I'll have to sneak around while you're with him? Let's face it, you won't go anywhere without Nicolas and I can't expect you to. But I can't give you what you want. Besides, I deserve more."

"But..." I stopped myself. Seriously, what did I expect? He was right. What I was asking, was for him to be my escape. Why not, Madeline had a Ricardo and Lawrence had Scarlet. Johannes could never be my husband, yet I wanted all the liberties as if he was. For me it was a dream come true. I'd get to raise Nicolas and have Johannes.

For Johannes it was a shallow and empty life. He'd be alone on holidays and at Christmas. He'd always wonder if my love was still true, or was Lawrence forcing his way on top of me? Lawrence was my husband. Could I be in love with the man I was living with, even a little? And what if Lawrence found out? I knew I wouldn't be able to do this and it was selfish of me to expect him to.

I reached out and placed my hand on his shoulder. He took it in his, holding it tight. "Johannes, I'm so sorry for putting you through this. I never meant to hurt you and I should have told you sooner. It's not like I've ever done this before."

"You said you thought of me?"

"Once I realised I was Rebecca, I thought of you every day."

He could tell I wasn't lying. I wanted to tell him that I had cried when I stared at photos. I wanted to tell him how it killed me to think he might fall in love, that someday he'd forget me. He'd hold her like he used to hold me, love her like he used to love me. I wanted to tell him all of that, but none of it changed the fact that I couldn't be there for him.

"I'm really sorry, Johannes."

"Me too." He let go of my hand and dropped his eyes. "What do we do now?"

I kissed his cheek. He didn't look up. "Good bye. I'll never get over you and when I get away from this man, and I know I will, I'm going to come looking for you. There's nobody else for me."

With that, I turned and left. As I started down the hallway I begged for his voice. If only he'd chase me. I never wanted to leave, but I couldn't be greedy. He was an amazing man and he deserved more. The man deserved the wife, the family, and the little house on the corner. And who was I kidding, he wouldn't be single long.

As the first tear escaped my eye, I hurried my pace. I needed the distance. By the time I rounded the corner, that single tear had incited a deluge. My stomach clenched, weakening my knees with each step. Could I leave Lawrence, leave my son? I couldn't, but could I walk away from Johannes? And then there was this child growing inside me. Should I have said something?

I was barely breathing. My limp body fell against the wall and I slid down it until I was a crumpled, sobbing heap on the floor. My chest had been crushed under the promise I'd made my sister.

"I'm sorry Johannes."

Chapter Forty-four

I closed my eyes and let my mind drift to the day I picked Madeline up from the hospital. It had been a week since Nicolas's premature birth. The boy had gained the required eight ounces and that allowed Madeline to take him home. Her slim figure had already returned, and I swear her body had bounced back better than before. She even had a little more hip. Lawrence had been busy as usual, having to deal with his lawyer. It was a meeting that couldn't be missed, not even to pick up a wife or newly born son.

Madeline was dressed and looking forward to getting home. From what I saw, the food hadn't looked that bad. Sure, the Jell-O was a little chewy, but it was tasty. I was in the middle of giving the room a quick once-over when she pulled a letter out of her pocket. There were three yellow pages, folder in half twice.

I had glanced over the contents of the letter. It was a will of sorts, simple stuff, wanting me to have visitation rights including one weekend per month. There was nothing about funeral provisions or what she wanted done with her personal items. I looked up at her hoping to see where she was going with this.

She told me it was nothing and that she'd talked to Lawrence about my going through the church to become Nicolas's Godmother. He agreed, assuming I'd fail. I was a flaky model. No church would accept me as a legal guardian.

But she knew that becoming Nicolas's Godmother would afford certain privileges. I'd have some say in Nicolas' life if anything ever happened, not that it would.

She was playing a dangerous chess game and I was a strategic piece, being moved into position. Again, Madeline told me the man wasn't dangerous, that things happen. At the time I assumed she meant a bus might strike her when she crossed the street. Now, knowing him better, I imagined him pushing her in front of that bus.

Years ago, at a little pond back in Chilliwack, I had promised to take care of her. In this letter she was transferring that promise to Nicolas. This folded letter might not carry the validity needed in court, so it was vital that I tried harder to accept Lawrence. Nicolas needed a family's influence in his life, her family.

She gave me the same lost eyes that I had seen twelve years ago. They were the ones that begged me to look out for her. Now it was her son's turn, so I repeated those words from years ago. I swore to watch out for her and my nephew until the day I died. Then for shits and giggles, I added, 'And beyond.'

I smiled and put a hand up to my cheek. Those were such simpler times. Where did it all go wrong? Was it the move to Paris, the accident, or the day Madeline drove off on her first date with Lawrence while I hung from a balcony, six floors up? The grin that had found me thinking about the past quickly dissolved as my tears ran the last of my mascara down my cheeks.

A couple strolled by me in the hallway. He was fumbling the keys to their hotel room in his hand. She looked a little too young for him. I remained seated, my back against the wall. The stare they gave me wasn't as compassionate as it was curious. I quickly grabbed a tissue from my purse and wiped at my cheeks.

They politely turned their heads and kept walking. She looked like she wanted to stop.

I worked my sister's wedding bands off my finger and tossed them into my purse, her purse. They were choking the life out of me. God, I hated him.

As hard as I'd tried, I'd failed that nine-year-old sister who had made those ripples flee to the shores of that pond. She feared Paris and I'd promised her everything would be fine. I'd promised to take care of her and her son.

I had failed her. I wouldn't fail him.

Chapter Forty-five

S till a crumpled heap on the floor, I willed myself to
my feet. I couldn't stay here forever. Where would I
go? My cheek throbbed and with the freezing fully
gone, I was a mental and physical wreck. I had no son, wore my
husband's handy work across my face, and I'd just lost the only
man I truly loved. I had only one person to blame, Madeline. I had
sworn to have her back, take care of her when she needed me.
Maybe I was naive, but I always thought she'd do the same. So
where was she when I needed her?

I looked down the hallway and hoped to see Johannes. He
would set himself down beside me and his arms would quickly
wrap me up like a blanket. I wouldn't speak. I'd just let him hold
me.

That wasn't going to happen.

Instead I made my way through the lobby, judged by
everyone that looked my way. Dark sunglasses poorly hid the eyes
of the woman I'd become. Beaten and alone, I looked as pitiful as
she did with every visit to the emergency ward. This was what her

life, my life, had become. It was people staring, forming opinions, and neither of us caring.

"Madeline?"

I turned, half protecting myself with my right arm. It was Ricardo.

"Shit." He reared back. "What the hell happened to you?"

"Save it Ricardo. I'm not in the mood."

What looked like an honest guilt started to consume him. "Tell me I didn't do this."

Telling him that Lawrence had found out about us would have sent him running for the hills. It might have made him change his ways. As fun as it sounded, I'm not that person. "Don't flatter yourself. This was all me."

"Why would anyone do this?"

"Shit happens, Ricardo. I'm already over it." Then I paused and took my glasses off. He needed to see the bruising, the stitches and the bloodshot eye. I was no longer the goodtime gal he was accustomed to. "This is what happens to the women that need lovers like you. It's as inevitable as a sunset, because at the end of the day, this is the reality."

"Reality?" That was the only word he heard. "He doesn't know, does he?"

"About you? No. This is more about bad choices, made for the wrong reasons. Now run along and forget about me. Go find somebody special and pray she never needs a lover like you. Pray she doesn't wind up looking like some deprived housewife. It's not always pretty. And for the record, what we had wasn't an adventure, it was merely a temporary escape."

He gave me an apologetic head nod and turned to make his escape, but I wasn't done with him. I grabbed his arm. "Hey. One question, only because I truly can't remember." Which wasn't entirely a lie. "What caused us to hook up?"

He took a step toward me. "We never talked much, but I'd have to say it was this Rebecca person. You were always jealous of her. You always talked about her, but never told me she was your sister."

"Why was I jealous?"

"She had beauty, an exciting life and what you called enough freedom to find herself. You said she followed her heart because she was blessed with the wings to do it. Where she had wings, you had been cursed with roots."

I put the glasses back on. "Thanks."

On the way to the car I stopped at a little corner grocery store. It sold milk, bread, and an assortment of wine. I grabbed an extra-large bottle of Merlot. After I paid for it, I talked the man at the cash register into opening it.

I drove through tears, safely reaching the cemetery, and parked on the grass. Madeline was jealous of me? We needed to talk, and damn if she wasn't going to get an earful. Death wouldn't save her.

I got out of the car carrying the wine. The bottle was a little lighter now, working well with the painkillers. The grass hadn't been cut since the last time I was here, and it pissed me off. This was the weekend and it looked shameful. I looked around for the groundkeeper. He might get an earful too. Lucky for him, the man was nowhere to be found.

When I sat, the bottle was half empty, or half full. Fuck the philosophy, it tasted good. I should have bought two. A long guzzling swig saw some of it escape down my chin. "Damn you Madeline. Look what you've done to us."

I wiped the dribble off my chin with the arm that held the wine. Sleeves were very absorbent. "I don't want to be you anymore. Shit, how many times had I wished for that? I thought your life was so damn good. Gotta tell ya girl, it sucks."

Another long guzzle of wine almost emptied the bottle and gave me a body numbing buzz. Maybe that was the pain pills. "I've tried to fix everything. Lawrence is such a shit. Why wouldn't you listen to me? Damn it, I tried to give you Johannes, but he wasn't good enough. Up yours, Maddy. You'd be damn lucky to have that man. He's one perfect man, a stallion. Now neither of us gets him."

The last of the bottle was poured down my throat, most of it swallowed without being tasted. "Instead you married the other end of the horse. Damn you Matts, you had a son. How could you leave him? He counts on me now. Me, the fucked-up sister. What were you thinking?"

I raised the bottle to my lips. It was still empty, so I drew my arm back and threw it. It shattered on her tombstone, the glass flying in all directions. A fragment of the thick bottom struck me across the bridge of my nose, splitting the skin open. The piece fell down my blouse. I reached up to feel the warmth pouring from the cut and I started to laugh. "Ya, I deserved that."

I untucked my shirt to let the large shard fall through. Then I pulled the grass back and while the blood dripped off the end of my nose, I scratched her name into the granite down by the ground. It took several minutes. When I was done, my shirt, hands and Madeline's tombstone were covered with blood. "Ha! Now that's what I'm talk'n 'bout."

The out-of-control laughter bellowed from me for a good five minutes. Tears flowed, and my mind was swimming when a hand landed on my shoulder. I looked back to see a cop, or whatever you called them in this country. I dropped the chunk of glass and put my hands in the air. "Got me. Don't shoot."

"Mademoiselle, vous vous sentez bien ?"

I fluttered my hand at him. "In English, man. Speak fuck'n English."

"Ma'am. Are you okay?"

I looked up at him. Blood peacefully streamed from the bridge of my nose and over a poorly hidden smirk. "No, but it's okay. I never was the normal one. That would have been my sister. She'd tell you if she was here." I barely got the words out before the final act of my melt down. "Wait, she is. She's right fucking here."

I don't doubt there was a part of the officer that regretted coming over. They honestly didn't get paid enough. He shuffled me to his car and drove me to the hospital. The man even stayed with me while I added to my stitch count. Once I'd been treated, he told me about the day he broke down.

"My son was three when he died."

Kevin Weisbeck

I immediately dropped my pity party and looked up to him. "I'm so sorry to hear that."

"It was two years ago, but it still feels like yesterday." He sighed and continued, "I saw that your sister hasn't been gone all that long. All I can say is that it takes time."

"I know. It's not fair."

"Tell me about it." He handed me a card. "I needed to go get help. I blamed my wife, my parents, myself. It was nobody's fault. I was just angry. These people helped me, and they can help you."

Unless they were lawyers, I doubted it. "Thanks, and I'm sorry about all this."

"Don't be. We all need to let it out eventually. How are you feeling?'

"I wanna barf, but I'd likely rip my stitches."

He laughed, and I followed suit. "Thanks for being there for me. And since you're still here, I gotta ask. Am I gonna get charged with anything?"

"No. I just wanted to give you that card and tell you that somewhere in that future of yours, everything will work out. It always does."

"You believe that?"

"I have to."

I reached up and touched the bandage. With the seven sutures to my nose, today's stitch-count was close to twenty. You'd think I was hemming a dress. Add the blackening eye and I looked like I was ready for trick-or-treating. For that reason, the nurse hadn't hesitated when I asked a favour of her. She wheeled me down to the ultrasound room. The story she gave her superiors was concerns for an internal bleeder. Turns out I was almost four months pregnant and Johannes's baby was a healthy one.

Back at the house, I had the bed to myself and no one to coax out of the tub. I slept more soundly than I had since the coma. The next day I went back to get my car and clean up the mess I'd made. I said my proper good-byes to my sister and put her rings back on my finger. Her identity couldn't be removed that easily.

Besides, Nicolas was my son and he deserved a mother. There was no looking back for Johannes. He had to do what was right for him and I respected that. My eyes glanced past Lawrence's office. There'd be no more rummaging through that room or my husband's suits for phone numbers in lipstick. The pictures I had were good enough.

The house received a quick appearance cleaning. I have no idea why I cared except out of habit, and because my son deserves a clean home. I finished up and took a second to walk around. The stairs, hallways and rooms that were so familiar to me now, had always been the dream of my sister, her warm fireplace on a cold day.

She could have it. It was time for me to make my move.

Chapter Forty-six

Outside in the driveway, the growl of gravel under the weight of Lawrence's sedan let me know they were home. My treasured solace was over. He walked through the door alone. I looked past him to the doorway and then outside. The car was empty. "Where's Nicolas?"

Lawrence dropped his bag at the door and slipped off his shoes. They landed where he'd kicked them off and I left the damn things there. He took a deep breath, filling his senses with the aroma of dinner. "Cooking a pot roast, are we?"

I stepped in front of him as he tried to make his way to the scotch bottle. "Where's my son?"

"It's good to see you too."

As he stepped around me, I could smell her. It filled my sinuses with fire. "You spent the weekend with Scarlett?"

Silence.

It was disbelief, despite my intent with Johannes. I followed behind him as he headed for the dining room. Scarlett wasn't the issue here. "Where is my son?"

"Relax, my son is still with my parents." He pulled out a cigar and bit the end off it. Then the man spat it on the floor, the very one I'd just cleaned. I didn't care. "We need to head over to my parents. They're expecting us in a half hour."

The fact that I'd prepared a dinner didn't bother me. The fact that this asshole couldn't even enjoy a weekend with his son didn't bother me. What pissed me off was Lawrence blackmailing me to get my son back. Nicolas could never follow in these arrogant bloodlines.

I'd have been smart to just grab my coat and go, but he was up to something. His mood was far too chipper. He was cocky and, pardon the pun, sex didn't do that for him. Money, however, was a different story.

"This weekend wasn't about teaching me a lesson or running off with her. What was it really about?"

He lit the cigar and took a drag, expelling the smoke in my direction. "I can't pull anything over on you, can I? You see, I had business to attend to."

"On the weekend? Who does business on the weekend?"

"The ones that want to win. If you wait until Monday, then all you are is an early bird. Sometimes the early bird doesn't find the worm because someone else beat him to it." He took in another drag and put a haze between us. "That someone works weekends."

Cryptic in his conceit, I had no idea what the hell he had done. "In English please."

The room got another infusion of wine-dipped smoke as he paced. "It means my latest investment is already paying off."

This was a good thing, wasn't it? His latest investment was that building. If it was good for him then it was good for Johannes. "How so?"

"Your husband's a genius. I simply bought a…" He stopped to correct himself. "Jon and I formed a separate Company that bought a building. My company owed a ton of money to that building owner and now it doesn't. I must thank Jon for that investment. And this weekend, I filed the papers for Chapter Seven Bankruptcy. They can't collect on their debts any more."

He watched my jaw drop. One of the tenants had been deep in arrears and that tenant was Lawrence. "Here's the best part. I'm thinking of putting in a bid for the bankrupt building with my company. I'm hoping to pick it up for a song. I'm sure I can breathe some life back into it. I mean the offices have been recently renovated. It's state of the art technology."

I couldn't believe it. What he was doing shouldn't be possible. To buy a company and kill it, just to get out of his debt responsibility. It was evil. "How could you have pulled this off without Johannes?"

"So now Jon is Johannes. Makes me wonder what you were up to while I was away." He took a seat at his spot at the head of the table. "I didn't need his signature. He's a minor partner. It's not like he had any say."

"I thought he signed up as a fifty-fifty partner."

"Fine print my dear, fine print. There was a clause. It was a twelve-hour window for either of us to buy an extra stake in the company. Any amount purchased would deem that person as having extra shares, control, and decision-making authority. It's all there in black and white."

"What's Johannes left with?"

"There's risk with any investment. You're never given a crystal ball. This one didn't go so well for him. He's likely lost everything and might have to draw from his personal account to cover legal fees."

"What?"

"Hey, I lost my part of the investment too, sort of." He laughed. "Ah, he's family. I'm sure I can cover his legal fees."

I wanted to kill him, maybe tonight in his sleep. The man lived for these moments, moments when his enemies realised their fate. I was the enemy. When did Johannes become an enemy? This was as bad as taking my son. "Lawrence, he's your brother. How could you?"

"My brother?" He stopped and let the words hang in the air. Then he crushed his cigar out on the table. "My brother? This guy comes into my life after having my real parents for all those years.

Then he tries to pawn his guilt off on me with a handful of cash? Is he serious? Shit, I'll take that cash and more. How much do you think I'm due for all those years in foster homes? He's getting off easy."

"I thought you were happy to have him in your life."

"Please. The man got my childhood."

"He didn't even know he had a brother. When he found out, he decided to do the right thing and share the inheritance with you. Even after he had realised you were rich, the man handed over half. And what do you do, you weasel both halves. What kind of monster are you?"

"Let me spell this out for you. I'm the monster putting a roof over your head while he tries to steal my wife."

"It's not like that. He's a friend."

"Look, I've earned my money and sometimes I am a monster. You used to appreciate that fact. If I didn't operate like that, you wouldn't have any of this."

I shook my head in disgust and started to walk away when he grabbed my arm. "Don't forget who you married. Now go get ready. My parents shouldn't have to wait."

I pulled away to a safe distance. Up until now his weekend had run like clockwork for him. This was textbook Lawrence and we had all learned our lessons. Now it was his turn to learn one. I wasn't Madeline. I was Rebecca and as hard as I'd tried, I couldn't play this game any longer. I'm sure my sister was up in heaven watching right now. She appreciated my efforts but understood my resolve. "I'm not going."

"My parents are expecting us, both of us. Now go get ready."

I stood there waiting for my courage to catch up. Could I do this? I needed my life back. Lawrence was too much for me. He was too much for anybody. The last few days had awoken parts of me that had died with the amnesia. Memories were back, and I couldn't ignore them. "Look, I'm not going Lawrence." My next words came out as a whisper. "I'm done with this."

I had expected a reaction, anger in the form of an ashtray, a chair, or a fist, flying in my direction. He remained calm, ignoring such blasphemy. "You're being foolish and you're going to make us late."

"This is all a lie. You have no idea what's going on, do you?" At this point I almost wanted his rage. I needed the reality. "Or, who I am?"

"You're my wife, Rebecca." The expression on his face didn't change. "Now go get your jacket."

Chapter Forty-seven

That comment swallowed me up in a wave of disbelief, but in hindsight, I should have seen it coming. Control was power and for Lawrence, life had been a game of chess. He played the game with me, Johannes, and I'm sure with his own parents. His job was to pay a finer attention to the details because it was in those details that he found weaknesses and opportunities. It was how he'd found my secret.

"Don't act so surprised, I'm no idiot. At first, I thought you were Madeline, but it didn't take long to figure out. You were too interested in Johannes, too wrapped up in Rebecca's life. Before the accident, you had always referred to him as Jon. Those were red flags. I started noticing the extra spices in the food. And you didn't dress the same. I mean you wore Madeline's clothes, but you wore them differently. You pushed up the sleeves and you didn't do the buttons all the way to the top on your blouses. The make-up was a little too colourful." He stole a quick glance at my chest. "And then there was the sex. I had to force you. Madeline never put up a fight. She always hoped it would bring us closer. She figured it might knock down the walls between us."

"How could it?"

"Exactly. She never understood. There weren't any stupid walls. This is just how I am. I never had it in me to be this loving husband everyone expects. I find emotions dangerous. They break people. It doesn't mean I don't have them. I just don't let them consume me. And for the record, Scarlett was more for you. When I realised who you were, I stopped wanting you, for Madeline."

"Wow." I pulled out one of the dining room chairs and sat. It felt good to have it out. "Well, now you know. I guess I should start packing."

He leaned against the table beside me and crossed his arms. "You're still leaving?"

I couldn't stop the blood from racing through my veins. It was surfacing a dangerous courage because I wasn't just leaving. "I want Nicolas."

"You know you're nothing more than an aunt, right? How do you expect to get my son?"

"I'm not leaving without him."

He grabbed me by the arm and pulled me off the chair. "You're not going anywhere, and neither is he. Now go get ready. We're going to be late." He let go and headed for the study.

But he knew I wasn't his wife. This should have been over. Thing was, Lawrence didn't play that way. He always had an angle. And as badly as I wanted to go, that wasn't a part of that plan. But I also had a plan, and that was not to spend another day in this lie.

I took a minute to collect my thoughts before chasing after him. He was sitting behind his desk. His eyes followed me into the room. They warned me, but I stood my ground. "You can't stop me from leaving, and you can't stop me from taking Nicolas. The world thinks I'm Madeline, Nicolas's mother."

"Look Madeline, I'm tired and we're running late. We can talk about this later."

"But I'm not Madeline, I'm Rebecca. Why doesn't this upset you?"

He sat back and studied me. There were so many similarities between my sister and me. "I just want to know one thing. If you weren't interested in being my wife, why would you want to stay with me? I mean, I'm your dead sister's husband. It sounds awfully weird that you'd want to be with me."

"It wasn't like that. At first, I thought I was Madeline. I had amnesia, I would have thought I was Mary Queen of Scots had you told me."

"Well your mother had no problem identifying you. She swore you were Madeline. I never knew your sister well enough to make the comparison. Why would your mother throw you into my life?"

"She was concerned for Nicolas. She never thought I'd get my memory back, so it wouldn't matter. Was it selfish on her part? Yes, and I still don't like the fact that she did it, but she thought she was doing the right thing."

"Think about what you're saying. You've lied to me for weeks and despite all the bullshit, you'd be a better parent for my son, your nephew?"

"I love him and can give him a better home."

"Give him a better home? You have nothing." Lawrence calmly pushed himself up from his chair. "Now Madeline, I understand you miss your sister, but stop being so foolish and grab your coat. We need to go."

"Don't call me that. I'm Rebecca."

He got up and walked over to a framed painting that sat on the wall behind the desk. It was one of my favourites. The morbid picture, crows flying to a dead tree, had a sky lit with all the hues of autumn. It was a Friedrich and for me it had two moods. There were days when the sky was a sunset and I knew that tomorrow would bring a new day. It was hopeful. Other days, the painting held a sunrise, extinguishing all hope from the start.

Lawrence hinged the painting forward, revealing a wall safe. That was a surprise. He dialled the tumbler right, left, and right again until it clicked. The door opened, and he returned to the desk. At that point I noticed the top drawer was partially open. He reached inside and pulled out a small tape recorder.

The tape was popped out of the machine. Then Lawrence walked it over to the safe, tossed it inside and slammed the door shut. "You are now Madeline from this day forward. You'll do well to play the part if you ever want to see Nicolas again. Now get your jacket and let's go."

"I'm leaving you. I don't need this, and I don't need you." I turned to leave, knowing that he might give chase. Physically he could beat me into tomorrow and I wouldn't stay. Tonight, with or without the black eyes, I'd be alone. "Good bye Lawrence."

"You don't need this, I agree. But I do. I need my wife, Rebecca. You're Madeline to everyone out there. You've got my family, my friends, and my co-workers all fooled. I mean don't be surprised, it doesn't take much. Now these people all see me as a successful man, with a successful life. My wife and child are a part of that and that's not going to change. Maybe in time we can work something out."

"I don't think so." I took a couple more steps.

"You should think twice. Leaving could be a little tricky. My poor Madeline, she's not coping with her sister's death or the accident. She is living with so much guilt. Johannes's arrival has triggered a sick need to be Rebecca. That way she doesn't have to deal with that guilt. She's telling me things like her mother is in on the conspiracy. I bet her father is too. I think it might be best if you take a little time to recover. I'm sure my doctors would like to observe you for a while. He could do that better from the comforts of a controlled environment."

"You want to have me committed? That'll never happen. My mother knows which daughter I am. They'd testify against you."

"And such bright testimony we'd hear. Hell, they almost missed their daughter's wedding. Can you imagine such a dysfunctional family? Did I mention, it's your mother's fault you're here?" He walked out of the study.

Again, I followed.

"Look, you gave that part of your life up. You had a chance to resurrect her and you didn't. Your parents buried Rebecca and they all threw dirt on her grave. The world says you're dead. You can't dredge her up now. I'd look like an idiot sleeping with my dead wife's sister. And then there's Nicolas. What would he think? You and I both know your parents can't help you. It's too late for that. At least I gave you a home." He opened the closet and grabbed my coat. "Now let's go."

I had an envelope of options. But like the courier that had delivered them, they had vanished. Entangled in my own web, I took my coat from him and slipped it on.

Chapter Forty-eight

The next morning, I awoke to the sound of the front door slamming while Nicolas climbed up on the cushion beside me. Dinner the night before had been sheer agony. Afterward, Lawrence had dropped us off and left to be with his whore.

I had fallen asleep on the couch while I waited for Lawrence to get home. We needed to talk. I couldn't let last night's argument end the way it did. Lawrence had played the game well and even trumped me with that damn tape. I hadn't seen any of it coming. One by one he had pulled my options from me.

"Mommy, sleepy." Nicolas touched the bandage. "Ouch."

"Hey Tiger, go grab me the book that Johannes gave you." I couldn't call him Uncle. The idea of him and Lawrence being brothers still put my stomach on the dance floor doing the jitterbug.

He didn't return with the book. After a few minutes I had to go check on him. I agonised my way up the stairs and peered into his room. Three trucks and a car were on the ruffles on the bed slowly trekking their way toward the headboard.

"Hey Tiger. Didn't you want a story?"

He looked back at me and ran for the door. "No."

The door slammed in my face and I found myself standing there as I fought off tears. How could I be upset? The kid wasn't even two. He had no way of knowing how rude that was. Earlier the front door had slammed when his father had left for work. That was also rude. This was how the boy would learn. I wanted to open the door and tell Nicolas he was acting poorly, but I didn't have the strength. Instead I turned and made my way back downstairs.

I sat in the chair by the phone and dialled Johannes. Love me or hate me, he needed to know what Lawrence had done. I was sure he'd know soon enough, but I'd rather he found out from me. The phone rang four times before I picked it up.

"Hello?"

"Hey Johannes, it's me. Can we talk?"

There was a devastating silence for several seconds and then a click. I listened as the dial tone hummed in my ear. He had just hung up on me. I knew he was upset, but this made everything a little more conclusive. Granted, kicking me out of his hotel room should have been final enough.

I set the phone down in its cradle. We had history and it wasn't always easy. I'd tried to hand him off to my sister. It took a while for him to get over that night, but he'd managed to see past it. Our love was strong, but this was different. This was betrayal. I'd slept with his brother while he mourned my death. Granted it was a little more complicated than that, but broken into its simplest form, it would be horrific.

I reached for the phone again and started to dial my mother's number. After six numbers I dropped the phone back down in its cradle. We were still too damaged. She was the reason I was in this mess and although her intentions were good, she had sacrificed me for her grandchild.

Because of that I could either live with Lawrence or get used to living in a sanatorium where the doctors would try to convince me I was Madeline. They'd use therapy, drugs, strobe lights and the odd jolt of electricity. Did they still do that?

I yelled up at Nicolas, "Hey Nicolas, wanna go visit Ingrid?"

He didn't come running so I had to think he was out of earshot. I dialled and got the machine. Should I hang up and dial again? Was she in the shower?

I left a message. "Hello Ingrid. I'm ready to talk. Call me when you get this."

I waited by the phone for a good hour before giving up.

Chapter Forty-nine

With no Johannes, Ingrid, or parents, I dragged Nicolas out to a matinee. He was anything but impressed until the cartoon started. The movie was something about a forest of wildlife trying to stop progress. It was a good distraction, for both of us. The popcorn and sodas were tasty, and I think I even nodded off for a couple minutes. When it was over I thought of staying for a second showing. Nicolas was restless. I knew I couldn't hide out forever.

We pulled into the driveway and sat there while I stared at the front door. Lawrence was already home. I prayed he was changing. Was he going out? This place wasn't *his* prison.

Nicolas unbuckled and climbed up on my lap for a hug. My little gaffer could tell I wasn't right and he finally decided to come around. I returned his hug with a big smoochy kiss. "I think a crimson butterfly just landed on your cheek."

"Butterfly?"

As we entered the house I heard Lawrence rustling papers in the sturdy.

"Go up stairs and put your jammies on, okay?"

"Where's butterfly?"

"It's still on your cheek. Get changed and check it out in the bathroom mirror."

Nicolas made his way up the stairs and I headed for the study. "Lawrence?"

He continued to shuffle papers into the safe. "What's with your friend coming to the house?"

"Johannes was here?"

"I'm not talking about him."

My next guess would have been Ricardo. Surely that stupid shit wouldn't come to the house with my husband home, would he? With the grace of a fox, I positioned myself closer to the doorway. "Who stopped by?"

"That Ingrid girl was asking for you. Hell, since when did I become your answering service?"

"She stopped by? Is she coming back?"

"I'm pretty sure that's a no." He pulled out a business card and handed it to me. "One more thing. I want you to see this man."

"What did you say to her?" I took the card and waited for a response. The card read Dr. P. Needham, Psychologist. The response never came so I dropped it. "What's this?"

"I need you to make an appointment with him. You can tell him how you're feeling. He's a friend of mine and it'll be confidential. It might help if you talk about things, like you know, being Rebecca. He's paid to be discreet and the sessions will help you accept your role."

"I thought you said we were keeping things under wraps? Who else have you told?"

"No one. Hell, I haven't even told my parents. There's no way I can. If this got out it would ruin me. Don't worry, this guy's okay."

"I don't think we should be sharing this." I had to believe it was a trap.

"You've got to get this straightened out. What do you think my investors would do if they found out I was screwing my dead wife's sister?"

"We're not screwing!"

"I know that, but we're husband and wife. Even if we're not, it's implied."

And what would his investors think? I think half of them would raise a glass. No, confessing this story to a doctor would surely get me committed.

He turned to the study. "Don't worry about supper. I'm heading out as soon as I get this done."

"Scarlett?"

"I know this isn't easy for you, so see that man. He can help you focus on your role as my wife. This doesn't have to be forever."

"No?"

"Couples get divorced. Some day that might happen to us. It's just that now is not the time."

"So, truce?" I asked.

"Whatever you want to call it." The darkness in his eyes stirred and I could tell he had an angle. There was always an angle. "Just make that appointment."

He was true to his word and left minutes later. I made my way to the kitchen and started dinner for my son. Nicolas had always loved grilled cheese sandwiches made the Canadian way, fried in a pan with ketchup for dipping.

As I got Nicolas set up at the table with his sandwich, there was a light rapping on the door. When I opened the door, a cheery-eyed blonde let herself in.

"I thought your man would never leave." Ingrid walked straight over and gave me a bone-crushing hug. Then she put a hand on my face and stared. "*Mademoiselle,* you look like hell. I can't believe you fooled me."

"Fooled you?"

"Yes, Rebecca." She pulled me in for a second hug. "God I've missed you."

Chapter Fifty

ngrid held me in her arms for what seemed like five minutes. When she let me go, her mascara was as messed up as mine. "Can't I come in?"

"I think you already are." I looked out into the driveway and closed the door. "Where's your car?"

"I'm parked around the corner."

"You got my message?" I handed her a tissue.

"What message? I just came from seeing Johannes."

"Word gets around quick. I'm pretty dead to most people."

"Like I'm most people." She laughed as she shook her head. "So, I drop by to check in on Johannes. He's looking over these investment papers, like he has a clue what any of it means. Much to my surprise, the man's a wreck. Said he's in love with Rebecca. I go Rebecca who, the only Rebecca I know is, well, dead. He says no, she's alive and she's living as her sister."

"I can explain."

She put her hand up. "Friends don't explain."

"You need to know, I never meant to leave you guys."

"I know this little guy had a lot to do with this." She ran her fingertips through Nicolas's hair. "Is that a good sandwich, my little man?"

I tried to continue. "It's just that my sister…."

"Don't. Unlike Johannes, I see why you're finding it hard to leave." She took one of Nicolas's toasted triangles. "This is a way of eating cheese I've never seen before. Being French, I'd like to try it. May I?"

Nicolas nodded. "Ketchup!"

"Ketchup? Are you sure? We don't do ketchup in France all that often. I think you Canadian transplants are a bad influence on us." She dipped it and took a bite. "Mmm, I may have to take that back."

I placed my hand on her shoulder. "Do you want one?"

"No time. Now that I'm past the sentry, we need to talk." She took my hand and pulled me to the couch. While I graciously sat like a lady, she flopped on one folded leg. I used to flop until I learned it wasn't proper. "Okay, you need to tell me everything, and don't hold back."

I held nothing back as I talked, as I got Nicolas in the tub, and as I shuffled him off to bed. The hours rolled by and before long it was nine. We cried, we laughed, and she talked me into letting my hair down. What was he going to do? He needed a wife. We enjoyed a glass of wine, but this couldn't last. Lawrence would be home soon. If he saw her here he'd freak.

"This has been fun Ingrid, but…"

"Oh, the dreaded 'but'. Do I smell fear?"

"No."

"Come on. He's slathered it all over you like duck fat. What are you afraid of, and how badly do you want to fix it?"

Fix it, was that even possible? Johannes's return couldn't fix it. Lawrence had worked his world into my life like tattoo ink into skin. I couldn't imagine how. Other than killing the man and dumping his body in the Seine, I'd never find freedom. "Okay, I'm listening."

"*Ma chére*, he's obviously got lots on you. He's holding the cards. You need to take them back. As angry as you've been with him, I doubt he'd be expecting an offensive." She thought for a second, her fingers gently tapping at her pursed lips. "So, what are his secrets?"

"Other than a lover, which is an acceptable provision in France, he has none."

"*Quelle crock!* Everyone with money has secrets." Ingrid got up and walked around the house, devising a plan. I waited in the living room, nervously keeping an eye on the front door. My fear began at a slower pace, but gathered momentum as she entered Lawrence's study.

"Rebecca…" She called me as if singing, "I think I found something."

I entered the room to a mess that sprawled from the bookcase to the desktop. Was she trying to get us killed?

She looked up from behind Lawrence's desk. "What?"

Chapter Fifty-one

Sitting in Lawrence's chair, feet up on his desk, Ingrid perused a hand full of documents. Books were stacked on the floor like Nicolas's wooden blocks, emptied drawers hung open, and she had moved the desk.

She looked up and smiled. "What are you doing tomorrow night?"

"Attending a funeral...mine." I looked over to see she'd opened the safe. "Shit! What have you done? Help me clean this up."

"In a minute. You said there was a bankruptcy?"

"Yes, and he plans on buying the company back, without Johannes. You see he bought the building with a company that he created with Johannes. He'll buy it back with his own."

"He can't, not if he was one of the owners who filed bankruptcy."

"I'm sure he has a plan." I started slipping the books back into place. "God, I can't believe you did this."

She ignored me. "Hey, what do you know about Foster's Holding's?"

"Who?"

"It's a company that Lawrence has odd ties to. Does he owe them a favour?"

"I've never heard of them, but anything's possible." I looked back at the door as I continued to gather books.

Ingrid kept her carefree demeanour as she continued to read. I'd always found it refreshing. Tonight, it would get us killed. "This man's got shit tucked away everywhere. Look at this." She held a birth certificate up to her nose before handing it to me.

I saw the name, Georg Faulkman. "Look. I get that you want to help, but we need to clean this up before Lawrence gets back. Where'd you get this?"

"The safe. Secrets never live on desktops, Rebecca."

"I know. I'm just…"

"Scared? I can tell." She grabbed a folder and handed it to me. "Okay, put this one in the bottom of the safe, birth certificate on top, near the front. I'll get these folders back in the desk."

"I don't mean to be all nervous, but I've never gone this deep into his life."

"You should. As a wife, it's your right."

"I've been warned many times to vacuum, dust and that's it. Hey, wasn't the desk drawer locked?"

"Please." She showed me the key she'd found. That was why she' had moved the desk. One of the legs had left an imprint in the carpet and that imprint had held a key. "There's no such thing as locked."

Papers carefully made their way back into desk drawers. Ingrid used a note pad to jot down tidbits she wanted to research later. "That box goes on top, to the left of the cash. I think someone's getting earrings. What did he do?"

"Huh?"

"Look in the box. When men like Lawrence screw up, they usually buy their wives something. The nicer the something, the bigger the screw up. This one had to be huge."

I flipped the box open for a quick peek. Each earring consisted of three strands of small rubies dangling from a larger single carat ruby. It dazzled, set in eighteen-carat gold. "I think this is what a snow globe to the side of the face gets me."

"Ouch. You never answered my question. What are you doing tomorrow night?"

"I don't know? What am I doing tomorrow night?" I was hoping the answer was something simple, like a flight to Offenburg for a concert. We'd done that the first night I moved to Germany. Ingrid, Marcus and Johannes had taken me to see the band Meatloaf. Those were good times.

"I've found a few things that sparked my interest, so I have homework. I think there's some good ammunition here, but it won't be easy on such short notice. My father should be able to help. Especially with this." She held up a key.

"What's that for?"

She held it closer, so I could see the engraving and a number stamped in it. "This is the symbol of the bank that my father manages, and this number, it's for the safety deposit box." Then she slipped it into her pocket.

"What are you doing? Put it back, Ingrid."

"If I do that, then how will we ever open the box?"

"Your Dad will help us?"

"Hell no, but I have my ways."

"But…"

Outside, a noise caught my ear. Someone had just pulled up. "Shit. That's Lawrence." I closed the safe and swung the picture back into place. "Get the rest of this cleaned up and hide. I'll stall him."

I left the office as Lawrence walked through the front door. I thought of the earrings. I should get the Hope Diamond for the beating I was about to receive. "What'd you forget?"

"I have to get a couple things from the safe."

I thought of Ingrid. I didn't hear papers shuffling. That was good. Had she found a good hiding place? "Why are you always in a hurry? Why don't you sit and relax? Can I get you a drink?"

"I'm in a hurry, because I'm in a damn hurry." I reached for his arm and he pushed me aside. "Let go!"

He made his way into the study. I quietly followed two steps behind and stopped in the doorway. As he entered, I waited for her scream. Lawrence's booming voice would drown it out as he lost it on her. Then I imagined the fight we'd have when she left. Would I get stitches this time, or would it be worse?

There was no woman's scream. Nor was Lawrence's shouting.

I was happy to see no toes poking out from underneath the drapes. Lawrence headed straight for the desk. The chair was out a bit and he shoved it back in. The first attempt didn't allow it, the second did.

He looked back at me. "Do you mind?"

"Pardon?"

"This is my office, Rebecca. Get out!"

"Right." I gave the room one last scan before heading into the living room.

Two minutes later, a passing breeze of old spice let me know he was gone. He didn't give a good-bye, have a nice evening, or a backhand. I shouldn't complain.

I ran back to the study. "Ingrid?"

She pulled herself out from under the desk. She looked like she'd just climbed out of a rabbit hole. "That was close."

I had to agree. "You scared the crap out of me."

"Are you're saying you've had enough excitement for one night?"

"More than enough."

"Okay. Meet me in front of this bank tomorrow morning. Make it nine-thirty." She handed me a business card as she made her way to the door. "Did I hear him call you Rebecca?"

"Yes, he knows."

"He's a twisted little man, isn't he?"

"I don't think he knew in the beginning."

"Doesn't matter. You're going to put on a dinner tomorrow night." Her smile grew as the gears meshed in her head. "Not to worry, I'll take care of the guest list and the details. You take care of the cooking. Make it for about twelve people, and don't tell Lawrence. I think we should make this a surprise party."

"Your master plan is a dinner party?" I didn't see it working unless Lawrence choked on a chicken bone, and I wasn't that lucky.

Chapter Fifty-two

All through the night and into the morning I wondered how throwing a party could bring me my freedom, but Ingrid was convinced and said she'd handle the details. She would tell the guests that it was a surprise, and that the guest of honour would be angry if he found out. Anyone who knew him would want to avoid that.

I got out of the car and took my place beside Ingrid. We were across the street from a large granite building, complete with pillars and plenty of steps. "What do you think we'll find at your father's bank?"

"Manages, *Mademoiselle* Trembley." Ingrid stepped off the curb and started for the front door at a hurried pace. Her stilettos played an authoritative tune against the aged sidewalk. I chased after her. "He *manages* the bank."

"Same, same." I was almost running. The tune from my heels on the cobblestones sounded more like Jenga tower collapsing. "What's the rush?"

"It's my father." She fluttered her hand at the thought as if she could erase it. "I mean it's me. He's such a professional, likely the only man on the planet who makes me…"

"Nervous?" Now this was a surprising turn of events. "You?"

"More like crazy. Now keep up and don't say a word." She held the door for me. "By the way, where's Nicolas?"

"Gramma and Grampa's house." The quiet thing lasted less than four seconds. She should have known better. "Which one is your father?"

"*Monsieur* Beauchamp is the one sitting at the desk over there." She discreetly pointed before shuffling me in the other direction.

"What the… Where are we going?"

She pushed me behind a counter and played the role of two customers filling out a deposit slip. On occasion she looked up at her father to see what he was doing. I'd also look up. He was sitting at a desk doing paper work.

"Why don't we just go see him?"

"I expected my father to be busy. He's always busy."

"Well he's not, so let's go say hi."

"That's not the plan."

I looked up again to see his secretary escort a young businessman to his desk. The man sat with hope and fear. "Great, now he's busy."

"Perfect." Ingrid stepped away from the counter and headed straight for the man. I obediently followed. "Remember, no talking."

"Gotcha." I'd do my best.

Her strut, like that of royalty, had been perfected on the runway. It was a nervous tick brought out by the only man she'd never measured up to. Looking past his client, he saw her and waved her on. He didn't have time for her now. She headed for a drawer behind the counter and grabbed a pair of keys out of it. Turning back to him she showed only one and smiled. He smiled, pointed to the ledger, and refocused his attention back to the man in front of him.

She nodded, signed the book, and started toward the back. "Come on. We've got a secret to find."

Her father looked beyond the client, this time at me, giving me a curious head nod. I smiled and nodded back before following Ingrid through the maze of corridors to the vault. Inside the vault, one of the keys quickly slipped into box fifty-seven. She grabbed the second key from her purse and with two twists the drawer slid out.

My eyes widened as I inched closer. "Do you know what we're looking for?"

"Anything unexplained like little black books full of names, notes on shady dealings, or with any luck, Cliff Notes to the man's insanity."

We lifted the cover, eager to see inside. We had expected documents, cash, and dirty little secrets. All we found was a single passport. It was an American one, never stamped. The picture was a man that looked a lot like Lawrence. He was thinner, his shaggy locks void of any distinguished grey, and he had a bad scar on his cheek.

"Does Lawrence have another brother?"

"Other than Johannes? Not that I know of."

"Then who is this Cam Bolen?" Ingrid quickly thumbed through it, before putting it back. "Well, Mr. Bolen, look's like we need to find your secret."

With the box closed, she slid it back into place and used the other set of keys to access hers. Inside that one she grabbed an emerald pendant. We made our way back through the maze and after putting the keys back in the drawer, she inched cautiously into his office. When he noticed her, he waved her in.

She delicately dropped a note on his desk, as if a secretary apologising for having to leave a message. He nodded again and continued discussing the securities of the bank. They were the safest anywhere, unless you had a daughter.

Outside the bank, she made her way over to a sitting area at the base of one of the pillars and we sat.

"I'll take it from here, Rebecca."

"How can I help?"

"The kind of people I need to see, are not the kind of people you want to know. Don't get me wrong, they're not dangerous felons, but they know everything about money, greed, and secrets."

"And they might know this guy?"

"Him, Georg or Lawrence, I'm not sure. I just don't want these people putting your face to any of these names. They may know Lawrence and word would travel fast."

"No, I get it." I winced as my stomach acted up.

It caused an awkward silence.

Ingrid noticed. Her eyes began pressing me like a mother's. "What are you not telling me?"

"What? Nothing."

"Come on Rebecca, the way you walk, your emotional mood swings, the belly bump."

I reached down, placing my hands on my stomach as if holding a basketball. It was starting. My eyes welled. Damn, I hated these emotions. "I have a belly bump?"

My comment was all the confirmation she needed. "I doubt anybody has noticed, but we were models. Belly bumps, be it from binge eating or a baby, don't exist. Tell me it's not Lawrence's."

"No."

"Oh my God." Her eyes lit up as the smile grew. "It's Johannes's?" Her excitement bubbled. She wanted to scream, throw a party, and buy a six-foot giraffe.

"Whoa. Nobody knows except for this homeless guy. It's for the best."

"Bullshit, Rebecca," she snapped. "I mean, I know this is hard, but you have to tell Johannes. The guy is mad about you, and he's the father. He has a right to know."

"He's also Lawrence's brother. I'm Lawrence's wife. Besides, I'm cursed, and he doesn't want to talk to me."

"Give him a chance. He's had a lot to absorb with you, his parents and Lawrence. And how are you cursed?"

"Don't you remember Billy?"

"What?"

"Billy."

"You mean that boy from Chilliwack?"

"He was my first kiss. I was nine and that boy swept me off my feet big time. I never saw it coming, I doubt he did either. He was all bullfrogs, snakes, and skateboarding. We wasted hours reading comic books in his fort. Billy loved Captain America and I liked the Hulk."

"What does this have to do with seeing Johannes?"

"When my sister and I left Chilliwack, we both wrote him. Madeline only wrote a couple of letters before giving up on him. Her crush wasn't that strong. I continued to send off letters, one a week for over a year. He never answered any of them."

"*Pourquoi?*"

"I'd broken his heart."

"He never wrote one letter?"

"It was no accident he didn't write. I later found out that instead of writing me, he took up smoking."

"But he was just a kid."

"Love does the strangest things to a person. We had tried smoking once. I told him it made him look cool. He must have remembered me saying that. I especially liked how he could French inhale, you know, up the nose.

I couldn't get the boy out of my head, so when I was twenty I tried writing him again. This time I got a letter back, but it wasn't from him. It was from his mother. Billy had died of Cancer at the age of nineteen. It was in his lungs, pretty rare stuff for someone so young."

"And you blamed yourself."

"That was why I had those Friday smokes and why there was a coffee can up on the rooftop."

"You were punishing yourself. What did you expect to achieve? You get cancer and join him?"

I shrugged. "A while back you said Rebecca was broken, and at the time, I was. I'm not broken anymore and I know that, but as far as Johannes goes, I still think he's better off without me."

"You need to let him make that call, Rebecca. He told me he was going back to Germany."

"Love's a lot of work and I don't have it in me right now. Sorry, Ingrid."

"No. Sorry is what you'll be if you never tell him."

I started the Mercedes and took off in the direction of my parents, but within minutes the car made an abrupt left.

It was in the direction of the hotel.

* * * * *

The walk from the parking lot to his room seemed longer than I remembered. It didn't help that I was walking like an inmate on death row. Scenario after scenario tortured me, dizzying my steps, and halting me on more than one occasion. We had shared a passionate kiss and I'd suffered the heartbreak of his rejection. It was unbearable, yet here I was.

What if he slammed the door in my face, again? Did I honestly need to go through that a second time? That being said, what if he invites me in? Could he forgive me? It wouldn't change the fact that I was married, or that I wasn't about to leave Nicolas behind. At least he'd know I loved him. He'd also know that he was going to be a father.

What if he understands and still wants nothing further to do with me? He had a plan to go back to Germany and forget about greedy brothers and estranged girlfriends. It was a plan I couldn't hold against him.

I stopped in front of the door and stared at it for a couple minutes. I was about to knock when a hotel cleaner stopped me. "*Un moment. Et je vais avoir votre chambre…* "

"No. This isn't my room. I want to talk to the man staying here."

She tapped on the door with her finger. "Room vacant. Man gone."

"Left, as in checked out?"

She returned a puzzled stare as she struggled for the right English. "I think left, as in airplane."

Chapter Fifty-three

My father always said that if you wanted something badly enough, you'd always find a way. During that talk, Madeline must have been listening while I stared off at a spider on the ceiling. She wanted a husband and she landed one. There was a need for a child, so she had Nicolas. And when she wanted passion, there was Ricardo.

All I ever wanted was to not slip through the cracks. I wanted a mother that didn't look at me with disappointment, a boyfriend that I could have shared comics with. These were simple dreams. Instead I ended up with hurt, guilt, and a passion for self-destruction. Damn that distracting little bug.

As for Ingrid, her father had been hard on her and this drove her tenacity. I'd hate to get on her bad side. Even before the first guest arrived she had me believing that this night would be my liberation. I was told to enjoy whatever my fate held, to embrace it because my only other option was a lifetime of fear and bruises.

We served drinks, and I set the table. Ingrid kept me in the dark for my own good. On the itinerary was a dinner that would pay homage to a man who had spent a lifetime building his empire.

The man was due a night like tonight for all that he had done over the years. My only role was to prepare the meal and act the part of a dutiful wife. It was a role I'd learned well.

I nervously twirled my hair with my finger as I looked around at the room full of strangers. They seemed an odd bunch. I leaned closer to Ingrid. "Are you sure you don't want to fill me in on something, anything?"

She put her arm around me and gave me an assuring hug. "Trust me, the less you know the better. You really have to look as surprised as your husband."

We all heard the car pull into the driveway.

"That should be your husband, *Madame* Trembley." Ingrid handed me a glass of wine. "Just sip it and remember, no matter what happens, you are Lawrence's wife."

"Okay." I took a mouthful and handed it back to her. "Lawrence's wife would never drink with house guests."

We shared a smile that lasted until the door opened.

"Hi Honey, I'm home." Some of the cars parked along the street would be familiar to him. That meant something was brewing so he'd be playing nice. Ignoring me, he scanned the people in his living room. These were mostly people he knew.

The dining room table had been set for twelve. Lawrence did a quick head count, as had I. We were two people short. It was a safe assumption that one may have been Nicolas. That would be wrong.

"Talk to me, Sweetheart. What's this all about?" Lawrence asked, "Did I miss a birthday or an anniversary?"

"Hi Darling, just a dinner party. You know your business partner *Monsieur* Debois."

Daniel Debois had been Lawrence's partner for just over ten years. Although he despised Lawrence, he never minded the money he'd earned from Lawrence's insights. I had only met this man a handful of times. He was often drunk, no doubt wishing to be anywhere but in this house. The man was always kind to Nicolas and me.

"You've also met Police Captain, Frank Delacroix."

Frank had also been by the house on a couple of occasions that I had seen. The man didn't drink, so his visits were often brief and confined to the study. Although he laughed at all of Lawrence's sarcastic comments, I never saw the man in a good mood. The closest he ever came was the brief smile he had when he left. There was always an envelope in his hand, thick with cash.

"Captain Delacroix had brought a friend, *Monsieur* David Latteur."

Passing by Daniel and Frank, Lawrence shook *Monsieur* Latteur's hand. "Any friend of Frank's is a friend of mine."

"I'm actually a co-worker," he admitted.

I introduced the man standing on his own. "And you know Dr. Pierre Needham. I met with him briefly today and asked him to join us. He seems nice, so I hope that's okay. You said he was a friend."

"Not a problem. I am glad to have you all here." He didn't have the option of saying no. He eyed Ingrid with a long nasty stare. She was the one behind all this. He walked up to her. "You seem a little out of place."

"Not at all." She turned to introduce her parents. "I would like you to meet my parents, *Madame* Marie, and *Monsieur* Alain Beauchamp. They live here in Paris. It was nice of you both to have us."

Lawrence shook their hands but purposely held Ingrid's an uncomfortable length of time. "You and Madeline are becoming quite the friends."

Ingrid replied. "We always have so much to talk about."

"Interesting. You'll have to share your stories some day."

"I'm sure we will."

Lawrence turned to the man on his left. The last time they had met was over the sale of his building. There had been, and still were, hard feelings, but they both understood that business was anything but personal. Michael Antoine had been freed of a dying endeavour, albeit dying only because of Lawrence. The payment was more than he'd expected, yet far less than it was worth. "Michael."

Michael kept the niceties to a minimum. "Lawrence."

The mood in the room thickened as Lawrence strolled past me toward his spot at the head of the table. I obviously didn't warrant a handshake, a hug, or any form of acknowledgement, so on that note I gestured to the table. "I think we can start dinner, so if we want to make our way to our seats."

Ingrid quickly ushered everyone to his or her assigned spot. Lawrence took his usual spot at the far end of the table, I at the other. To Lawrence's immediate right there was an empty setting, followed by Dr. Needham, Ingrid, and her parents. On Lawrence's left side we started with another empty setting, his partner Daniel, the Police Captain Frank Delacroix, his friend David, and then Michael.

The two empty plates segregated Lawrence, much like an imaginary wall. Wanting to know who the wildcards were, he questioned me. "So, neither of these plates are for Nicolas? Are these two on their way?"

I opened my mouth, but Ingrid answered before I could say anything. Only she knew, which was for the better. "Yes, on their way and running fashionably late, I'm sure."

From her smile I could tell that the evening was rolling out exactly as planned. She told me earlier that she'd expect Lawrence to be cordial, simply because he'd have a significant mix of people in front of him. She also told me that the cordial wouldn't last long after he started to figure everybody out. Ingrid and her parents would soon be deemed as insignificant. I'm sure I'd be grouped into that mix. The rest of our guests were friends and associates, and under his control. That would relax him.

Lawrence's favourite dish was duck and although I couldn't stand the greasy fowl, I felt obligated to give him a gourmet meal. It could be his last. When I brought it out, he not only smelled the savoury aroma, but trouble. He eased his demeanor to the defensive. I had to admit that I enjoyed watching his mind scramble to find the angle. In his world there were always angles. Ingrid brought out the mashed potatoes and the Brussels-sprouts. I quickly grabbed the rest of the food and joined them. I didn't want to miss a thing.

Raising a glass of water, I read a speech that Ingrid had handed to me earlier.

"I've brought you here tonight to celebrate what I call new chapters. If I've learned anything, it's that life is unpredictable. We have all had changes in our past and have further changes on the horizon. They say that to embrace change, you should focus all your energy to the future, never looking back. Change is as inevitable as our next breath. It's how we survive. So, to changes."

Everyone touched glasses and the dinner began. We were still two guests short. Lawrence's eyes swept across the table to find mine. Dark and sinister, he knew I was up to something and he openly welcomed me into his world.

Chapter Fifty-four

Ingrid looked over and her wink was sinister. Born near the end of September, she was a Libra. People born under the sign of Libra stood for justice, but they were also about compassion. She must have had a touch of Virgo in her.

I brought my hand up to my face and let my fingertips find the new seam on my cheek. It reminded me of lying on the floor, watching the snowflakes float amongst the sea of red. Three hours ago, I had pulled seventeen stitches out of my not-yet-healed flesh, stitches that should have been left in a lot longer. They had to come out so that the makeup could soften the disfigured ridges. War paint could only do so much. Thankfully, Lawrence's friends knew better than to ask questions.

The knocker tapped against the front door and Ingrid gave me a subtle head nod. It was okay to get up and greet our latest guest. I opened the door to see an adorable young woman with long wavy *scarlet* hair. I showed her to the chair at Lawrence's right. She was much prettier than her pictures. Her skin was unblemished except for a few freckles.

Unsure of this strategy, I looked over to Ingrid to see her twirling one of her earrings. The frown in her eyes motioned me to look back at our newest guest. I didn't see it at first, and then I couldn't miss them. She was wearing the ruby earrings, the earrings that I thought were meant for me. What did I get for losing my child, healing this face of Frankenstein, or being dumped by the one I truly loved? Perhaps, all I got was the revenge. Thinking of the hurt that I'd put Johannes through, maybe it was all I deserved.

Scarlett turned to Lawrence and gave him a nervous, but energetic smile. I'm sure she was hoping he'd hold her chair or welcome her with a hug. He didn't.

"*Bonjour.*"

Lawrence remained silent as he studied her. The game had changed. Scarlett turned a distressed look to Ingrid because she was the woman who had said that she'd be welcome. Ingrid, now enthralled in Lawrence's anxiety, politely kept her eyes to herself.

I doubt there had been any intent to get his girl harmed. She was here to unsettle Lawrence and learn a few values. Men like this weren't worth it. They only brought heartache and trouble.

Ingrid turned to Michael, remembering that her party had a purpose. It was time to get started. "Hey Michael, I heard you just sold your—"

Another knock on the door hushed the room. Ingrid looked over to me, puzzled. My eyes darted to the empty plate and back to her. She shook her head. That guest wasn't expected yet. As I got up, I looked to Lawrence. Our confusion had placed a smile on his face.

I swung the door open to see Johannes. He gave me a hurt glance before walking past me. My eyes shifted over to Ingrid. There was terror in hers. Johannes hadn't been invited.

"Lawrence, what the hell did you do to our company?"

"Yes," Lawrence replied. "By all means, come in. We were only sitting down to have a meal."

Ingrid got up from her chair. "Johannes, *sie müssen wirklich verlassen.*"

"No. I'm not leaving until I get answers. My apologies to everyone else, but this is important." He looked back at me, as if I'd been in on the betrayal.

I grabbed his arm and pulled him toward the front door. "We need to talk, come."

"Not now." He noticed the new ridge on my nose and paused briefly before pulling his arm free. "I just heard rumours that you filed bankruptcy on our company today, that this great deal of yours has gone bad."

Ingrid got up. "Trust me, Johannes, this is not the time."

Lawrence made a mental note. "Look, I'll also lose money, so let's get back to the subject at hand. Were you invited tonight?"

He looked around. "No."

"Then maybe we should talk tomorrow. Come by my office, say around nine."

"Why would you do this? We were partners." He stepped away from me and past Ingrid. Was he daring Lawrence to stand up and fight? "We're brothers."

Lawrence cleared his throat. "It's business."

"What happened to our Company? I thought you said we got a good deal on it."

Ingrid interceded, "Can we talk, tomorrow?"

Shaking his head in disgust, Lawrence looked over to his friend, Captain Frank Delacrois. The look was meant to get him off his paid ass and do something. Frank remained seated.

He turned back to Ingrid. "And what business is it of yours? If you like, you can join us tomorrow at nine. I'll give you both a rundown on the particulars."

"You know what? This works too." Ingrid dropped her hands to her lap. "I did a little digging for my friend, Johannes. Seems it was never a good deal. There were tenants holding back rent. Michael tried to get the money through litigation, but these tenants had connections. This caused quite a few cash flow problems. Any idea who these tenants were?"

"This conversation is over." Lawrence tried to manage his anger as he spoke, "It's the middle of dinner and I don't think this is appropriate table talk."

"I don't care." Johannes took another step forward. "I'd like to know."

"Get out of my house," Lawrence demanded.

Ingrid continued, "It was the offices of Daniel Debois and Lawrence Trembley. Their firm owed close to two year's rent on eighteen offices. It's one hell of a cash flow dam and Michael couldn't evict them due to a loophole."

"I think you should leave with him." Lawrence chuffed.

"You did this, Lawrence?" The colour drained from Johannes's face. "You had this planned from the start, didn't you?"

Lawrence said nothing.

I was truly dumfounded and looked the part. No wonder Ingrid had held back. "What did you do, Lawrence?"

"I simply unloaded some debt."

"Let me see if I got this right." Johannes's anger was bringing the blood back to his face. "You crippled our building by forgiving the debt that you owed, and then you declared bankruptcy? How could you?"

"That can't happen with a bankruptcy," Ingrid's father piped up. "Moves like that would be illegal without your consent. Shareholders, even the ones that aren't fifty-fifty partners need to be informed in writing before transactions like these can take place. You knew that, didn't you Mr. Trembley?"

"Of course. I know how a bankruptcy works." Lawrence sharpened his glare. "There's no proof that I didn't tell him. He likely lost the note. And I think you should mind your own damn business."

Johannes started for Lawrence and Ingrid's father stopped him. Chairs slid on the hardwood as everyone but Lawrence got to their feet.

"Lawrence, was this a bankruptcy?" I had to ask. As a wife I'd be implicated. He'd also mentioned something about putting in a bid. "Or is the building for sale?"

"Not any more."

"That's right. Someone's already bought it," Ingrid offered. She looked around and shrugged. "What? I do my homework."

I looked to her." What are you saying?"

"Cam Bolen bought it." She made deliberate eye contact with me. "I found out yesterday, Madeline."

"There we have it. It wasn't a bankruptcy. I bought it, I sold it." Lawrence leaned back in his chair, giving her a chance to concede. "I've done nothing wrong. Cam Bolen bought my building. He got one hell of a good deal too. So when did losing my shirt become a crime."

"Cam Bolen?" Had I heard that right?

Chapter Fifty-five

It was no surprise that he had lied to me. I was merely a wife and honestly, I wasn't even that. "Why did you tell me it was a bankruptcy?"

Lawrence lit a cigar and the glow matched the fire in his eyes. "Because as always, you weren't listening. I found a last-minute investor, nothing illegal, nothing shady. My brother and I made an investment that went south quick. It even surprised me to find a buyer so quickly, but I've never been one to look a gift horse in the mouth. We didn't get much, but at least we have something. We'll settle tomorrow Jon. I'll write you a cheque."

Johannes was morbidly intrigued. "What kind of cheque are we talking?"

"I'd rather talk about it tomorrow."

"And I'd rather know today."

"Okay. After legal fees and my commission, it'll be a little over eighteen thousand Francs."

Johannes slumped. "That's not even a fraction of what I gave you. My parents worked hard for that money. But this isn't even about the money. We were sharing our parent's legacy. How could you do this?"

"He can't." Ingrid answered.

"You're still here?" Lawrence took another puff. "It was my company. I think I can."

"Oh, you can sell it. It's Cam Bolen. He can't buy it."

Her father was the first to raise an eyebrow. "Do you know Mr. Bolen."

"That would be difficult. *Monsieur* Bolen does not exist." Then she added, "He was our final guest."

Now I was confused. We saw the passport, saw the picture on that passport. "If he doesn't exist, then how can he be here?"

"I spent the day calling in quite a few favours," Ingrid answered. "They were all leading nowhere. The man was a phantom. He didn't exist. I mean he did, but nobody knew him. I was taking a break, a glass of wine on a patio, when it hit me. You see I used to do anagrams when I was a kid. Dad got me started on them to bolster my I.Q. I'm not sure if it worked, but it sure helped me find this Cam fellow."

Again, the explanation lost me. "Anagrams?"

"Yes, Madeline. You take a word like 'tar' and turn it into 'art' or 'rat'—the same letters, different words. I was looking at Cam Bolen and playing around with the letters. Then I remembered Johannes telling me about his long-lost brother. This Mac Noble Agency fostered him. Imagine my surprise when I scrambled the letters of Cam Bolen into Mac Noble. It tossed a few red flags in the air. Then I found out that this agency also helped kids find jobs."

Johannes turned to Lawrence. "Weren't you one of those kids?"

"He was." Ingrid announced. "And when he left the agency, he got a most fortunate job at the Department of —."

Lawrence cut her off as he got to his feet. His chair teetered on its back legs as it slid back. "You little bitch, who do you think you are? You enter my house, eat my food, and run your damn mouth on things you know nothing about. You need to leave, now!"

"But..." She looked over to me. "I was invited."

"Where was this job?" Johannes asked.

"The Department of Records," Ingrid answered.

"Who the fuck are you, anyway?" Lawrence demanded.

I watched in amazement as the vein in his temple started to beat harder. Was she going to kill him? Was that her plan all along, to anger him until a massive heart attack dropped him?

Lawrence put his hands up. "You know what, it doesn't matter. Dinner's ruined. Get the hell out of here." He turned to Captain Frank Delacroix. The man remained seated. "All of you, get out!"

Monsieur Latteur positioned himself between Ingrid and Lawrence.

Ingrid's father also moved closer to her. "I think we need to settle down."

Lawrence turned to me because I had started all this. "What do you think you're pulling, inviting these people into our house? You have three seconds to get them out of here."

I stood there, mouth open. I still had no idea what they were talking about. What I did know was that Ingrid had forced my hand. There'd be no staying here after tonight. "I, uh..."

Ingrid's father stepped forward. "Don't blame her. I know you don't deal directly with me, but your firm deals with my bank." He pulled his wallet out and placed a business card on the table. "We've already started a full investigation on this venture." He slid the card toward Lawrence. "I'll be expecting your full co-operation."

Lawrence picked it up and started to read. As he did, his face paled. He looked up at them and opened his mouth to say something. Nothing came out. The shocked look caused his partner, Daniel, to grab the card. His face also drained to a ghostly grey.

Scarlett looked around the table and then back to Lawrence. "What's going on? This isn't a party. Who are these people? Who's Madeline?"

Kevin Weisbeck

"I'm his wife. And how exactly do you know Lawrence?"

Her words were timid. "Why, I'm his girl—"

Lawrence slammed his fist on the table. "Don't answer her you idiot."

"Yes Scarlett, best not to upset the man." Ingrid reached past her father and slowly lifted the last vacant plate, revealing an enlarged photocopy of a passport picture with the name Cam Bolen under it. It was the one that looked a lot like a young Lawrence. There was also a snapshot of Lawrence kissing Scarlett in front of a hotel. "I think upsetting him is my job."

"That's it, Frank." Lawrence grabbed his friend by the shoulder and shoved him toward her. "I want these people out of my house." He turned to Alain Beauchene. "I'll see you on Monday. For now you can take your wife and your stupid kid and get out."

Police Captain, Frank Delacroix remained frozen as he stood there. "I'm sorry, Lawrence. I can't help you with this."

"I mean it Frank, you owe me."

Mr. Latteur stepped forward, pulling out his badge and a folded sheet of paper from of his jacket pocket. Earlier, Ingrid had convinced him that a search warrant for Lawrence's safe and safety deposit box was necessary. "Frank, I advise you to take this man into custody."

Frank spoke softly as he slowly reached for his cuffs. "Yes Commissioner."

Lawrence lunged against the table as he fired his glass at me. I flinched as it drifted past my head and landed down the hallway in pieces. "You bitch. You think you're going to get away with this? After all I've done for you."

Ingrid snapped. "Done for her. Look at her face."

Commissioner Latteur held up the passport picture of Lawrence, a.k.a. Cam Bolen. "Do you know this man, Lawrence Trembley?"

Lawrence didn't answer. His secrets, no longer secrets, were about to ruin him. Then, as if a light went off, Lawrence

244

turned to me. His eyes became black pools of hatred. "You're going down with me, Bitch."

Lawrence glanced over to the study and wrestled himself free from Frank. "This wife of mine is a fraud. I found out yesterday that she's not who she says she is. Did you know she killed her sister? Now she's been pretending to be my wife."

Frank followed him. "Where are you going Lawrence?"

"To get the proof."

He paused at the entrance of his study for effect. "This woman isn't my Madeline. She's Rebecca. And if that's not enough, she's been seeing my brother behind my back."

Ingrid held up a copy of Lawrence's birth certificate and tore it in half. "This is fake. You're no more Johannes's brother than you are mine."

Lawrence ignored me. "For months they've been preying on my feelings. Scarlett was all a part of it. She's a plant. They've been holding me captive in this marriage, planning to ruin me if I didn't go along with them. She wants the house and my son."

Johannes grabbed the two pieces of the certificate. "This is a fake?"

"I'm sorry, Johannes," Ingrid answered. "He's not your brother. He's an opportunist. This was all made up."

"I can't believe you're all buying their bullshit. It's all a scam." He turned to me. "You're good, but I have proof."

"It's true," Dr Pierre Needham weighted in. "He recently brought it to my attention. There's a taped confession."

"Go get it, *Monsieur* Trembley." Commissioner Latteur signalled Frank to keep an eye on him.

I looked over to Johannes. He was looking back at me confused, quiet. I wanted to hold him. I had to look away.

Lawrence returned with a tape recorder and a tape. He pushed the play button and cranked the volume. I closed my eyes and waited for my confession. Ingrid was good, but she'd overlooked the fact that I had spilled my true identity on that tape. If they found out I was Rebecca, they'd see it as me plotting against him. If they still believed I was Madeline, they'd see me as not right in the head? Either way, I would be considered unfit to be Nicolas's mother. We'd both go down.

At first there was only silence. My stomach churned as I waited. Then there was a click as the machine clicked off.

Lawrence swore and fumbled the tape over, pressing the play button again. And again, we waited. It was quiet for a second before starting.

Baby we can talk all night...

"What the hell?" He forwarded the tape and pushed play one last time.

...that I would love you to the end of time, I swore I would love you to the end of time...so now I'm praying for the end of time, to hurry up and arrive. 'Cause if I have to spend another minute with you, I don't think that I can really survive...

The song played for close to a minute before Ingrid broke our silence. "You like the band Meatloaf. Uh, what's your point? You still hungry?"

Ingrid must have recorded over the confession while I had prepared supper. This was a twisted joke, more for me than anybody. Meatloaf was the band that she had taken me to see. Call it the sweet taste of revenge.

I was looking at her when the tape recorder sailed across the room. This time it caught me off guard. I zigged when I should have zagged, and it struck me in the shoulder.

"Tell them who you are, you conniving whore." Lawrence slipped past Frank and shoved me to the floor. When I looked up, Frank had him pinned against the wall.

Ingrid came running over to me. "Shit. Are you okay?" Her eyes and one of her hands dropped down to my belly. If no one had noticed before, they had now.

"What?" Johannes asked, "are you pregnant?"

The hurt in his eyes crippled me from saying anything. He automatically assumed it was Lawrence's and I couldn't say otherwise. To say anything now would put us all in jail.

"Let go of me Frank, I'm not going anywhere." Lawrence pulled himself free again and headed for the bar. "I think a drink is in order."

I couldn't stop staring at Johannes. Not only had I cheated on him with this asshole, but I'd brought their lives together. Now his inheritance was gone, and the woman he loved was pregnant with another man's child.

Lawrence looked back at us as he opened the cabinet. "Does anybody want to join me in a drink?"

Chapter Fifty-six

I was the first one to see the gun. Lawrence levelled it at my head and the puff of smoke was immediate. It was larger than I would have imagined and had my mind swimming in confusion. I didn't hear the bang.

The shot whistled through my hair, freezing me, and cracked the hardwood frame of the cabinet that normally held our good china. I heard that impact as I looked back to see the splinters of wood landing on the floor. The scent of singed hair sat on the sides of my tongue overpowering the lingering cigar smoke.

A second shot, fired at Johannes, also missed shattering glass in the kitchen. Johannes started to inch toward me, but Lawrence kept the gun on him. "Stop right there brother or the next one won't miss."

Johannes nodded as he raised his hands. Lawrence quickly turned the gun toward *Commissioner* Latteur. He already had a hand inside his jacket.

"Before you get any crazy ideas, you and Frank need to pull your guns out and drop them on the floor."

Frank dropped his gun to the floor first, followed by *Commissioner* Latteur. He put his hands up to shoulder height and took a step toward Lawrence. "You do realise, this is a mistake? You don't have to escalate this. Right now, there are a few fraud charges. I'll tell you how the courts work. You'd be out in less than five years. Shoot one of us and it becomes life."

"I'm out in five." Lawrence shrugged. "Doesn't sound bad, except to what? I've lost my child, my house and my reputation?" He trained the gun back in my direction. "This woman says she's my wife. That's a lie."

Johannes inched toward me. "You don't need to do this."

Lawrence readied a third shot and snarled, "Stay away from her."

He trained the barrel of the gun back to my left eye and it paralysed me. The first two shots had damaged furniture. They were warning shots. This one wouldn't miss. "Lawrence please."

"Please what? You've won. You get my house and my child." He started toward me, firming his grip. "Thanks to you, I'll be looking at a life sentence."

I tried to correct him. "*Commissioner* Latteur said five years."

The gun left me briefly. I watched as another puff of smoke left the barrel. The accompanying wet thud of a bullet hitting flesh stopped my heart. I watched helpless as Johannes fell to one knee and then to his side.

"Johannes!"

I was on my knees beside him in seconds. A searing pain had his eyes squeezed shut. He opened his mouth to talk There was nothing but a groan. A red stain quickly grew on his starched white shirt. I touched the spot, felt the saturated warmth.

"So there. I think we can all agree that it's more than five years now." Lawrence moved over to me as he trained the gun on the others. "If you don't want this to get any worse, then you'll do as I say."

"Just don't kill him," I begged.

Pain shot through my shoulder as he grabbed my arm and jerked me to my feet. "Why not, my Dear? Do you love him? Would you miss him? Things might go a whole lot better if you just admit it."

"You're crazy."

"Whatever. Admit you love him and I won't put another slug in his chest."

"Why are you doing this?"

"So that's a no." He raised an eyebrow. "Suit yourself."

He aimed the gun at Johannes again and my world flashed before me. There was Rudesheim, Rommer Square and the old lady who spat at the tourists in Sachenhausen. I remembered the flattened baguette that we fed to the rather large ducks. "I beg you, Lawrence. Don't! I say whatever you want me to say."

He stood there staring at Johannes, holding the gun, and letting his mind spin. "Change of plans." He grabbed a handful of my hair and dragged me toward the door. "We need to go."

I dug in my heels. "I'm not going anywhere with you."

He jerked me from my stance and in seconds I was out the door, thrown in the car, and we were peeling out of the driveway.

Chapter Fifty-seven

We both remained quiet as he drove. I thought of
Johannes and hoped he would be okay. I couldn't
imagine the world without him. Lawrence likely
blamed the man for everything that had happened. Before long, we
were leaving Paris headed west on the A14. I had heard the sirens
but, like lost children looking for their parents in a crowd, they
were nothing more than faded cries.

"Lawrence, slow down. You're going to kill us."

He kept his foot mashed on the gas pedal.

"Where are you taking me?" I asked.

His eyes remained focused on the road.

"Look, you've got the gun and you're driving. What does it
hurt to tell me?"

His eyes shifted from the windshield to the rear-view
mirror. "That was quite the stunt back there."

"You didn't leave me a lot of choice."

"I know you think I'm an ass, and you're probably right,
but I too had no choice. Life seems to deal me cards I don't like.
It's always been my nature to change them."

"My sister, was she one of those cards. Did you love her?"

"I loved her very much." He paused as if remembering her. "She was one of a kind."

"I agree." That was a first.

"Madeline was more than just an obedient wife. She understood me. And even though she didn't always agree with everything I did, she went along with it. The woman put her trust in me. She was the only one who believed in me. I knew she'd always be there for me, not just when the times were good."

"I'm sorry I'm not her."

"Me too."

"So where are we going?"

He looked over at me. "Have you ever heard of a *Sûreté integrée*?"

"Where?"

"It's more like a what. It's a failsafe or a 'plan b'." He looked at me in frustration. Madeline would have known this. She understood the game.

Me, I hadn't been jaded enough to want to learn the game. I preferred an honest approach. "A failsafe isn't a place, Lawrence. My question was, *where*, are you taking me?"

He kept his eyes trained on the road. "Was life with me so bad you couldn't just accept it? We could have set ground rules. I mean, your sister had no problem with the arrangement. Damn it, you're identical twins and yet you two are nothing alike."

"And you need to accept that fact." It felt good to say. I wasn't my sister. My whole life, I had wanted to be her, wanted her life. It was stable. She was our mother's favourite. Madeline had a husband and a child. Her life was perfect.

But I'd learned that her perfect wasn't mine. And to hear Ricardo say she'd always wanted to be like me. It made me wish that we'd talked more. "For the last time, tell me where we're going?"

"Okay. We bought a property a while back."

"We?"

"Your sister and I had bought it before the wedding." He hesitated. "It's a couple hours away."

The gun was in his left hand. He kept it pointed at me, casually, without intent. I stared at it, hoping for the sirens to get louder. I was sure the search blanketed the city by now. The police were interrogating his parents, and there were squad cars parked outside his office.

Had they set up roadblocks? That would take too long. There were dozens of routes out of Paris. I didn't know France all that well, but I knew we were heading west. We had just crossed the Seine River and taken the north exit toward Courbevoie. I made my mental notes as the road signs and landmarks passed.

"First chance I get, I'm running. You know that, right?"

"I know you're thinking about that, now." He took his eyes off the road and looked over to me. They were calm, looking past me as if I wasn't there. "I'm hoping that you'll come around, that you'll become more like your sister."

"I'm not her. If you let me go you can have your *sûreté integrée*. I don't need to know where this thing is."

"If it were only that easy." He put the signal on, exiting into the parking lot of a storage facility. The car stopped. "Stay put. I'm a better shot than you think."

I waited while he went into the trunk and returned with a brown attaché case. He set it on the hood and glanced at me through the windshield, before dialling the brass tumblers that kept it locked. The tabs popped open and he pulled out a set of keys and a card. The card was swiped through a box on a post and the front gate started to lumber open.

He tossed the case in the back seat and got back in the car. Inside the compound he drove up the centre lane. At the end of it there was a patch of gravel—storage for RV's, boats, and cars. He backed the Mercedes beside a dusty white BMW. "Get out."

"No."

"Suit yourself." Shaking his head, he grabbed the attaché, unlocked the other car, and threw the case in the back seat. Then he opened both trunks and started to change. His suit became casual pants and a golf shirt. He pulled out a dress. "Change or I'll kill you and leave you in the trunk of the Mercedes. I'll give you three seconds to decide."

I sat quietly, as if defying a parent—one, two...three. My door opened, and I was pulled out of the car. I felt the cold steel of the gun pressed against my stomach. "Do you think it would have been a boy or a girl, had it lived?"

I let the warm wave of fear rush through my body before taking the dress. The gun pressed harder. Did Lawrence think it was his? I took the dress.

Brown and drab, the dress was my size. I stepped behind the cars to disrobe. "Was this for...?"

"Madeline picked it. She had accepted that some of my dealings were a little dangerous. I had made a few odd friends and even more enemies. There was always a chance that the banks or an associate might get an upper hand. That was why we had a back-up plan."

"It sounds like she was okay with that."

He shrugged. "She was okay with it, almost better than I was. She liked her insurance."

Madeline had known a lot more than she had ever told me. I thought the guy was an ass. That was just the surface. "What about Nicolas?"

Lawrence quickly shuffled our past lives in the trunk of the Mercedes, including his wallet, less the money. Credit cards, clothing, and ID's were no longer required. I was handed a purse and told to get in the BMW. I sat and had to look inside. There was a wallet with money, house keys and make-up. There was also a passport and it had a name.

No longer Madeline, I became Anastasie Colombre Léone. "Why this name?"

"It can pass as French or foreign. I chose Anastasie because it means resurrected, and Colombre means dove. It was meant for your sister." Then he added, "and you need to start calling me Benoit."

"And Nicolas? Are you just going to leave him behind?"

"I will for a couple of weeks." He flashed me a third passport. It had a small boy's picture in it. Nicolas would become, Théo René Léone.

"It means reborn gift from God. Once the dust settles, I'll find him and bring him home…to our home."

"Why don't we get him now?"

"You need a couple weeks to adjust. I don't need you screwing this up by calling him Nicolas. I'm sure I'll find him with my parents."

I was speechless.

We pulled out of the compound, no longer Madeline, and Lawrence Trembley. We were Ana and Benoit Léone. The transformation of our lives had only taken minutes and it finalised as we exited through the threshold of the compound.

I turned to him, seeing the gun still in his left hand, but resting on his lap. "What if I don't want to play?"

Chapter Fifty-eight

Lawrence focused his attention on the highway, but I could tell my sister was in the back of his mind. She was the one who should have been sitting in this seat. This was their day, not ours.

Before long we passed through Houilles, Sartrouville and got back on the A14. I stared at the picture in my passport. It was my sister and she looked almost happy in it. What was going through her head when she agreed to all this? Was this why the will, why the need for me to become Nicolas's Godmother. She wanted to keep me in his life. None of that mattered now. It all changed the moment the trunk on the Mercedes closed. Not only was Rebecca dead, but Madeline and Lawrence had vanished as well.

The silence in the car was ominous. It wasn't awkward. Instead, it allowed me to think of what my life as Anastasie might be like. I also thought of my parents, Johannes, and Ingrid. These were the people that would be torn from my life unless I stopped him. Granted Nicolas's eventual kidnapping would deposit him back into our lives, but doing so would crush the hearts of both grandparents. None of that mattered to Lawrence. He had been groomed to put himself first.

"What makes you so sure I'll do this?" I asked.

"Because Nicolas means everything to you. You would have walked away when your memories returned if it wasn't for him. You want him in your life." He looked over. "I'm betting on it."

"But, you hate me. How do you propose we…?"

"Nicolas needs a mother. You do that well because you love the boy. We can work on the rest. Ground rules are easy to draft up."

I wanted to ask about Johannes. Did he feel any form of remorse? Did he wonder if Johannes was okay? I looked over, trying to read him. I couldn't ask. I wanted to make a call, just a quick one to see if he was still alive. Was he in surgery? Regardless, this wasn't the time. "Slow down. It's not the damn Autobahn."

The corner of his mouth turned upward in the allusion of a smile.

"You don't think I'll try to escape some day, steal my child and go to the police?"

"I have a passport and an established life. People know me, where we're going. They've even met you a couple of times."

"Madeline?"

"Who do you think helped me pick this place. You see, they have no reason to think we're anyone other than Ana and Benoit, and no reason to arrest me."

He had it all figured out. Madeline wouldn't have given him such grief. She was in on it. She would have enjoyed her new home, meeting the neighbours, raising her son somewhere new. I'd have no choice but to do the same.

"I'm not saying this will be easy for you, Ana. You'll need time to wrap your head around this. I can give you a couple weeks."

"I don't think I can do this."

"I'm hoping you can." He tapped my leg with the gun. "We'll move into the house and I'll let you make it your own. You can change things, wall colours, furniture placement, even the yard. Do it for Nicolas. Heck, we'll get a swing set for him."

"Don't you mean Theo? He's not even two yet."

"Good catch, and he'll grow into it."

He pulled out and passed three cars.

"Can you please slow down, unless this is how you plan on killing me?" I hoped it wasn't. "What about your parents? Aren't you going to miss them?"

"My options are limited. If I hang around them, I go to jail? This day had always been a possibility. I'd hoped it would never happen, but it did. Now, we have to make the best of it."

"You said they'll have Nicolas. How can you just take him?"

"I've lost almost everything. I won't lose my him too."

"Say I agree to all this." It wasn't like I was rich with alternatives. "I won't do it as a prisoner."

"I don't want you to be one. I want you to be the mother of our son."

"And a wife?"

"A figurehead only. I don't expect us to be intimate. You're no Madeline. I'll take a mistress and you can do whatever, as long as you're discreet. Can you do that?"

"You'd be okay with me seeing somebody else? You gave me shit every time I looked at Johannes?"

"A wife shouldn't be sleeping with a man's brother. No reputation can survive those kinds of complications."

"What a load of shit. He wasn't—"

"I was protecting my name. You weren't being discreet. My co-workers were running to me with stories like you were some whore. We couldn't have that."

"We need to trust each other."

"I agree."

"Answer me this then. Where are we going?"

There was only silence. He was letting me into his world, but it was conditional. I watched as the A-14 merged with the E-5 and again I wondered about Johannes. Was surgery his going well? How was Ingrid holding up? Then there was the look in my father's eyes when he found out I wasn't Madeline. He had his little Rebecca back, only to lose her once again. I'd have to get a message to him, but how?

I looked down at the wallet he'd handed me. I flipped it open and counted the money. It was enough for a week's worth of groceries. How far could I get with that? I had a driver's license, a credit card, and a library card. It was white with red letters—Médiathéque de Val de Reuil. That was interesting. The library was in Val de Reuil. I'd heard of that place, from Madeline. Slipping the license out of the slot, I looked for the address. We lived in Val de Reuil on Rue du Bac.

Lawrence looked over and tightened his grip on the gun.

We needed to work on the trust thing.

Chapter Fifty-nine

I had figured out where he was taking me and although he didn't say a word, I could tell that this wasn't sitting well with him. I wasn't that good at playing the role of Madeline and the sooner he figured that out the better. Call it a compromise. He was right however, about Nicolas needing a mother. We both knew that, and my playing the role well could buy me a few liberties.

He continued to drive faster than he needed to. It made me wish we were there.

"Val de Reuil? Is it nice there?"

"It's quiet."

"And Madeline was okay with this? She liked the place?"

"We had spent a few weekends there, got to know the locals. They all think we're from Bordeaux."

"I know nothing about Bordeaux, and neither did Madeline."

"She learned, studying maps and pictures."

"Is it a good place for Nicolas? Are there schools nearby, a park handy?"

"Your sister thought the place was perfect. There's a park, a school, and we're a block away from L'Eure."

It felt odd to hear him talk freely about this, but the man knew he had to play nice for this to work. It was compromise. "What's a L'Eure?"

"It's a small canal. The kids all swim in it in the summer."

I decided to push him, see if he had it in him to trust me. "How many people live there?"

"Just under fifteen thousand."

"What else?"

"There's a golf course just down the street from our house."

"You've gotta like that. See this trust thing is good."

"Enough already."

"Can I call the hospital?"

"No."

"Can I at least call my parents?"

"No."

"You know we'll never pull this off if you can't trust me."

"After what just happened at dinner, trust will be a work in progress."

"But it's hard for me, not knowing. You want me to adapt. That would be a lot easier if I knew how Johannes was doing."

"Look, nothing is easy. I've worked hard for what I had, including lies, creating personas, and convincing people that I was someone else. I haven't always been proud of what I've done, but Madeline was okay with it. Like me, she never wanted to lose the finer things. This place was never meant to be our home. It was an insurance policy. We're cashing in that policy because of you. If you have to wait a few hours to find out about Johannes, live with it."

I shouldn't have been surprised that my sister was like this. She never wanted to be without. That was why the man in a fancy car could sway her into a quick marriage. It bothered Madeline that her family was treated poorly, even lied to, but not enough to stop the wedding. Sadly, she was weaker than I ever thought.

"You'll get a lovely home and you'll never have to work. You want trust? Here's some trust. We own a strip mall, five stores. They're three blocks from the house. Four have been long-time tenants. The other is on a six-month lease. The house and the mall are paid for."

I said nothing. I didn't want his trust any more. I didn't want this to work. Hating him was easier and leaving him when he let his guard down, was still the plan.

"Did you know your sister and I used to talk about you? You and I aren't all that different."

"What?" It pissed me off that she had talked about me with him.

"She used to tell me how she was her mother's favourite and that she never worked that hard at it. She just knew what people wanted to hear. You were the opposite. When your mother wanted a grandchild, she gave her one. I wanted a wife that would make me look good and she played the part to perfection. But you, you're a rebel to the bitter end. You don't care what people want. You're Rebecca Harrows, a free spirit."

"So? Why is that a terrible thing?"

"It won't get you anywhere. I bounced from foster home to foster home as a free spirit until I realised how it held me back. People bend over backwards for people like your sister. And as a free spirit, we're considered unstable, even a liability. I figured it out and so should you. Stop being a liability. You can have it all if you play the game, starting with Val de Reuil."

"What about love?"

"There's always a trickle, seeping in from somewhere. It's poison."

"I had love and it wasn't poison."

"What, you mean Johannes? Look what that got you. He didn't even attend your funeral."

"He had his reasons."

"Of course. Face it, love is blind. Did he know you were Rebecca when he stormed our dinner party? I'll wager you both talked about it before he got there. If that were the case, why'd he come to see me? Why didn't he come to rescue you?" He shook his head. "But hey, what do I know about love."

"It's complicated."

"Love should be anything but complicated." He pulled out to pass a slower truck. "Slow down, Lawrence."

"Benoit, and I'll make you a deal. I'll make the call when we get to the house. I know you're concerned about him. I'll talk to your Dad, get as much information as I can, and forward it to you. I'll also tell him you're okay, but to forget about you."

"Why would you do that?"

"Where's the trust?" He wheeled the car past the truck and back into his lane just in time. A passing car leaned on the horn. "It's called a truce. Our kind has to stick together."

"Our kind?" I wasn't anything like him. I was confused, rebellious and riddled with unwanted baggage. Lawrence was the one that had died as a child, trading his free spirit for lies and deceit. No, I wasn't anything like him.

"Aren't you tired of going without?" He asked.

"Aren't you tired of lying to get what you want? Isn't it exhausting not being able to trust anyone?"

"Not if I get what I want."

"If you say so, now slow down."

"We need to get there before dark."

"Why?"

"I have things to do."

With that the conversation was over. He had revealed enough to deserve a truce. There was trust. He saw us as similar people and acknowledged the fact that this was my fault. Sure, there was anger, but we moved forward because he and my sister had devised a plan. He liked sticking to plans. That and it was all he had left of her.

Back at the dinner party my belly bump had been revealed. Had Lawrence done the math? Again, I had to push this trust a little further.

"You know don't you, about the baby?"

Chapter Sixty

W hy would you bring that up?" He raised the gun to my face and gently stroked the contour of my jaw. His eyes dared me to continue. "You don't have anything to tell me, do you? Anything that might upset me?"

It was safe to say he knew the child wasn't his. It was also safe to say he had issues with that fact. He wouldn't want confirmation, because that would force his hand. "No. I guess I don't."

Again, he pulled out to pass two vehicles. The first was a car, the driver not wanting to pass the semi-trailer truck in front of him. We were on a hill. Lawrence is such an ass.

As we passed the car, a lorry in the oncoming lane came into sight. Lawrence pressed down harder, trying to squeeze the last couple horses out of the engine. I closed my eyes and thought of home. Would I ever see them again? Would I ever get a chance to hear one of my father's silly stories about Chilliwack?

I let the silence calm me. The engine's sudden drop in revs let me know we were past the truck and back in our own lane. We were also travelling too fast for my liking. I kept my eyes closed and mentally put some distance between our worlds. There was no need for us to talk, and no need for me to see where we were going. He didn't want to know about the baby. This concluded our session in trust building.

On occasion, the engine revved, sucking me back into the seat. After a moment, the revs would drop, and the seat would release its grip. We weren't dead.

I let myself drift off to Johannes's world, opening my eyes on occasion to catch a road sign or a marker. The Val de Reuil exit came and went. I looked around. It was quaint.

"Was that…"

"Val de Reuil? Yes."

"But…"

Lawrence remained silent, did a shoulder check, and pulled out to pass. I let my eyes close. I'd get no answers, even if I asked.

Minutes later, the car slowed, and my eyes popped open. The highway was distancing itself in the rear window as dusk settled over France. A sign read *Forêt de Rouvray*—Oakwood Forest. He had mentioned that he wanted to get something done. I now had to accept the fact that I was that something.

There was a part of me that had known this was too good to be true. I had ruined the man's life. I had cost him his home and was pregnant with another man's child. This was a man he hated. He'd also hate this child. How could he live with such an encumbrance? The answer was simple—he couldn't.

"What happened to Val de Reuil?" I waited through the silence before continuing. "I mean we drove past it, right?"

More silence.

The man had promised me a fresh start. He'd said I could change the wallpaper. How stupid was I to believe him? This was the same man that had told Johannes they'd make a few dollars on an investment. He had also told me we were going away for the weekend. That was before he struck me with the snow globe.

"So where are we going?"

The silence continued as he turned off the main road and onto a dirt one. The trees were getting taller, now. I watched as they passed. I've always loved trees. They take me home, make me a child again. Would I be killed and buried amongst them? I only wondered because I was hopelessly in denial. How could Madeline have loved this man?

Pebbles danced off the underside of the car while Lawrence kept a consistent eighty kilometres per hour. I wanted to tell him to slow down, but it seemed moot. At least he could answer one last question for me.

"Are you going to kill me?"

There was only the car's growl of tires along the gravel.

"Answer me you fucking asshole!"

He was calm. "You're a free spirit. You'll always be one."

The look in his eyes was admiration. I was strong, unwilling to change. But this was a bad thing. I couldn't do the things that he did, the lies, deception. I'd screw things up, and there was no plan 'C'. Free spirits were a liability.

Lawrence kept his eyes to the road, steering wheel in one hand, gun in the other. Trees passed us in a blur. In the sky, the blues had given way to the darkening night sky as the canopy of the forest closed in on us.

I wondered about the house, the one I'd never see. It would be the one that Nicolas would grow up in. He'd go to school here and get a library card like the one in my wallet. Nicolas would get the story that I left them for another. It would be easier that way. The police would get the same story, if they even came looking. Lying was what he did, and he did it well.

In time they'd find me, my rotted remains dug up by animals and found by hikers. And who would they find? Would it be Ana, Madeline, or Rebecca? My parents would have talked to Ingrid and changed the tombstone back in Paris. That is, and always will be, their Madeline. God, I'd put them through so much and it wasn't even over. Unless the police found my body and identified me as Rebecca, they'd keep looking for me. They'd be hoping I was safe, but in the furthest recesses of the mind, they'd be imagining the worst.

Again, I let my eyes find the passing trees. Unlike me, they were survivors. They had stood tall and firmly rooted their whole lives. They'd endured weather, animals, and mankind. The forest was their home, and nothing would change that. There was no mistaken identity, no amnesia. Their existence was simple, fearless, and they were the true free spirits.

I let them enchant me. My mind needed to pull from their strength. They were my big brothers, protective and loyal. Because I trusted them, I slowly reached across my body. I grabbed my seatbelt and pulled it to the latch. It quietly clicked into place as I masking the noise with a phoney cough.

But I wasn't under the forest's spell when I latched my belt. And I wasn't under the forest's spell when I found the strength to grab the steering wheel from Lawrence.

The car darted right and was promptly overcorrected before sliding off the road on the left-hand side. Tossed around by the underbrush, the BMW escaped the ditch and shot across the road one last time. Tires slid over the gravel like a child's eraser over a misspelled word.

One of the tall oak trees had to be a hundred years old and a couple feet thick at the trunk. We struck it and the tree sheered through the driver's section of the car in an explosion of glass and torn steel.

Branches hammered at the doors, the windshield, and tore through the roof. Dirt and leaves washed over me, suffocating me as the car dug into the ground.

When we came to a stop, all I could smell was the freshly churned earth. It reminded me of all those times planting a garden as a child. The soil was dark and rich. Madeline would sprinkle in the carrots and I'd take the peas. Together we'd get the tomato plants in their cages. Dad would always stand by and supervise with a beer in hand.

I shook the thought as reality began to resurface. Dirt had come in through the opening of the car and half buried me under clumps of sod. I hurt all over, but none of the aches stood out as urgent. I moved my neck around and managed to look over to the driver's seat. Lawrence wasn't there.

That side of the car had been peeled open and violently emptied. I unlatched my belt and pulled my legs free. Climbing out the left side of the car was like crawling out of a cave. The tree was still standing tall, scarred and unmoved.

I staggered over and leaned against it as I searched for Lawrence. His bent and twisted body was tucked against a freshly exposed rock. He was face down and bloodied by the impact. I made my way over to him and rolled his body over. His skull was half-exposed, and a branch had torn a large opening in his chest. I looked up in relief and quietly let the first muddy tear flow. It stung as it trickled down my face.

This nightmare was over.

Chapter Sixty-one

My body wouldn't stop trembling as I took a seat at the kitchen table. Johannes sat in the chair across from me. The man had sounded confused over the phone but said he would come and he did. He had no way of knowing what he was walking into and I had no way of explaining anything over the phone. I'd disguised my voice and told him that my name was Ana. I needed to talk to him about a woman named Rebecca. Hearing that name, the man came. This was what we called love.

"I can't believe it's really you." He couldn't stop staring at me. "What happened, Rebecca?"

"It's Ana. You need to start calling me that, especially out in public."

"What?"

"I'm the woman who called, Anastasie Colombre Léone." I slid an open passport toward him. "My husband, Benoit, died a week ago in a tragic car accident. It's just me and my son now."

"You mean Nicolas."

He was sleeping in the other room. The house was half the size of the one in Paris, but I was adapting. There were two modest bedrooms, a bathroom, and a large back yard. I'd bought a swing set. It was quaint. I slid a second passport toward him.

"He's Théo now."

"Why are you doing this?"

"After this accident, I remembering everything, and this time I had a say in what happened next. I decided to choose this life for my future. Rebecca had already died, and Madeline, she'd spend the rest of my days in court, or in jail if they ever found her. Lawrence had so many shady dealings? Did you know my sister knew about his shenanigans?"

"No."

"She helped him pick this place. That makes her an accomplice. If I go back to being Madeline, it makes me an accomplice. If they could prove any of this, I'd rot in jail. I don't think I deserve that, nor does Nicolas, I mean Théo. He needs a mother."

"You could be Rebecca again."

"Rebecca was just as guilty. She should have left him when she realised. There'd be motive for all that crap he said at the house. They might even believe his death was murder. There'd be an investigation and you'd be implicated. So would Ingrid. Whether I was Madeline or Rebecca, I'd have to come up with answers I just don't have."

"Did you kidnap Nicolas?"

"No. I had his grandmother's consent. She knew what her son was, what her husband is. She also knew what her grandson would become if he stayed.

We talked, we cried, and eventually we both agreed that Théo would be better off with me. I promised that I'd call her whenever I was in Paris. We would do a quiet lunch, so she could stay in touch. Her husband could never know. She'd become Auntie Catherine.

"And your parents."

"I've filled them in as well. They know everything. I'm not saying they're happy about it, but they're starting to get used to me being the one that flies left of centre. They'll be coming over for dinner in the next few days. I'll always find ways to keep them in my life, although it won't be easy."

He sat there absorbing, processing, and trying to understand where he fit in. I let the gears turn while I poured him a cup of coffee. I thought about bringing up how Lawrence died? I wasn't proud of myself. Johannes never asked, and I never offered.

"This isn't ideal, but for the first time I'm the one in control, albeit living the life of Ana. Regardless, I'm happy. I have Nicolas, my memories as Rebecca, freedom from a torturing husband, and no lawyers trying to have me thrown into the deepest dungeons of France."

"So who's Ana?"

"More like what's Ana's. It's just a name. Think of me as a second version of Rebecca, or even a third. I'm the one without the baggage, the guilt or the past."

"No past?"

"I'll always have the memories, like the day with the ducks and that flattened baguette."

He took my hand and placed a gentle kiss on the back of it. "I've missed you."

"You can't imagine how I've missed you." I bathed in the warmth of his eyes, so sincere, so loving. "I've hurt you so much." I let my open hand land on his chest. It was strong, chiselled and still a bit tender from the gunshot.

He flinched before taking my other hand in his and giving it a gentle squeeze. His eyes dropped down to my tummy. "You mentioned a car accident. Is the baby okay?"

"Your baby is doing very well." My eyes instantly welled. I put my coffee cup down, my hand shaking it as if the ground was moving.

Johannes's strong arms enveloped me. I thought of Frankfurt, my friends, and all those times I had woken to his smile.

I let my forehead rest against his chest. "What do we do now?"

He let go of me and stepped back. Then, without saying a word, he turned away. "This is the hardest thing I've ever had to do, but it's something I must do."

My heart sunk. Why do I keep expecting more? Because I was born a rebel, staring at a spider on a ceiling while I stumbled through life making messes. But this wasn't his mess. He still had his life and it was a normal one, albeit lost in a world of Rebecca and Madeline. It was all he knew, all he had ever wanted. He had never wanted an Ana.

But me, I needed this new life and I needed Anastasie. She was a simple woman. She had a home, a modest business, a cute little boy, and another child on the way. What more could I want, other than the man of my dreams to share it with. Was that selfish? I imagined it was.

Johannes turned around to face me again. His face was sober—German sober. He was looking for Rebecca, but that woman had died. Madeline was also gone. I had no choice but to brace my self for a life without him. I was Ana now.

The man took a step toward me and dropped to one knee. He took my hand and, not having a ring with him, gave my knuckles a gentle kiss. "Ana, would you—"

"Yes!"

Epilogue

Chilliwack – December 24, 2015

I stood at the window and watched day turn to night while winter continued to drift down from the sky. For the last eight hours God's dandruff had turned our driveway into an impassable sea of white. The trees, and we had many in our yard, looked full again, except instead of the green leaves of summer, they carried the weight of millions of tiny little snowflakes.

Thankfully, everyone had arrived for supper hours ago. I walked back into the living room, where chaos abounded, and looked for a place to sit. My granddaughter saw my silent plea for a spot and squished over on the couch. "Over here, Gramma."

I took the spot and set my plate of goodies down before rewarding her kindness with a hug, and half of my Nanaimo bar. They were her favourite Christmas treat.

My Johannes sorted through the gifts under the tree, handing them out as he read the tags. With his red Santa hat, he had his hands full. Our old farmhouse was full with my parents, Theo and his wife Annette, our daughter, Rebecca, and her husband Pierre. Oh, and the smiling girl that sat beside me with chocolate on her chin, was Rebecca's daughter, Madeline. She'd recently turned four, but there were days when I swore she was in her teens.

Little Madeline's pile of gifts was spreading like dandelions on a wind-swept hillside. "You better start unwrapping Maddie, or you'll never get finished."

That was all she needed. Within seconds paper tore and her tiny mouth gasped. It was funny how each gift was perfect, and just what she'd always wanted. I stole the occasional glance at Johannes. The man still looked as handsome as the day he stepped on my baguette. He looked back at me for a second and my heart began to palpitate, which, at my age, scared me a bit.

The last three decades had given us an exceptional brood. Their hearts were pure. Even Theo, who had lost his father at such an early age, grew up to be a man that any mother would be proud of.

Johannes married me a year after the accident. It was a respectful amount of time, we figured. He adopted Theo and Rebecca, secretly his real daughter, right away. After five years in Val de Reuil, Johannes and I decided to visit Chilliwack. He loved it so much, we moved that year. My husband also saw how badly I missed it.

It truly was a kinder environment for children with all the ponds and acres to roam. We sold the house and the strip-mall to buy a farm with a golden retriever. A second house sprouted onto the property the following year, for my parents.

Ingrid and Marcus eventually had a daughter. Sienna was three years younger than our daughter Rebecca, who was born five months after that fateful dinner party. We're still the best of friends and once a year we manage to meet up somewhere.

Last year they came to our farm. I took them to the pond and walked Ingrid through the first decade of my life. Little Sienna loved the horseback riding. I imagined it wouldn't be long before she'd want a pony of her own. Yes, the years had been kind.

"Gramma, are you okay?"

"I'm sorry dear. Was I drifting again?"

She giggled. "Uh, huh."

We'd all come to accept my drifting. My thoughts became clouds, rolling along and wandering off to the past, the present, and even the future on some days.

"Look what I got." She held up a doll. Then she gave me a run down on her whirlwind moment of present unwrapping. Being the sole granddaughter, she did quite well for herself. The others started cleaning up paper, picking away at the turkey, and snacking on chocolates. Little Madeline and I nibbled at my plate of goodies, sitting back with our feet up on the coffee table. I'd spent the day cooking and felt the break was a deserved one.

"Hey Gramma?" Madeline sounded concerned. "I think I..." Her pause came with a scan of the room, looking for her mother.

"What is it, dear? You can tell me."

"If I tell you, can it be a secret?"

That took me back a few years. "I don't know. We don't generally keep secrets in this family, Madeline."

"Do you have any secrets, Gramma?"

I smiled as I shot her a wink. "Maybe one."

Other Books by Kevin Weisbeck

The Darkness Within

A victim of his own bad choices, Johnny Pettinger is stranded following a plane crash in a remote mountain wilderness. His injuries are serious, but they're not the only factors preventing him from getting home. In order to do that, Johnny needs to shine a light on the very reason for his being there, the ***Darkness Within***.

The Divine Ledger
Coming in June 2018

Detective Violet Stormm is a woman on a mission. She'll do anything to catch the man responsible for a series of gruesome murders. Victor Wainsworth is the man doing the killing. He's fuelled by a ledger, a book that not only holds the names of his next victims, but clues to the ***Eve of Humanity***.

(This is the first of five books in the ***Eve of Humanity*** Series)
(This book also introduces the ***Violet Stormm*** Detective Series)

Kevin Weisbeck

About the Author

Kevin Weisbeck is a Canadian author, born in Kelowna, British Columbia and currently living in Okotoks, Alberta. He's had several short stories published in magazines and newspapers, and currently has one in McGraw-Hill's iLit Academic Program.

He can usually be found on the couch with his laptop in front of him and his Ragdoll cat, Franklin, on his shoulder. It's not an ideal writing set up, but Franklin doesn't mind. Otherwise Kevin enjoys hiking, kayaking, camping, photography and golf (when the weeds and water don't get in the way).

2

Made in the USA
Lexington, KY
14 May 2018